DOUBLE TAP

Peter McGarvey

Cliffhouse
PUBLISHING

PETER McGARVEY

Cliff House Publishing
Toronto

CliffHousePublishing.com

Copyright © 2016 by Peter McGarvey

Publisher's Note: This book is a work of fiction. Names, characters, places or incidents are either the product of the author's imagination or are used fictitiously, and any resemblance to actual persons living or dead, events, or locales is entirely coincidental.

Edited by Amy Mark

Cover Design by Lesley Stodart

Author's Photo by Marcus Ames

ISBN: 978-0-9881396-9-5

FOR MY BROTHERS

WILL and DOUG

Books by Peter McGarvey

FICTION

Dark Sunset

Hair Trigger

Bloody Sunset

NON-FICTION

Baffled by Travel Guide to Toronto & Niagara Falls

The 10 Second Guide to New York City

ACKNOWLEDGMENTS

Many thanks to Peter Halasz, Arleen Mark, Brett Randall, David Warren, Sandee Brown-Davidson, Helena Aalto, Lesley Stodart, Robert J. Sawyer, Don Hutchison, and the Second Tuesday Gang for your help and support.

Special thanks to Brian Irving, Steve Carlson, and Promod Sharma for generously lending me your names.

DOUBLE
TAP

Double Tap (definition)

"In the double-tap technique, after the first round is fired, the shooter quickly reacquires the sights for a fast second shot. This skill can be practiced by firing two shots at a time, taking time between the shots to reacquire the sights. With practice, the time between shots grows shorter and shorter until it seems to the observer as if the shooter is just pulling the trigger twice very quickly."

~ Wikipedia

"There are known knowns; there are things we know we know. We also know there are known unknowns; that is to say we know there are some things we do not know. But there are also unknown unknowns — the ones we don't know we don't know."

~ Donald Rumsfeld

MY MENTAL ELF

Interlaken, Switzerland

Everything I'm about to tell you is a lie.

That's the first one.

To say I *need* intensive analysis is akin to saying the National Rifle Association *dislikes* gun control.

"Your mental elf," Monique said.

I was hardly listening. Instead, I was busy fantasizing about the inside of her thighs barely hidden by the hem of her short skirt.

What would my analyst think of that?

But wait a minute, Monique *is* my analyst — Dr. Monique Vessier, founder of the Vessier Clinic. It's an exclusive facility in Interlaken, Switzerland, where the fucked up like myself come for healing, as long as they can afford it.

Monique leaned forward in her leather chair and balanced an arm languidly on the armrest. She was holding a leather portfolio filled with pages of expensive paper on which she made notes with a platinum finished fountain pen.

"I would like to talk a little about your mental elf," she repeated in her seductively smooth voice.

My mental elf? Is that a little creature nestled on the top of my head that causes my complete lack of empathy toward all human beings?

Probably not. More likely it was just her thick French accent mangling words like "health" and turning them into "elf".

The French are allergic to the letter H.

I should've been used to it by now. I'd been in her capable care for the past three months. Together we were working hard on my "mental elf", especially my paralyzing fear of heights.

As a professional contract killer, it's not good to have a paralyzing fear of *anything*. My acrophobia had almost gotten me killed when some rotten bastards tried to drop one of the largest office buildings in downtown Detroit on me. With only seconds to escape, I froze because I was scared shitless to free-fall down a twenty story elevator shaft.

Obviously, I managed to survive, but my fear of heights is much stronger now. Every night, as regular as murders on Motown's east side, I have a nightmare about falling. Each morning I wake up feeling like a bug that hit a windshield at seventy miles an hour.

My partner Wilma suggested I get some help. Since we'd earned a shitload of money from our last job, I decided to make an effort to face my phobia.

Hence the cure.

The Vessier Clinic specializes in helping people deal with acrophobia. Their cure rate is over 90% and costs an astronomical amount of money. Hundreds of thousands of dollars converted into francs were being drained from my Swiss bank account.

While Rip Hunter is my professional name, I'd chosen Brian Irving as the nom de plume for my treatment. My new mustache and goatee made for a more continental look. Thin wire-rimmed glasses completed the air of the wealthy venture capitalist I was claiming to be.

Honesty is not one of my stronger characteristics. Almost everything I'd told Monique had been made up, most of it on the spur of the moment. Although I suspected my dishonesty was an impediment to any chance the treatment would be successful, on the positive side, I was giving Monique one hell of a case study to present at psychiatric symposiums.

I remembered an old joke about two analysts meeting for the first time.

One says, "Hello," while the other thinks, "Hmmm, I wonder what he meant by that?"

Back to my *mental elf.*

"Brian, you are not being completely 'onest with me."

Monique glanced down at her portfolio. Flipping back a few pages, she scanned her notes and looked up at me. She cocked an eyebrow and fixed me with a stare.

Gotcha!

"There is a discontinuity to what you 'ave been telling me in our sessions." She continued to thumb through her notes.

Although an expert liar, I'm not used to having someone make detailed notes on everything I say. Lies are just one of the tools of my trade and normally only for short term use.

She frowned in disappointment. "If we are going to make progress, we 'ave to be 'onest with each other.

Honest?

I'm not sure I can even spell it.

And what could I tell her? That I'm a professional killer for hire? That I work with a partner who'd kill me if she even suspected I was telling the truth to a third party? Wilma wouldn't care if said third party was obligated by medical oath never to reveal what she heard from a patient.

"And what makes you think I'm not being honest?" I asked nonchalantly.

"First of all, you are not who you claim to be. I checked. There is no record of a Brian Irving or a Bartlett 'edge Fund."

Fucking Google makes any false ID only skin deep.

A phony identity should be disposable. Use it and throw it away. I wasn't going to spend good money to buy domain names and then set up and maintain false cover sites. Now my frugalness had come back to bite me in the ass.

"So ... who do you think I am?"

She shook her head. "I don't know. I was 'oping that you would tell me so we could work together on 'elping you with your problem."

"But you must have some idea."

"I think you are a man who operates without boundaries. A dangerous man."

She had that part right. There were a dozen different ways I could kill her by using the objects on her desk. I seriously considered it and then recalled the previous night's dream. It was one of those nightmares — an arms flailing, hair flying, free-fall through the never-ending darkness that left me in a heart pounding, cold sweat.

Coincidently, this is the same way I feel after watching an Adam Sandler movie.

If she can help me ...

Monique tapped her pen against the top of the portfolio. We were at a demarcation point. Either I could continue to waste my money and her time by telling lies, or I could take a leap of faith and start telling the truth.

Telling the truth, however, would involve talking about Wilma, and that would be extremely dangerous. Wilma, at the best of times, is be unpredictable. There was no telling what she'd do if she learned that I was spilling our dirty little secrets to a shrink.

How would Wilma find out anyway?

She was on a round-the-world cruise. At least, that's what she'd said when I told her I was going to vacation in Europe. After our last adventure, we decided we needed a break from the business for a while. What we didn't say was that we really needed a break from each other. I had fucked up badly during that little caper and had almost gotten us killed numerous times.

On the plus side, I did get laid quite a lot by a pair of beautiful women and we ended up with millions of dollars to put into our 401Ks.

But I digress. Let's return to therapy.

I pointed to the pad Monique was holding. "You might as well throw all that out." Then I proceeded to narrate the fantastic tale of my career as a contract killer and how I'd met Wilma.

Once I got started, it just flowed out of me. She canceled all her appointments for the rest of the day and we continued until 7:00 that night. I was exhausted from all the truth-telling.

Monique, on the other hand, was vibrating with excitement. Her eyes glowed as she rushed to get every word down on paper. I could tell she was aroused. Little Rip stirred as I began to imagine the velvet smoothness under her skirt. My tale full of bullets, blades, and chainsaws had moved her in a way that I certainly did not expect.

She shook her hair loose and stood. I took this as my cue to get up from the couch. In one fluid motion, she yanked her dress off and was on me before I could even budge.

Over the years, I've had many different kinds of sexual relations. Analyst sex is definitely the best.

The floodgates of repression were flung wide open and I got a real taste of French culture.

GANGBANGED BY
INSATIABLE FREUDIANS

The Vessier Clinic was located on the upper floors of the Victoria-Jungfrau Hotel.

Nicknamed the VJ, this is one of Europe's finest hostelries. The two original hotels, the Victoria and the Jungfrau, were across the street from each other. When they merged, the street was enclosed in an atrium which now forms the lobby.

I had a three-story suite in the hotel's south wing.

Monique wanted her patients to feel comfortable and pampered. She said it helped with the therapy. And it certainly seemed to be working.

I felt we'd made a breakthrough the previous evening.

My therapist worked very hard to get to the root of my problem. And although I had been skeptical about it at first, the cure was indeed getting results.

I hadn't felt this good in months.

Sadly, my desire died when Monique whispered the details of the immersion process that would have me conquer my fear of heights forever.

It would start simply enough with me climbing onto a chair and jumping off.

Simple enough.

Next, I would move to a step ladder and do the same.

No problem.

The final step of the cure would have me bungee jumping out of a cable car — five hundred feet off the ground.

What the fuck!

I stiffened, and not in a good way. Monique had to work extra hard to calm my fears.

~

My typical breakfast was an Egg McMuffin. Although Interlaken has a very nice McDonalds, the breakfast buffet at the hotel was nothing short of magnificent, and the view of the Alps from the dining room was breathtaking.

There was plenty of time for a leisurely breakfast since the day's session wouldn't begin until after lunch. I loaded my plate with sausages, cheeses, sweet rolls, eggs, and cold cuts. While I gorged myself, I gazed out at the mountains and imagined what it would be like to dive head-first from a cable car.

Booooinngggg!

The idea of it almost turned me off my breakfast.

Almost.

Three thousand calories later, I poured myself a cup of coffee and headed for the hotel's reading room. The only occupants were wealthy Teutonic businessmen. In the past, the room would have been blue with cigar smoke. Now it was only thick with hubris.

Newspapers from all over the world hung on split bamboo poles nestled in wooden racks. I bypassed the *Wall Street Journal* and *Financial Times* and selected that day's edition of the *International New York Times*.

European newspapers featured stories about the real world, in contrast to the Detroit papers which only reported the latest murders or city hall shenanigans. Since Motown had gone bankrupt, our hometown papers have been in tight competition to see who could feature the best hard luck story of the day.

I casually flipped through the *Times*, skipping over items about wars, ballets, and atrocities. I stopped when I saw a small headline about the black widow killer, a story I'd been following with particular fascination over the past few weeks. Someone was murdering philandering husbands on cruise ships. Interpol suspected it might be the work of one person, a woman they dubbed 'The Black Widow'.

The latest killing had occurred on an Italian ship sailing the western Mediterranean. A security cam photo of the murderer accompanied the article.

While it was hard to tell from the poor quality of the picture, I was certain it was my business partner Wilma. She couldn't go without killing for too long. It was an itch she would just have to scratch, so this made sense, at least to me. Sightseeing and sunning herself in a deckchair wasn't Wilma's style. The challenge of randomly stalking victims in a confined space would appeal to her pent-up appetite for excitement and danger.

Everyone has to have a hobby.

Although I don't share the intensity of Wilma's homicidal urges, I was glad to see she was productively spending her time honing her skills.

My urges are more pragmatic and profitable. I thought of my therapist. Once my cure was complete, the good doctor would regretfully help no more patients. She would disappear along with my case file.

~

Monique's tone was different that afternoon. The fear and wonder of last night's confession-fest was replaced by a subtle arrogance. While a condescending attitude is a national characteristic of the French, hers was more haughty.

Monique was blatantly telling me that she had something on me.

And that was not a good thing because …

In psychiatric terms, she'd hit the mother lode. She was officially treating that rarest of all creatures — the homicidal psychopath. And what was even rarer was that *this* psycho was revealing the unvarnished truth.

While yesterday's session had been liberating, this one left me feeling as if I had been gang-banged by a bunch of insatiable Freudians. Monique's talking cure had turned into mind rape. And when she wasn't baring my psyche on the couch, she was joining me there for a bit of horizontal therapy.

At the end of our four-hour session, we lay there totally spent. Instead of feeling satisfied, I felt empty.

Monique ran a finger along the bridge of my nose and tapped me right between the eyes. "I know what you are thinking. You 'ave little thoughts of 'ow to kill me, no?"

I let my silence speak.

"I 'ave put my notes safely away, along with all the details of your life. If anything were to 'appen to me, I am sure the police would be very interested."

Monique put her right nipple into my mouth with a harsh laugh.

Instead of feeling aroused, I felt cold.

"I thought you were going to help me."

Her chuckle was cruel, exactly like Wilma's while she merrily dismembered some poor sap.

Monique stroked my chest and let her hand trail down to my groin. Little Rip stirred — curse him.

She turned on her side to face me. "You are more than a patient to me now," she laughed. "You are a career."

Visions of being shackled to this leech danced through my sex-addled brain. Monique would suck and suck until she drained every last thought from my *'ead*. And then she would toss me to the police when she shared her findings with the world.

Her success would mean book deals and appearances on *The Tonight Show*. Monique and Jimmy Fallon would share a laugh at my expense as she seduced America into making her book a bestseller.

Who knew where that would lead. Maybe a movie version of my life. I wondered who they would cast as me. My preference would be Robert Downey Jr. Hollywood being what it is, however, would offer the part to someone like Seth Rogan. And Lindsay Lohan, in a career-reviving role, would play Wilma.

Monique cut off my chain of thought by rolling onto her back and pulling Little Rip along for the ride.

It was time for more *bon coup*.

THAT'S ALL FOLKS!

Our therapy 'sessions' went on for almost a week.

Monique assured me we were making progress though I suspected the only progress being made was filling up the final third of her book. Still, I have to confess the sex was great. Monique liked it lusty and loud and screamed various profanities in French, a tongue that I had not entirely mastered.

After one particularly strong climax that almost cracked my teeth, she whispered in my ear that the talking cure was over. It was now time for the immersion part of the treatment.

The immersion part of the treatment ... leap with wild abandon into thin air ...

My gut clenched painfully, and Little Rip withdrew into a safe place. No amount of urging on Monique's part could coax him out. She finally gave up with a disgusted sigh.

A cloud of impending doom followed me back to my suite.

At the beginning of our therapy, Monique had driven me out to the cable car station at the base of the Schilthorn to show me where the final exercise would be held. She'd explained in a soothing voice how the cable car would stop about 150 meters above the parking lot, followed by a literal leap of faith that would mark my cure.

150 meters?

That didn't sound too bad until I converted it into feet.

450!

She had laughed at the horrified expression on my face and told me many of her patients actually enjoyed the experience so much they went right back and tried the higher 200-meter leap.

200 meters?

I could barely keep control of my bowels at the thought.

"You will leap into death and then you will rise up into a new life."

She made it sound so religious, or like a Batman movie.

Monique assured me every safety precaution is taken. Seventy of her patients had successfully made the leap and were now completely unafraid of heights. She promised when it was over I would be able to climb mountains, stand on the top of tall buildings or, at the very least, clean out my eavestroughs. I would have a life without fear.

But at what cost?

To achieve freedom, I had sold my soul to this harpy. Now I was going to pay a terrible price — my anonymity and my freedom.

Will they arrest me here, or wait until I'm back in the States.

Or maybe the cord will break and save me a lot of grief.

I imagined the horror of looking back at the trailing end of the severed cable. Would I feel satisfied that my fears had finally come to fruition? Or would I just shit my pants?

~

The next morning, the cable car was waiting to take me to my doom.

Monique was practically dancing with delight. Not only was she going to turn me into a New York Times bestseller, but she was also going to cure my fear of heights.

There's no stopping this woman.

Or so I believed.

While her assistant hooked up the bungee cord, Monique explained what was going to happen.

"We will go up in the air and the operator will stop when we reach the correct elevation. You should stand in the middle as we climb. I find it is best if I jump first to show you 'ow safe it really is."

Monique traced a finger along my arm.

"Once I 'ave returned to the car, my assistant will 'ook you up. The best thing is to stand in the doorway and just let your body fall forward. I assure you it is quite exhilarating."

She made a diving motion with her hand and then bounced it up and down.

"When the cable reaches its full length it will snap you back upward. This will 'appen a few times. Once you have stopped bouncing, we will pull you up. It is a very simple thing, yes?"

I nodded and trudged after her.

With a loud whir, the gondola started to rise and the wind buffeted us through the open door. The higher we climbed, the colder it got. Even if I hadn't been scared beyond belief, I would still be shivering. But the view was spectacular. The snow-topped peaks of the surrounding Alps reminded me of donuts frosted with powdered sugar.

Donuts ...

Monique sat down and tightened the harness around her ankles. The assistant pulled it snug and locked it into position. Then the good doctor moved carefully to the doorway and looked down to gauge the height. A few moments later, she held up her hand and we stopped.

The car swayed like a hanged man.

Monique motioned me forward for a better view. I inched toward her.

She seared me with a contemptuous look before taking a final glance at the cord.

Monique paused in the doorway and with a final smirk, dove into space.

I watched the cord unravel behind her.

Her assistant watched the cord as well, first in fervent admiration, and then in growing panic.

The cable stopped unwinding, but there was a considerable amount of it still neatly coiled on the floor.

This cannot be good.

Monique's assistant shrieked as she sank to the floor in shock.

With what little courage I had left, I crawled to the door and peeked over the edge. A wave of dizziness almost made me vomit.

In the parking lot below was a tiny dark blot. I watched the blot get bigger as we descended toward terra firma. The blot became a splat

Emergency vehicles had raced to the scene even before we reached the ground. The Swiss are very efficient.

I staggered to my feet and beheld a scene out of a ghoulish cartoon.

Dr. Monique Vessier had planted herself head-first in a huge crater. One leg stuck straight up, pointing in the direction from which she had come.

I tried hard not to laugh, but my first thought, as always, was for myself.

This is not good.

An accident like this would attract all kinds of attention.

I touched the fake passport tucked safely inside my jacket. It would hold up; it had been crafted by an artist. But it was the only identification I'd brought to Switzerland and, as a material witness, the authorities hold it until the investigation was finished.

The assistant was still hysterical and I pretended to comfort her while I worked hard to keep a grim expression plastered on my face.

Then I remembered what Monique had threatened the day before — my hidden case file would surface if something happened to her. Since nose diving into a parking lot from 150 meters up indeed counted as *something,* I had good reason to regret my decision not to bring a second set of false ID.

I watched CSI Zurich argue about the best way to pry her from the crater. I was tempted to suggest they use a posthole digger.

"Silly damn thing, is it not?" I hadn't noticed the detective who'd come up beside me. His trench coat and pork pie hat made him look a lot like Inspector Clouseau from the *Pink Panther* films.

He politely offered me his hand and introduced himself as Jurgen Nurst, an investigator with the Kriminalpolizei Bern.

His eyes were soft and full of sympathy, but I sensed, despite his comical appearance, the man was no fool.

He offered me a lift back to the hotel and casually interrogated me. I recounted the morning's events in a voice choked with phony emotion. At one point, I pretended to break down completely and he stopped asking questions.

"How could this have happened?" I sobbed.

"Sadly, it has happened before."

I suspected his regret was more about an inefficiency of the process that allowed it to happen than about the death of the good doctor. To the Swiss, any lack of efficiency was obscene.

When we reached the hotel, he requested my passport. He explained it was "only a formality".

After I had handed it over, he suggested I get some rest. He would drop by the hotel later that evening to take my formal statement.

But my thoughts were on the case file Monique had hidden like a ticking time bomb. I would have to tear her office apart to look for it.

~

I'm fucked.

From my hiding place in the stairwell outside Monique's office, was an officious policeman guarding the door. Nurst was doing it by the book.

Damned efficient Swiss.

There was no way I was going to get inside that office and look for my dossier. And at some point, the file was going to pop up like a piece of burnt toast. The jig, as they say, was up. I was headed for prison.

If Swiss jails were half as beautiful as their hotels, I was in for a treat.

~

When I heard a knock on the door around dinner time, I expected it to be Nurst and a gaggle of Swiss policemen. He'd probably discovered that Brian Irving was as fictitious as Richard Nixon.

Instead of the constables, it was the room service waiter Claude pushing a cart loaded with food. This was extremely odd because I didn't remember ordering dinner. And after the tragic events of the day, I didn't really have much of an appetite.

Claude wheeled the cart into the dining room and put the covered plates on the table. He set out silver and linen before raising the covers on each plate to reveal my dinner, the one I didn't remember ordering.

"Heimisches Kalb, Lauch, and Eierschwämmchen," he told me. "Veal, leek, and chanterelles. An excellent choice, sir. The veal is from a local farm."

Claude pulled the cork from a bottle of wine. He poured a small amount and offered it to me. It was excellent. I nodded with an approving smile. I wondered if it had been sent by Nurst, as the last meal before he arrested me.

I added a generous tip to the room service check.

"Bon appétit," he said with a smile and let himself out.

"I'm starving," Wilma said as she came down the stairs wearing a hotel bathrobe.

This might have been a surprise except it was my partner, and she had long ago since ceased to astonish me.

Wilma poured herself some wine while reading the label. "Drouhin Clos Des Mouches 2009." She took a sip and an expression of pure bliss filled her face. "Exquisite." She dug into the meal, pausing now and then to refill her glass.

I watched her eat. The pleasure she took from the food was sexual. Despite the tragic events of the day, Little Rip started to rise. To discourage him, I recalled Monique's legs poking out of her crater. But the image aroused him even more.

When she finished, Wilma flopped down on the couch and sighed. "I hadn't had anything to eat all day."

"I thought you were on a cruise."

She smiled as if remembering something particularly evil. "I got bored and decided to see what you've been up to."

I shrugged. "Not much. Just trying to get over my fear of heights."

"Oh, yeah? And how's that going?"

I thought of Dr. Vessier. "Not so well," I admitted.

Wilma picked up her purse. She set it on the coffee table, fished around inside for a moment, and pulled out a leather portfolio. I recognized it immediately.

"Looks like she was helping you work things out."

I didn't bother asking how she got my file. I was just relieved that Nurst wasn't reviewing it.

"You've been a bad boy, Rip." Wilma's voice had a nasty undertone that made me pray she didn't have a saws-all in her bag.

"But it was for a good cause," I pleaded.

She smiled. "Yes, the betterment of Rip. I can respect that. But did you have to pick a therapist who's as psychopathic as we are?"

"I thought it would help."

"You're lucky the unfortunate Dr. Vessier had an accident then."

An accident?

During our drive back to the hotel, Nurst revealed the color coding on the two bungee cords had been mixed up.

I looked at Wilma.

I knew it wasn't a mix-up.

"I took a lovely sequence of photographs of Monique's swan dive into eternity. I think I'll post them online."

"How did you know she was going first?"

Wilma shrugged. "I didn't. But either way …"

She was a cold bitch, which was exactly what attracted me to her in the first place. She was a particular kind of woman, the kind who would cut off your ear, make you eat it, cut your stomach open, take it out, and then make you eat it again.

A woman like that was rare.

"So it all worked out well then," she said. "For *both* of us."

"Well … maybe not. I'm kind of stuck here while they investigate the accident. I only brought one set of ID with me and, once they take a closer look, I'm fucked."

Wilma shook her head sadly. "You can be so stupid sometimes. Don't you ever plan ahead?"

"I wasn't planning on any of this."

Wilma reached into her purse. She pulled out a white envelope and handed it to me. Inside was a clean set of identification — passport, driver's license, credit cards — everything for the well-dressed man on the run.

She got up from the couch and looked down at me severely.

"Promise me, no more therapy."

Wilma headed toward the stairs, stripping off her robe.

"Time to get dressed and go for a walk before that policeman actually puts two and two together."

And that's my partner Wilma. She always covers my back.

LOTS OF FOLKS OUT THERE
STILL NEED KILLING

Wanting to leave an impossible trail to follow, three days later Wilma and I arrived in our hometown of Detroit after multiple planes, trains, and automobiles.

After the breathtaking beauty and civil order of Switzerland, it was a challenge coming back to the Motown vibe. It didn't help that a bitterly cold wind greeted us. Although it was only mid-October, winter was already on its way. I couldn't imagine how the city would pay to have snow carted away when there wasn't even enough money to fix traffic lights or fill potholes.

Bankruptcy had sapped much of the Detroit's Mojo. A palpable sense of depression made people walk slower, heads down, the weight of their hometown's failure carried hard on their shoulders. There was the inescapable feeling that anything of value was about to be sold at a giant municipal yard sale.

While the city had suffered a devastating reversal of fortune, I had faith it would come back from the brink bigger and better than ever. Because if it didn't …

On a more positive note, the troubles had not affected our business at all. When I logged into our email, I found some business 'proposals' waiting for our special attention.

It appeared that lots of folks out there still needed killing.

~

It was time for us to go to work again. I opened one of the messages at random. It was from a former client, a well-known restaurateur who appreciated the way in which we had turned his partner into a baked Alaska. He wanted to introduce me to a friend of his, a woman he'd code-named Laura Petrie. She desperately needed our services.

Our clients use the names of television characters from the 60s and 70s. I'd always loved the *Dick Van Dyke Show*, so I decided that was as good a reason as any to give Laura a call and set up a meeting.

It felt nice to be going back to work again after such a long break.

~

I arranged to meet Laura at Cliff Bell's for a drink at 3:30 that afternoon. It was usually crowded but because it was early, we had the place almost to ourselves.

Women who use our services generally act like they've just stepped out of *The Real Housewives of Grand Rapids*. They have one thing on their minds: their domestic situation. Hubby had strayed from the kennel and now they want him put down. Once the life insurance money is collected, they can settle back into their routine of cocktails and shopping. For the most part, I find them dumpy and opinionated.

Laura was neither. She wasn't a stunning *Penthouse* type of beauty, airbrushed tits and ass, but she was beautiful nonetheless. Laura carried the unmistakable feel of some life-altering tragedy. I could see it in her face and in the very slight roll of her shoulders. Still, she was a striking woman and perfectly proportioned.

Little Rip stirred like an Irish Setter at the sound of a bird gun.

Laura nodded when I waved at her from my table in the back. She crossed the room radiating the kind of gloom that would kill house plants. I wondered what it would take to make her smile or, better still, make her scream with passion.

Whatever it is, we're a long way from there.

She sat down but didn't offer me her hand.

Strictly business.

"Our mutual friend said you can kill someone for me."

She didn't mince words or waste time, two qualities I find extremely attractive. Most potential clients danced around the **K** word as if saying it out loud might give them herpes. Not Laura, though. She got right down to it.

Silently I waited for her to continue.

17

She took a photograph from her purse and pushed it across the table. A stern-looking gentleman in his late fifties stared back at me. I felt a twinge. The face was vaguely familiar, I just couldn't remember from where.

"Who is he?"

"My father," she replied.

An inheritance issue.

The last time we'd been hired by a disgruntled heir it had not gone well.

Slipping the photo into my pocket, I smiled reassuringly. "When would you like it done?"

"No, he's not the ..." She shook her head. "He's already dead. He was my father and I want you to kill the person responsible for his death."

A tear was forming in the corner of her eye. I found it alluring. She possessed two things that really turn me on — beauty and an air of tragedy.

"And who might that be?"

The tear let go and trailed down her cheek. "I don't know."

Resisting the impulse to reach over and gently brush away her tear, I took her hand in mine.

She pulled it back. Laura obviously didn't like to be touched.

"I'm sorry, I don't think I can help you. I need an identified target. If you can locate the person responsible, I can do the job.

On the stage, a small jazz quartet was setting up for the evening. I hoped they weren't going to play. It would destroy the intimacy of the moment. Modern jazz is one of my pet hates. To me, it sounds like pointless noodling combined with endless repetition. That leaves me grinding my teeth. It's like being hit over and over by a mink-covered wooden mallet.

Eventually, it actually starts to hurt.

I stood up. "Talk to the police. Maybe they can help."

This, of course, was a useless suggestion. The Detroit PD is so underfunded that half their cars don't have working radios or headlights. If you want justice in Motor City, you have to hire people like us. But while I'm an excellent contract killer, I'm not a detective.

If Laura wanted vengeance, she would have to bring me a target.

Too bad, though. She was an attractive woman and playing white knight for her might have brought me other 'benefits'. She sat there looking fragile and, if I was capable of it, I might have even felt sorry for her. I was impaled on the horns of a dilemma. One part of me wanted to walk away while the most primal part of me wanted to swoop Laura into my arms and become her tool for retribution.

But there was nothing I could do for her. Wilma and I don't have the skill it takes to track down unknown killers.

Laura looked dejected as I walked away.

It was hard to leave her there alone, but I knew if I looked back I would not be able to resist trying to help her.

WELL I'LL BE DIPPED IN DOGSHIT

Since it was nearby, I decided to stroll over to the Fox Theater.

I could lose myself in the crowd while I waited for Wilma. Street crime had become so rampant lately that it was prudent to travel in large groups for safety. Not that I worried about being mugged. But with the cost of bullets being what they are, it's a cheaper alternative.

Outside the Fox, desperate theater goers were trying to score rush seats for that night's performance of *The Book of Mormon*. They had more chance of passing through the eye of a biblical needle.

I called Wilma, who was parked nearby, and waited patiently for her to pick me up.

As she drove me home, I looked at our devastated city — street after street of empty lots, graffiti-decorated warehouses, and bombed out factories. Detroit now looked like post-war Tokyo.

When Laura had left the club, Wilma snapped a few close-ups with her trusty Nikon. I took the camera and looked at Laura's face once again. I saw the trail her tears had left.

"It sounds like you had an emotional encounter," Wilma said brightly.

I shook my head. "She was looking for Sam Spade."

Wilma nodded in understanding. "So who's next on the list?"

"Jethro Bodine," I replied.

While *The Beverly Hillbillies* was not as intelligent or urbane as *Dick Van Dyke*, that show always made me laugh, especially the antics of Jethro, that loveable lamebrain with the goofy grin.

Our Jethro was having an issue with his next door neighbor who had a big dog that liked to shit on his roses. He wanted us to send Rover and the owner to doggie heaven.

Whoever said our work was all glitz and glamor.

"I'll call him in the morning."

~

Wilma's condo on the river was outfitted with a kitchen that Gordon Ramsey would have been comfortable in. Tonight she was cooking her famous smothered pork chops. The fragrance of caramelizing onions was almost sexual in its intensity.

We rarely hung out together when we weren't working, but I was still shaken by my Swiss Miss adventure and asked if she'd cook dinner.

She'd given me one of those new ice tea flavored beers. It had a subtle bouquet of elephant piss, with just the right note of rotting garbage. After two sips, I poured it down the drain and looked around for somewhere to bury the bottle. Grabbing a Michelob from the fridge, I swallowed half of it in one gulp just to kill the taste.

Standing in the kitchen doorway, I wondered if this was what *ordinary* domestic life was like.

Wilma poured a stream of heavy cream into the pan. The sight of it set off the juices in my mouth. She swirled the cream into the onions with the assured confidence of a cook who could debone a leg of lamb with the same ease that she could arc-weld a victim's legs to a steel girder.

"Did Laura share any details about her father's murder?"

"I didn't let her get that far. It was a lost cause."

She smiled and pointed to Little Rip with her spatula. "Nice to see you resisted temptation for once."

Frowning, I remembered that I hadn't given Laura back her photo. I took it out of my pocket. Laura's dad stared at me disapprovingly.

Damn, he looks familiar.

I *had* seen him somewhere.

"She wanted us to find and kill whoever handled her father's death."

Wilma glanced at the photo. "Well, that should be easy enough."

"No, it isn't. We're not detectives."

"We don't have to be. All we need to do is look in the mirror."

Taking a closer look, I got what she meant.

Flipping through the tattered pages of *Rip and Wilma's Greatest Hits*, I found Laura's father.

No wonder the picture was familiar.

The last time I'd seen him, his face was contorted in terror.

Holding up my index finger in what I hoped was a Sherlockian gesture, I frowned.

"The Judge."

Wilma nodded.

~

It had been three years ago on a cold winter evening outside the State House in Lansing when we'd last seen Laura's father, Judge Walter Armstrong. At that time, he was no longer a judge, after having been elected as a state senator. We'd been hired to kill him as revenge for a client who had suffered an unusually severe sentence when Armstrong was still judging.

Our client only had two stipulations in our contract: it had to be painful and it had to be messy. We made sure it was both. His death made headlines for a few days before being chased off the front page by a scandal involving an aide to the governor and some boy scout diddling.

The Judge disappeared into our extensive portfolio of successful business projects. I tried to remember who'd hired us to do the Judge, but couldn't. Too bad I didn't keep notes on that sort of thing.

But that would be insanely imprudent.

My thoughts turned again to Laura and her desperation to find and bring vengeance upon her father's killers. Most of all, I remembered the tight sweater she had been wearing.

What would she have thought if she knew that one of her father's killers had been sitting right across the table from her?

That little piece of knowledge wouldn't have helped my chances in the romance department.

Oh, the irony.

And then a Grinch-like idea began to form in the back of my mind. It was born of lust. Laura's fragility and vulnerability had aroused something inside me.

What was it that the late Dr. Vessier had told me?

I am a man who operates outside of boundaries.

"We should try to help Laura." I drew the words out slowly like it was a developing thought.

Wilma looked at me like I'd just pissed on her pork chops which, by the way, smelled delicious.

"Sure. Why don't you two go out for a drink? You can just blow your brains out in front of her."

Wilma could be unduly harsh sometimes.

"No, hear me out on this. She wants us to find the person responsible for her father's death."

"Yes, and that would be us."

"But we're only the *instrument* of destruction, the *weapon*. Someone else was *responsible* for pulling the trigger."

"Don't confuse semantics with ethics," Wilma said. "We were hired to do a job for a client who trusted us to get it done with no blowback."

"But we don't have a rule that says once the job is finished we can't be hired to kill *that* client."

Wilma scowled and shook her head. "There is no rule for that. It's common sense. We don't bite the hand that feeds us. It would be bad for business if we got a reputation for double-dipping and offering our services to our victim's grieving friends and family."

She had a point. I tried to think of a counter argument. Wilma could tell I was reaching.

Menace slipped into her voice. "You're not going to let it go are you?"

"But what if we were lied to by our client when we were contracted?"

"I don't care. We were hired to do a job. We did it. They paid us in full. End of story."

End of story.

Prophetic words indeed. It would have been better to let it go at that point and move on to the neighbor and his shitting dog.

But I didn't.

And that was a huge mistake.

~

Instead, I got busy over the next few days. Jethro's problem was an easy one to resolve. We made it look like his neighbor had slipped on his dog's shit while out walking the pooch. The poor man broke his neck in the process. The incident went to the top of the *Weird Death of the Week* column in many national newspapers. There was even a human interest angle when his kindly neighbor offered to adopt his grieving Doberman.

Cha-ching!

While the doggie and his master had been a distraction, I was still obsessed with playing hero for the Judge's daughter.

If I helped her, it would go one of two ways. Laura would either fall into my arms and let her father's avenger ravish her. Or, she would think of me as the foul creature she'd hired to avenge her father's death which would haunt her forever.

Guilt can be a bastard.

I'm happy I don't suffer from it.

Straining my memory, I tried to remember the circumstances of the Judge's death. Vague recollections of the person who contracted us swam deep below me. I attempted to draw them closer to the surface.

Fuck it. Just leave it alone.

This itch was quickly becoming an obsession, so to distract myself I turned to the more practical matter of moving canine carnage money to my offshore account. After spending a few delightful minutes online reviewing my deposits, I saw how my balance had ballooned from nearly nothing six months before to a healthy seven-figures.

Suddenly I had a thought — if I checked *when* I'd deposited the money for the Judge's contract, it might jog my memory. From the newspaper stories, I knew the date we had killed the Judge. Once I had the date, I tried to recall what else we had been up to around that time.

Then in a blazing red flash, it all came back to me and I realized we could go after the Judge's killer without violating our Code of Ethics.

~

"We didn't get paid in full."

Wilma looked at me skeptically and paused.

It wasn't often we were stiffed by a client and when we were, we usually ended up making them a stiff.

This one, sadly, had gotten away.

"Eddie Haskell," Wilma said the name like she had just sniffed a turd.

We had spent time trying to trace him, but he'd dropped out of sight. I couldn't remember the client who'd referred him, just that he'd been really scared and had offered to pay the outstanding balance.

While that was very noble, we just let it drop and chalked Eddie up as an uncollectable debt.

It drove me crazy that I couldn't remember the client who recommended Eddie.

Our business is a chain. One customer recommends us to the next and so on. Eddie Haskell had referred someone to us, and I remembered we'd demanded 75% up front because of the Eddie connection. After all, we didn't want to get a reputation as pushovers.

I tried to recall who the referral was but came up empty. All I remembered was the job was smooth and we were paid in full. Eddie's lack of payment had changed Wilma's attitude toward ethics.

Killing Eddie would satisfy two debts.

"How are we going to find him?"

It would take time and a lot of effort but, what the hell, our pride was a stake. No one could make suckers out of us. Plus there was another consideration. We weren't the only contract killers in the yellow pages and Laura would likely turn to one of our competitors to get satisfaction.

That would not be good because they would come after us.

We had to locate and kill Eddie Haskell.

It would not be easy, but I had a plan.

A VISIT TO SANTA'S WORKSHOP

As I mentioned, false identities play an important part in our business.

They protect our clients and, more importantly, they protect us. A client expects anonymity and so do we. False IDs ensure this. If sometime later the customer has buyer's remorse or a severe case of conscience and confesses, there's no way they can lead the cops to us.

To make it even safer, Wilma never meets clients face-to-face. That's my responsibility. I sit down with the customer to get the details and collect the initial payment. When the job is completed, I pick up the balance. My client meetings are typically short and to the point, and are always conducted in public places.

I have what cheap fiction calls *an average face*. Two minutes after you meet me, you'd have a hard time describing exactly what I look like. I use particular mannerisms to draw attention away from my face, and being able to vary the pitch of my voice also helps.

Security cameras, however, cannot be so easily deceived. The post 9/11 spread of CCTV in public places has become the bane of our existence. We'd already made a guest appearance on CNN when one of our projects went slightly awry. Luckily, the footage was too blurry to make out many details. But digital surveillance technology was getting better every day.

We need to continuously stay ahead of the curve.

Detroit is full of inventors and engineers. This town was built on innovations of men like Henry Ford.

Maker Faire, a kind of crazed science fair on steroids, is held every year in Dearborn. I'd spent an entire day there a few years ago. That's when I met Steve Carlson. He was demonstrating a miniature working model of a

V-8 engine he'd built from scratch. During our casual conversation, I got a distinct feeling Steve was corruptible.

~

A few days after we met at Maker Faire, Steve invited me to his secret lair in a loft just off the Eastern Market. It was like visiting Santa's Workshop, or Q Branch in the James Bond films.

Steve had been an engineer with GM for forty years and had worked on all kinds of special projects, including one where they were developing a stealth option for the Corvette to make it invisible to police radar. Unfortunately, it never made it to market.

When he retired, Steve decided to supplement his GM pension by meeting the needs of an elite group of customers.

Over the past few years, he cooked up a few things for us, including a device that overrode the onboard computer in a target's Lexus. It allowed me to stop the car and lock its doors at a level crossing, which was unfortunate for the loan shark inside. A speeding Amtrak train turned him into turkey stuffing.

Several months ago I'd complained about the CCTV issue. Steve gleefully mentioned he had a solution. It was simple, efficient, and quite elegant — a device, designed to be worn as a necklace. It was made of LEDs that put out infrared light which turned the wearer's head into a glowing sphere when viewed by a security camera.

When I put one on and looked at the result on a monitor, I was shocked. From the neck down, I was me. But from the shoulders up, I resembled *Little Helper*, the robot assistant with the light bulb head from the old *Gyro Gearloose* Comics.

It was a practical solution to our CCTV dilemma.

~

I was wearing Steve's LED invention when I met Laura in the lobby of the Guardian Building.

"What made you change your mind?"

We were standing there like tourists who were admiring the domed ceiling and chatting casually.

I didn't really have an answer to that question so I just winged it. "Your story moved me. It bothered me that I couldn't help you."

Laura looked at me.

I melted and Little Rip took over like a horny autopilot. I had a hard time focusing on the conversation.

"My father was a decent man who never hurt anyone."

She slipped me a thick envelope. From its girth, I could tell there was $25,000 in it. This was the down payment to seal our deal.

Sneaking a look at her tight purple turtleneck, I hoped this job would come with extra dividends.

"What happens now?"

"I get to work and find your father's killer."

"Do you give me updates or something?"

"It's better we keep contact to a bare minimum. I'll let you know when I've located the person responsible and then you can decide how you'd like me to proceed."

"I've already decided. Why do you think I contacted you?"

From the bitterness in her voice, I knew what she had in mind but I asked anyway. "How would you like it done?"

Laura looked up at the tiled ceiling far above. "Come up with something creative. And I have to be there when you do it."

"Sorry," I said. "It doesn't work like that. I don't run excursions. It complicates things."

She considered this and then reluctantly nodded.

"When it's done, I'd be happy to take a picture for you," I added as consolation.

Laura looked like she was going to cry again.

"Thanks," she said gratefully.

~

A few minutes later, Wilma and I were zooming up Michigan Avenue. She ignored a series of broken traffic lights.

Someone had been stripping the signals of their copper wires and the city didn't have the money to replace them. The police suggested we treat any intersection with non-working lights as a four-way stop. This, however, was just a suggestion and was virtually ignored by most of the anarchists who regularly braved driving in downtown Detroit.

The only rule that applied when approaching an intersection was Darwin's *Survival of the Fittest.*

Wilma had a method to her crazed driving. She was trying to beat the lunchtime rush at Slows Bar-B-Q.

We got our orders and settled in at a table in the back. Wilma looked at my Triple Threat Pork sandwich and frowned.

"Maybe you should cut back a little on the calories," she suggested.

Defiantly, I took a massive bite of bacon, pulled pork, and ham and let the sauce dribble down my chin.

"Disgusting," she muttered and took a dainty bite of her *Yardbird* sandwich.

Wilma did have a point about cutting back on the calories, though. Europe had not been good for me in that respect. Normally I'm a pretty active guy but during the months at Monique's clinic, I'd resisted all desire to work out. Plus I'd gobbled down all those sausages, cheeses, and pastries. The net result had been a thirty-pound weight gain.

Wilma, on the other hand, was in great shape. She followed a religious regimen of exercise and diet to keep fit and trim.

From the look of disgust on her face, I could tell what she was thinking. She didn't need a fat slob slowing her down. If we found ourselves in a situation where we were being chased and I was puffing along behind her struggling to catch up, she would turn around and put a bullet between my eyes.

"How are we going to find the guy who hired us to do the Judge?" she asked between nibbles.

Poking petulantly at my *Triple Threat* I struggled with the desire to wolf the whole thing down.

"We'll find him by going backward."

"That should be fun, considering our clients use fake names."

But a celebrity can't hide behind a false ID.

BLESS ME FATHER,
FOR I HAVE SINNED

Ste. Anne de Detroit is the oldest church in the city and was established just a couple of days after they began construction of Fort Ponchartrain in 1701.

Over the years, the church had been built, destroyed, and built again. It now stands in the shadow of the Ambassador Bridge.

I'm not a religious person, but I do know how to play one. I made a reasonable approximation of crossing myself as I entered the sanctuary and then headed for one of the confessionals along the side.

Monsignor David Blake heard my confession.

"Bless me, Father, for I have sinned."

"How have you sinned, my son?"

"I took another man's life at the request of a grasping toady of a parish priest who wanted to move up the chain of command."

A sharp intake of breath was followed by a long pause.

"Aren't you going to give me my penance, Father? Don't I have to make a Hail Mary pass or something?"

~

Monsignor Blake had contracted us when he was still Father David, a low-level functionary in the diocese. He lusted after higher office in the church. We helped him out when a bishop's position was up for grabs. It was a rather convoluted scenario involving Wilma dressed as an alluring altar boy and ended with his chief rival re-enacting the martyrdom of Saint Sebastian.

I certainly improved my crossbow skills that day.

Several former altar boys were taken in for questioning, although Fox News speculated it may have been radical Muslims. In the end, it was tossed, along with thousands of other cases, on the growing stack of the Detroit police's unsolved crimes.

~

Monsignor Blake wasn't happy to see me, and I couldn't blame him. No one wants a ghost from the past rudely intruding on their path to the Vatican. He was very upset with me and the circumstances of my visit. From the stench, I gathered he was treating the confessional as his own personal outhouse.

I decided to not keep him in suspense.

"Listen, Dave, what we did is all water under the bridge. Don't worry, I'm not here to blackmail you or anything like that. Your past sins are *your* past sins. But I need to know who you referred to us after our little mission on your behalf."

There was an even longer silence.

"This is the last you'll ever hear from me. I just need that name. There'll be no blowback on you. I promise."

I could feel him shaking through the wall between us. I wasn't sure if it was from fear or anger.

Finally, he blurted out the name. I went cold.

The name was familiar to me.

~

"Bobby Barbarra," Wilma repeated.

"Yup. Ain't that something."

I tried to remember what false name Barbarra had used. I thought it might have been Boo-Boo Bear. I also couldn't remember who we'd rubbed out for Barbarra. After a while, details like this tend to blur.

Barbarra, as they say, was *all mobbed up*.

We try to avoid mob hits if at all possible. They tend to attract a lot of unwanted Federal attention. But we'd obviously done something for Barbarra at the recommendation of Monsignor Blake. Not that it really mattered anymore. It was all ravioli down the river since Barbarra himself had been whacked a few months ago.

He'd been sitting in his Cadillac on Grand River sipping a Slurpee. Someone rode up on a motorcycle and put six shots in his head, leaving a big hole in the structure of Detroit's underworld. The void had been neatly filled by Joey Rizzolio, Barbarra's second in command, who then ascended to the top of the heap and now ruled what was left of the city's mafia kingdom.

"Why don't we see if Joey knows who Barbarra recommended us to."

That idea had about as much appeal to me as sticking my hand in a bear trap. While the old-time mob had faded over the years, they could still be nasty if poked.

"The last thing I want is to be beholden to Joey Rizzolio," I argued.

"And what's the worst thing he could ask of us in return? Kill someone for him?"

She had a point. If he did ask us to kill someone, I would just double our usual fee and then offer him a fifty percent discount out of respect. Mob guys love to be respected. It makes them feel all warm and fuzzy.

Dealing with made men has other benefits as well. They still have a modicum of honor, which I find charming, especially these days with all the thieving politicians and hedge fund managers out there.

Plus most of them are excellent cooks.

~

We didn't have to track down Joey Rizzolio. He held court at a private table in the back of an Italian restaurant near the Eastern Market. The place had a long history in the annals of the Detroit mob. Al Capone even ate there when he visited our fair city back in the 1930s.

It's never a good idea for a total stranger to approach a mob boss's table in a restaurant. They tend to be a little touchy about that sort of thing. It's an easy way to get shot by jumpy bodyguards.

There is a certain etiquette to meeting mobsters. It needs to be done in a very specific way.

Luckily, I knew a guy who knew a guy who knew a guy who knew Joey Rizzolio. I asked my guy to speak to *his* guy to see if *his* guy could talk to Rizzolio about a meet. It took a couple of days to set up. All this back and forth can be time-consuming, but I was finally invited to sit with him at his table.

~

"This is the best fucking olive oil in the world," Rizzolio told me as he ripped a loaf of bread in half and dipped it into the plate in front of him. I thought about commenting on stereotypes, but he was having such a good time playing mob boss to the hilt, I decided to stay silent.

"So, Rip," he laughed as he stretched my name out savoring its absurdity.

The apes sitting on either side of him joined in his laughter. They apparently found my name amusing and I let it go. My name was a good icebreaker. The humor it provoked would disarm them and make them feel superior. Maybe they wouldn't take me too seriously, which was fine with me. I didn't want them to feel I was a threat in any way.

Rizzolio was wearing a $5,000 suit. I loved the fabric but hated the double-breasted cut. The tailoring made him look six feet wide, which I guess was the effect he was going for.

Mob life had obviously been good to him. He had six more chins than either of his bodyguards, both of whom looked like prime contestants on *Extreme Weight Loss*.

I wondered if their layers of fat might act as natural body armor.

Even with my recently gained pounds, I felt svelte next to them.

Rizzolio dabbed his oil-coated fingers on a napkin and motioned to the waiter. "Double order of Spaghetti a la Roma for the twins, and I'll have a Veal Scaloppine a la Tosca."

He didn't bother to ask me if I was hungry, which was just as well. I didn't want to spend any more time with them than was absolutely necessary. The food arrived within five minutes and they spent another five slurping it down.

I drank a glass of Chianti while trying to avoid the constant spray of tomato sauce and meatballs.

When he was finished, Rizzolio pushed his plate away. "So what the fuck can I do for you?"

"I don't know if you remember me from a few years ago, but I did a little favor for your predecessor Mr. Barbarra."

At the mention of Barbarra's name the bodyguards laughed. It was a grunting sound that reminded me of the Vienna Boar's Choir.

Rizzolio's eyes narrowed. He shook his head thoughtfully, pretending he had brains.

"I remember you. You're the one who put Gato in his grinder."

And it all came flooding back to me — Gato Tapanari and his meat packing plant. We'd dressed in butchers' clothing for the occasion. He'd gotten on Barbarra's bad side over some unpaid gambling debts. Wilma deboned him and we turned him into sausage meat which, I believe, was sold in excellent butcher shops around the mid-west.

"That's right," I replied.

He looked at me with respect and the two apes stopped snickering at my name.

"My business works on referrals. I know that Mr. Barbarra referred us to someone else, someone who didn't have the sense of honor that you do."

Rizzolio remained impassive.

"He did not meet his full obligation to me, and now I must seek him out and ask for restitution."

I felt like a character from *The Godfather*.

"I might be able to help you with your obligation," he whispered.

I knew what was coming

"But ..."

And he explained what he needed from me.

HE GIVES PSYCHOPATHS A BAD NAME

Wilma laughed when I told her, but it wasn't a happy laugh; it was a weary one.

"How do you manage to take a simple task like a contract killing and turn it into such a complicated thing?"

I had just finished explaining about Joey Rizzolio's *little* problem.

"Tommy Souer?" she laughed again at the mere mention of his name and then repeated it once more in case she hadn't heard me correctly.

~

In the somewhat tiny community of Motown contract killers, Tommy Souer was well known. In fact, he gave psychopaths a bad name. As a hit man, he'd always been out of control and wildly undisciplined. There was no subtlety to Souer. He was a full-on, blunt-force trauma. With each killing, he got loonier. Finally, he went completely over the edge and was now certifiably batshit crazy.

Since no one would hire him anymore, he went on a personal vendetta against the 'powers of oppression'. Souer became a one-man death squad.

The previous summer he rode his bicycle past a sidewalk café in St. Clair Shores and mowed down six patrons with a machine pistol. Later that same week, he dropped a hand grenade through the open moon roof of a Bentley Continental while it was stuck in downtown traffic. The grenade went off in the lap of a software executive. Another time he stole a live cobra out of the Detroit Zoo and set it loose in one of the downtown hotels. His piece de la résistance, however, was poisoning a keg of beer in one of the private boxes at a Tigers game. That one killed the top traders of the city's leading investment firm.

If it had been any place other than Detroit, Souer would have been apprehended within fifteen minutes. But our Keystone Kops couldn't even get a solid lead on his whereabouts. In the meantime, his stunts just got wilder and weirder. Eyewitnesses said he even cackled like a Batman villain.

In the past, when Souer was still mostly sane, he'd done a lot of work for the mob. I suspected turning Bobby Barbarra into mush was included. But now he'd become a big-time liability for them. The mob needed Souer gone, along with the heat he was bringing down on them.

Tommy Souer was the type of target we hated the most — unpredictable. Before he went completely round the bend, he'd been a very resourceful and ruthless killer.

And that made him an extremely dangerous adversary.

~

"He's attempting to make a warped political statement, isn't he," Wilma said.

Souer was a man with a mission — to scare the living shit out of the privileged class. He appeared out of nowhere, did his mischief, and then disappeared back into the woodwork.

How the fuck were we going to catch him?

Just thinking about it made my ears buzz.

"Where the hell do we even begin to search for him?" she asked.

"We don't. We make him come to us."

~

The Motor Industry Ball was the social event of the fall season. The guest list included only the absolute cream of the city's movers and shakers. It was being held at Cobo Hall in a week and would make a target too tempting for Tommy Souer to resist.

While Wilma and I were technically millionaires now, we were nowhere near the social strata eligible for an invite to this soirée. We did, however, have a slight edge that might get us invited.

~

Our good friend Promod Sharma had recently moved out to a building in Troy where he was sandwiched between a gynecology clinic and a firm of litigation lawyers. On the surface, Promod appeared to be a high-end insurance broker but his real bread and butter came from his talent as the world's preeminent computer hacker. He started out as one of our satisfied customers and quickly became a valuable resource. Promod was one of the few people who knew about our dirty little business. In fact, he knew most of our secrets.

At one point, after he'd betrayed us, we'd thought of killing him, but decided to keep him alive.

That's how talented he is.

Promod blanched when he saw us in the anteroom of his elegant new office and shook his head. "Whatever it is, the answer is *no*."

The last time we'd seen him, he wasn't looking so hale and hearty. He was in the intensive care unit at Henry Ford Hospital after being stabbed in both lungs. He looked much better now, especially since he'd lost sixty pounds due to hospital cuisine.

"You can't say *'no'* to us." Wilma flashed a sardonic smile.

His eyes widened with fear.

Wilma had taken his treachery very personally. She'd really liked him. Not that Wilma exactly *liked* anyone. She had tolerated Promod because she respected his unique talent. Now she would be happy to turn him into Kibbles 'n Bits and feed him to a hungry St. Bernard.

I didn't really care. I was more reasonable. Plus having Promod in our bullpen was expedient. Like right now when we needed his expertise.

I sat down and Wilma stood behind me glaring at Promod. I smiled in a vain attempt to lighten the mood.

There is nothing uglier than a betrayed woman.

"This is a friendly visit ..."

Promod leaned forward. "I thought you guys never wanted to see me again."

"Well, it's true we were a little upset about that unpleasantness last time, but let bygones be bygones I always say."

I don't always say that. In fact, the idea of an un-avenged double-cross is abhorrent to me, but saying it to Promod made him relax a little.

"So what do you guys want from me now?" Caginess crept back into his voice.

I smiled. This was the old Promod we knew and loved, always searching for an angle that would benefit him. Even after he'd turned on us and almost gotten himself killed, he still had the audacity to ask for a share of our windfall. He wasn't content that we had left him alive.

"Nothing too difficult," I explained. "We need to get onto the guest list for the Motor Industry Ball next week."

"That's impossible," he gulped. "They vet the hell out of that list. The planning committee knows every invitee personally. I could get you into the Rose Garden at the White House easier than I could do this."

Wilma took a Bowie knife from her purse.

Promod looked at it in alarm.

"I don't care if you have to blow everyone on that committee." Wilma's words were carefully measured. "Use your skills and get us on that list."

The threat was palpable and hung in the air like a ripe fart.

I changed the subject. "So, what have you been up to?"

Promod squirmed a bit, reluctant to talk about his new enterprise, but eyed Wilma's knife warily and said, "I've worked out a way to scam a clearing house." His eyes gleamed with malfeasant joy.

For the next ten minutes, he explained about moving fractions of percentages of basis points over hundreds of millions of transactions. It was complicated and we didn't really understand most of what he said, except when he got to the bottom line. He had amassed $20 million in three months.

The scam would run for another month and then shut down. In the unlikely event a snoopy auditor ever discovered his scam, the trail would be cold and the amount of loss to each individual company so tiny they wouldn't be motivated to pursue it. They would just tighten up whatever loophole he'd found and move on.

Even though Promod had made a lot of money, I was confident he would continue to help us with our *special* projects. He was motivated by more than money.

Impossible challenges inspired him.

Promod finally got back to our problem of how to get into the Motor Industry Ball.

"Let me work on this for a few days. I'll try to come up with something."

Wilma put her hunting knife away, and I got up and shook his hand.

~

"I need a drink," I told Wilma when we were back in the car.

I was tense after our meeting with Promod and didn't know why. I had the unsettling feeling we were getting in too deep. One impossible thing was piling up on the next and it was becoming too complicated. My thoughts led me back to Laura and her tight turtleneck sweater.

Little Rip reminded me that I had not given him a workout since Interlaken.

"Drop me off at the Motor City Casino."

The Radio Bar would be quiet at this time of day and chances were good it would be filled with lady conventioneers out for a jolly time.

PEACH PIES AND MINT JULEPS

I found a table as far from the noise of the gaming floor as possible and ordered a salad, with a double gin Martini on the side.

While I waited, I looked around the place like a lion surveying the savannah. There were a couple of gazelles sitting at the bar and they weren't bad looking. The turn-off for me was that one had an annoying bray of a laugh and the other snorted along in unison. In my experience, women in pairs were usually hard to pick up and this duo looked like they had been drinking for a while. A woman sat alone at the other end of the bar, elegantly dressed and radiating sophistication. I figured she was a high-class hooker. I passed on her as well.

Then my perfect prey entered and looked around. She headed for a table near me. I presumed she wanted to get away from the din of the casino as well. She was a striking ginger who was maybe an inch or two taller than me. She picked up the menu and looked perturbed as if nothing captured her fancy.

Gazing at her, I became deeply entangled in a fantasy where she and I were recreating the Battle of Vicksburg. It was an odd thing to imagine, but I went with it anyway.

I tried to catch her eye by shifting in my chair but that didn't work.

She closed the menu and signaled for the waiter. I detected the honey dulcet tones of a Southern accent when she spoke.

I decided right then she was going to be my entertainment for the afternoon.

Once the waiter left, I got up and crossed to her table. I deliberately did not sit down but stood a respectful distance so she wouldn't feel threatened.

"Excuse me. You aren't from Atlanta by any chance, are you?"

Large, liquid green eyes looked up at me. She smiled.

Ahhhhh those southern gals.

"No, I'm not. I'm from South Carolina."

South Carolina?

I tried to remember something conversational about the state.

"From Charleston," she added.

I remembered why I love southern women — they're so open and friendly. They haven't developed the hard cynicism of their northern cousins.

It must be all those peach pies and Mint Juleps.

Since I knew nothing about Charleston, I cast around for a safe topic and decided on that old reliable, the weather.

"You must find it cold up here then." I casually slipped into the chair across from her.

"Yes, it's freezing. Is it always like this?"

"Well, it warms up a bit in July and August, but most of the time we shiver."

Her laugh was the tinkling of a crystal wind chime.

"I hope you don't mind if I join you," I added as an afterthought.

"Not at all. My name is Mandy Shugar."

She extended a hand. I wasn't sure if I should shake it or kiss it. I opted for a firm handshake.

I would save the kissing for later.

"Rip? I knew a boy named Rip once upon a time. He used to come up from Savannah and take out my older sister Charlotte." Her face clouded. "Poor boy, he was killed in a terrible tractor accident." Then she smiled again and I melted.

Little Rip was singing *Sweet Home Alabama* at the top of his lungs.

If I played my cards right, it was going to be a beautiful day.

~

We spent a relaxing lunch together making casual conversation. Every word bathed me in sweet syrup.

The south was more formal and there was a certain etiquette for relations between men and women.

Must be all that old time religion.

And bourbon.

41

All was prim and proper above the table, but down below Mandy's shoeless foot slid seductively along the inside of my thigh. Her dexterous toes gripped Little Rip in a most provocative and forward manner while she smiled sweetly and carried on a leisurely conversation. Below the Mason-Dixon Line, things were coming to a head so to speak. Before it got too far out of hand — or foot — I put some cash on the table and we rushed to her room.

~

Mandy was a regular polecat and I soon discovered the real meaning of eat a peach.

She must have been in a major sex drought because she couldn't get enough. When she was mostly sated, I rested my head on her belly and took a few minutes to catch my breath.

"Oh, darlin', you are so good," she drawled seductively.

That made me feel special, even though I figured she probably used that line on every lover she'd ever had.

I watched her breasts rise and fall and couldn't resist the temptation to reach up and squeeze one of her nipples. She moaned with a distinctive southern drawl and pushed my face down.

The North shall rise again!

~

Two days and eight room service meals later, I managed to surface for air. I can't believe I'm saying this, but I'd had enough sex.

Thank God Mandy had a convention to attend. She was a tourism marketing executive for the city of Charleston.

When I finally found my cell phone tucked between the pillows, there were over a hundred missed calls. Most of them from Wilma.

I promised Mandy we would hook up for her last night in town on Friday evening. She was flying back to Charleston first thing Saturday morning.

Little Rip was in a coma but I had every confidence he would struggle back to life by Friday.

He was a trooper.

COSTCO

"Have a nice time?" Wilma asked.

If she was pissed off, she didn't show it.

"Very nice, thank you."

We had an open partnership and occasionally found ourselves in bed together. Our sexual relationship was mostly to scratch an itch. Long ago she'd accepted my hyper sex drive. It didn't bother her unless my libido threatened to get us into trouble. My last three relationships had gotten us into such deep shit that Wilma tended to take an interest in *who* I was sleeping with.

"A southern belle?" she snorted.

Wilma banged on the horn. "Fucker!" she screamed at the pickup truck that cut us off.

She's a very aggressive driver. I, on the other hand, liked to let things roll off my back. Not Wilma though. Several times I'd had to restrain her from shooting other drivers who'd pissed her off.

We were on our way to see Promod. It was early evening and I-75 was clogged with office workers trying to escape from downtown before it got dark and the zombies came out.

Wilma struggled to get her anger under control.

"I hope this isn't going to take too long," she snapped. "I have to get to Costco before they close. I need toilet paper."

~

Since Wilma usually went to the store in Novi, I was hoping she would drop me off at my place on the way back instead of forcing me to endure another trip to Costco.

I discovered shopping at Costco is a religious experience for Wilma when I made the mistake of going with her one time. It had taken half the day. She pushed her cart slowly through the store examining every item. When she was finished, I had to rent a cube van to take her purchases home.

The spare bedroom in her condo is filled with gigantic packages of coffee, bottled water, mixed nuts, and Corn Flakes. Her freezer is crammed with double cut pork chops, submarine-sized beef tenderloins, and boxes of jalapeno poppers.

~

Promod sat behind his desk with a smug look on his face. I knew he'd been successful in getting us into the Motor Industry Ball.

"Like I told you, it was impossible to get you on the guest list. It's just too incestuous."

Wilma started to reach into her purse.

Promod held up his hand. "I did the next best thing, however. I got you security accreditation for the event. With all those rich folks and that crazy guy running around, it was relatively straightforward. You're official representatives of WR Security Consultants LLC assigned to provide personal protection for a group of high-ranking General Motors executives."

He gave us a pair of very official looking laminated passes with our pictures on them. I didn't bother to ask where he got the photos.

"It's formal dress, so break out your best party clothes." He adjusted his tie. "Now if that's everything, my wife is waiting dinner for me."

I took the passes and shook his hand.

"I won't be seeing you guys again soon, will I?" he asked hopefully.

Wilma flashed an evil smile. "I don't see any reason why you should."

Unless you fuck us over again.

~

Promod walked us to the parking lot and we stopped next to his car.

He was now driving a Bentley Continental, which was quite a step up from the Lexus he used to have.

I admired the car's sleek lines, leather seats, and walnut trim. "Nice."

"Yeah, I got a real deal on it last fall. It'd been in a small accident or something."

I looked more closely. The burn marks and blood stains were barely noticeable.

~

Wilma dropped me off and with a crazed look in her eyes headed to Costco where she would fit right in with the other shoppers.

Since I hadn't been home much lately, I decided to order pizza, put my feet up, and watch TV. But I found it difficult to relax. I was restless and uneasy as if someone was watching me.

I went into my study and checked the security cameras concealed outside. Everything looked fine, but this didn't ease my concern. The house was a secure fortress with steel shutters, armor plating in the walls, and bullet-proof glass that would block anything short of a tank round. And still I felt vulnerable.

I still had the unshakeable feeling something bad was relentlessly bearing down on me.

Wilma was the one who usually had this kind of feeling. She referred to it as her *spidey sense* and it had saved our asses on more than one occasion.

What was bothering me?

Mandy Shugar!

Usually, a good bout of old-fashioned sex clears my head but, if anything, my tryst with Mandy left me feeling more uneasy than before.

Now that Little Rip wasn't doing the thinking, I realized Mandy had fallen into my arms *too* quickly. I was charming, but not *that* charming. Logic would have told me Mandy was just a little too accommodating.

I called the hotel and discovered she'd checked out.

Something dead sloshed in the pit of my stomach.

A quick Google search showed there was no phone number or address for Mandy Shugar in Charleston, or anywhere else for that matter. I checked their tourist association website. Mandy wasn't listed there either.

She was a ghost.

I hoped she wouldn't come back to haunt me.

But I feared she would.

MOTOR CITY MADMAN

I was genuinely perplexed.

I thought about calling Wilma to see what she thought of Mandy's subterfuge but decided that might not be a good idea. Wilma's paranoia would likely boil over and she'd want to go to ground while we figured out what was going on. And if we did that, I would never be able to play avenger for Laura Petrie and have her fall into my arms.

It is important to keep one's priorities straight.

~

There was much to do before the big night.

To make an impression at the Motor Industry Ball, I would have to rent a tuxedo, an elegant one like James Bond would wear and not some powder blue monstrosity that would be embarrassing at a senior prom. A Paul Smith number would have just the right air of casualness yet make a powerful statement. And it was the kind of thing the hired help would wear.

I showed the tailor my security credentials and asked him to let out the left side just a little to allow for my *special* equipment. I touched the area under my arm and he got the point.

~

"If we couldn't get on the guest list, there's no chance that Tommy Souer could either. That means he'll show up as one of the hired help, like a cook or a waiter." I'd been giving it some thought and even Wilma was impressed.

"But we have no idea what he looks like."

"That's right, but I know someone who does."

~

Joey Rizollio was in his secret hideout, still flanked by the two sides of beef he called his bodyguards.

The hideout was upstairs in a strip mall in Plymouth. From the outside, it looked shabby and threadbare, the kind of place an accountant with a gambling problem might use. On the inside, it was all expensive wood paneling and leather furniture.

Rizollio was fluorescent red from exercising on his stationary bike. He looked like he was about to pop a head gasket.

He mopped his face with a stained towel and slumped into his massive chair. "A fucking description of Souer?" he repeated. "He looks like a cock-sucking weasel. Does that paint a picture for you?"

I didn't dwell on the image that popped into my head.

"Looking like a cock-sucking weasel isn't going to help me pick him out in a crowd, especially at the Motor Industry Ball. Everyone there will look like that."

Rizollio laughed and opened one of his desk drawers. He rooted around until he found what he was looking for. He pulled out a file, slapped it on the desk, and flipped it open. While his hands were as large as catcher's mitts, he had incredible dexterity. He plucked out a page and passed it across to me. It was a blurry photo of a man.

"My security camera takes pictures of everyone coming in and out of this place."

I was glad I'd put on my garland of infrared diodes before dropping in on Rizollio. When he got around to looking at my picture, he would have a bit of a surprise.

I looked down at Souer's picture and smiled. He really *did* look like a cock-sucking weasel. His eyes were set tight against a blade of a nose that had one of those bulbs on the tip. It might have been cute when he was a kid, but now just made him look freakish.

We would have no problem picking him out in a crowd.

"Can I get a copy of this?" I asked politely.

Rizollio passed it to Thing One who silently crossed to a color copier and made me a print.

When I showed the picture to Wilma later, she just said, "Yikes!"

~

The big evening finally arrived and we headed for Cobo Hall dressed to the nines and armed to the teeth.

"We need to get him quickly because whatever he's planning, it's going to be nasty and we don't want to get caught in the crossfire."

Wilma's sleek black number seductively adhered to her curves. I wondered where she'd stashed her gun. Mine, a Kimber .45, was tucked safely in a form-fitting shoulder holster. The tailor had done excellent work on the tux jacket and the bulge didn't show.

Wilma and I flashed our credentials at the rent-a-cop guarding the side entrance. He nodded and gave us each a radio.

The large kitchen area was hot and crowded and with hundreds of people preparing trays of food. The prep area was separated from the bourgeoisie by a set of purple velvet curtains. Waiters scurried in and out, adding to the behind-the-scenes chaos.

I parted the curtain and peeked out at the reception.

Cobo Hall was filled with the cream of Detroit society, although in today's tough economic climate they were more like spilled milk. Among the flower displays and food service areas, the cognoscenti of Motor City were in full mingling, air-kissing mode. They'd already formed into cliques based on where they fit in the social food chain and without missing a beat were filling their engorged bellies with the finest edibles.

I shivered from the icy layer of unabashed entitlement hanging in the air over their heads and motioned to Wilma.

"We should circulate."

"Sure," she replied with the same enthusiasm reserved for cleaning her toilet.

Wilma was less than impressed with Detroit's social elite. Her portfolio had lost a lot of value during the recession and I knew she'd love to literally extract a pound of flesh from some of these one-percenters.

~

The plan was to move in quickly, scoop up Souer, and spirit him away without attracting any attention. Wilma and I split up to cover more ground.

I wandered through the crowd playing the part of a security person to the hilt. My radio earpiece was alive with mostly useless chatter.

The Big Three automakers had the usual over-the-top exhibits of their latest motorized hardware. Strategically positioned spotlights made each car gleam like precious metal. The effect, however, was lost on this crowd. In their jaded eyes, Detroit steel was for the working class. They preferred automobiles built in Bavaria or Milan. It was kind of ironic since most of them had made their money betting on the success, and more recently on the failure, of the American auto industry.

"GM!"

Wilma's hiss burrowed into my brain through the earpiece.

I scanned the hall. When I saw the General Motors logo hanging from the ceiling, I moved quickly in that direction.

What the hell would the security guys monitoring the CCTV think when they saw two bobbing blobs of light converging on the Ford display.

I quickly found out through my headset.

"Set One to Hall Three. We're getting intermittent interference on the monitors again."

I listened to these sad sacks with amusement as a short, heated discussion followed about the *shit* equipment they were forced to work with.

Wilma tilted her head in the direction of a Cadillac bathed in so much illumination I expected Jesus to emerge from the backseat.

Disguised as a waiter in an ill-fitting tux, Souer carried a tray of canapés. No one noticed when he slipped a small object into the Caddy's trunk. He turned smoothly and walked away nonchalantly keeping his tray extended so the Raptors could continue feeding.

I went to the trunk, leaned in, and fished around until I found the object he'd left, a concussion grenade like the cops use in hostage situations. Souer had attached a small radio-controlled detonator with black electrical tape. The bomb wouldn't do much damage, but the resulting flash and shockwave would create panic in the hall. This was when he'd unleash mayhem on the unsuspecting crowd.

I looked for Souer but he'd disappeared.

"Two One," Wilma's voice ordered through my earphone.

I tapped it to switch to the secure channel we'd pre-programmed.

"He's heading for the kitchen. I'm on him."

I stuffed the grenade into my pocket and headed in that direction. "I've got his little surprise. He's going to detonate it with his cell."

"Roger that."

I caught up with Wilma. She was watching the door to the men's room.

"He's just wheeled a food cart in there."

"That's not very sanitary."

She didn't laugh and neither did I. Time was of the essence.

Having the grenade in my pocket was unnerving. Although the damn thing was designed to create a distraction, it still packed a powerful punch and would kill me if he set it off now.

We slipped silently into the washroom behind him. Souer didn't notice. He was kneeling beside a food service cart. A Thomson submachine gun and a shit-load of spare magazines were on the cart's metal shelf.

Wilma zapped him with a Taser. She'd dialed back the charge so it wouldn't completely disable him. We needed Souer to be docile so we could get him out of there.

Like a swooning lover, he sagged backward into her arms. She lowered him to the ground and rooted around inside his jacket for the cell phone.

An immobile Tommy Souer looked up at us in awe.

"A Tommy gun?" I mock-scolded him. "Really, Tommy?"

He attempted to twist his mouth into a smile.

"I admire your style," Wilma grinned. "It's a shame you went nuts. We might've been able to work together."

We lifted Souer to his feet and I nodded toward the machine gun on the food cart.

"Planning to go out in a blaze of glory? That's a beautiful touch. Kill as many of these weenies as you can before you get drilled. Nice ..." I drew out the last word. "Unfortunately, we can't let you do that. You're an inconvenience to your former employers and reflect poorly on them."

The truth dawned on Souer.

"Rizzolio," he slurred.

"I'm afraid so. He has something we need and, in return, he asked us to take care of a little problem for him."

Wilma pinched his nose shut and Souer's mouth flapped open as he tried to breathe.

I shoved the concussion grenade down his hatch.

Clutching his throat and gagging, Souer staggered away. Wilma and I followed.

Turning blue, he stumbled through the busy kitchen desperately trying to get someone's attention.

Wilma hit the speed dial on Souer's cell phone which he'd conveniently pre-programmed with the detonator's number.

The result was directly out of *Looney Tunes*.

His tux ballooned out and then tore completely open in a brilliant flash. That really got everyone's attention, especially when bits of Tommy Souer sprayed the main course.

While chaos ensued in the kitchen, we casually strolled out into the reception where no one was aware of anything amiss. Heads turned, however, at the sound of screams coming from behind the curtains.

"What's going on?" an elegant, gray-haired woman asked as we passed.

"I think dinner might be a little delayed," Wilma replied. "The beef tenderloin was overdone."

"But I understand the dessert is to die for," I added.

We faded into the crowd and slipped out of Cobo Hall before the cops arrived.

RANDY YAMAHAHA

When I told him about Tommy Souer's unfortunate detonation, Joey Rizzolio laughed so hard I thought he'd get a hernia.

It was mid-afternoon and the Italian joint was empty. The two bodyguards were nowhere in sight and Rizzolio sat with his back against the wall watching the door. He didn't invite me to sit.

I assessed his flab trying to figure out how many bullets it would take to make a dent in him. I was running out of patience and just wanted our business to be over.

"You fed him an explosive cannoli," he laughed again.

I'd been over the story twice now and he wasn't getting tired of it.

"Rip, you got some style. I could use a guy like you."

I shook my head respectfully. "Sorry, Mr. Rizzolio, I prefer to be an independent contractor."

At first, he frowned and then smiled broadly. "But I can call on you if I need you again for something special."

"Of course, Mr. Rizzolio. Anytime. I would be honored if you did."

"I suppose I need to keep my side of the bargain," he said. "The guy you want to talk to is Randy Yamahaha."

~

"Randy Yamahaha," Wilma repeated as we cruised up Gratiot.

My meeting with Rizzolio had stressed me out. Every muscle in my neck had contracted, setting off a killer headache. I don't know what I'd been expecting, maybe that Rizzolio and his goons would have the person I was looking for trussed up and ready to take away. Instead, all I got was a name. And it was a weird one at that.

Randy Yamahaha?

I rubbed the back of my neck.

Wilma pulled into the parking lot of a liquor store on Mt. Elliott where Lightbulb Lugosi was smoking an e-cigarette. Lightbulb was our ears and eyes on the street. He knew everything that was happening on the east side of town.

~

"Randy Yamahaha?" He exhaled a plume of vapor. "He's strictly small time, man. Why the fuck would you be interested in him?"

I slipped Lightbulb a twenty dollar bill, which told him to mind his own business.

"He disappeared a while ago. I don't know where he went but like I said, man, he's small potatoes. He tried to be big time once but just ended up annoying everybody. Maybe someone killed him. He was a pest."

"Lightbulb, you're not telling me anything I don't already know."

Information was his currency and I could see he was digging deep trying to recall anything he could about Yamahaha. It was killing him to come up dry like this, so I finally passed him a hundred dollar bill for his effort.

~

"I'll call Del in the morning," I told Wilma when she dropped me off at my place.

I took a couple of Advil and washed them down with a tumbler of Bourbon. I should have gone to bed right away but couldn't stop tossing Randy Yamahaha into the blender in my brain.

Rizzolio had given me a photo of him and I vaguely recognized Yamahaha as the one who had contracted us to kill the Judge. But there was something more. I stared at his face once again. It was ordinary like mine. Nothing jumped out, but I couldn't shake the feeling that I'd run into him before.

And then I had a revelation. Our paths *had* crossed before he contacted me to do the Judge.

Yamahaha had tried to lift my wallet when I was going in to the Fox Theater one evening. He was the world's most inept pickpocket. I caught him red-handed and duck-walked him into the alley next to the theater. Since I didn't want to miss the first act of *South Pacific*, I just twisted his wrist until it snapped.

I took his wallet looked at his driver's license.

Randy Yamahaha?

It had to be a made up name, though why anyone would choose an idiotic alias like that was beyond me.

I left him howling on the ground.

My lasting impression of our brief encounter was *loser*. The show, however, was delightful.

Some *Enchanted Evening* indeed. You just can't beat Rogers and Hammerstein.

~

I set up a meeting with Detective Sergeant Delbert Newell of the Detroit Police Department. Del was as sharp as razor wire, but we had him by the short hairs over a long unsolved murder.

While I waited for him to show up, I thought about Randy Yamahaha and why he would contract us to kill the Judge. It was funny that I hadn't recognized him after our previous encounter outside the theater, but the two occasions were separated by five years. I also had a vague recollection that Yamahaha showed up to our meeting wearing a beard.

I wondered if he'd remember me.

~

"Why the fuck do you do this to me every time?" Del sat down across from me and picked up the menu.

He was a vegetarian and always objected when I insisted on meeting in restaurants where they served meat by the ton. He'd lost some weight since I'd last seen him. He had been at least 350 pounds but was now down to 348.

Del was perspiring profusely even though the temperature outside was frigid. There were sweat stains under the arms of his jacket and I wrinkled my nose at the smell.

The waiter came to take our orders. Del asked for the mac and cheese. I decided on a meat platter.

"All that smoked shit will give you stomach cancer," he said after the waiter left.

I doubted that cancer would ever have a chance to kill me.

"So … Randy Yamahaha?"

"Is a loser."

"Yeah, that's what everybody tells me. But I need to find him."

Del pulled out some sheets of length-wise folded paper and smoothed them out on the table, careful to avoid getting mustard on them.

"According to his sheet, he's a real non-entity. Shoplifting, petty theft, fraud ... "

Del scanned down as he read. His eyes widened in surprise. "He's currently doing a nickel in Sawmill Grove for shoplifting."

"Sawmill Grove?"

He nodded his head thoughtfully. "For shoplifting?" He continued to nodding. "Yeah, from Neiman-Marcus in Troy."

"How the fuck does anyone get five years for shoplifting?"

There was something really wrong here and we both knew it. You don't get hard time in Michigan's most notorious supermax prison just for shoplifting. Most shoplifters get a lifetime ban from the store and maybe, if they're really unlucky, community service.

"I don't know. I didn't send him away. Talk to the Judge about that."

Del pushed over Randy Yamahaha's rap sheet and I put it in my pocket for bathroom reading later.

"From what I read, this guy's really hinky. Yamahaha is a nickname they gave him after he was busted for stealing one of them electric bikes. He tried to escape on it when our guys showed up. The thing had a top speed of fifteen. Even a Detroit PD car could catch him."

I wasn't so sure about that. The last one I'd seen ended up on concrete blocks with its wheels missing while the cops were responding to a call. It's probably still there.

Our food came and Del spent the next few disgusting minutes consuming his lunch. As he slurped and slopped, I ate smoked brisket and tried to make sense of why a loser like Yamahaha would be serving such a severe sentence in a place like Sawmill Grove.

He must have really pissed off the wrong person.

WORM ON A HOOK

At this point, you may be wondering about Wilma and me.

Almost 20 years ago we'd bonded over a discussion of Nietzsche and arson in a bar in Ann Arbor. While we understood the concept of rationality, we never applied it to what we did. Rationalizing was for those who felt guilt for their actions. Guilt, or any other emotion, was not one of our flaws.

Long ago we'd come to terms with the fact that we are high-functioning psychopaths. We'd do what we do even if we weren't paid. But instead of getting into a car and randomly crisscrossing the country killing hitchhikers, we applied basic business principles to our predilections.

So far it's worked out well. We make a good living, but we're not greedy. There are plenty of high-end contract killers and assassins who operate in the million dollar category, but we skew toward the middle class who are sadly underrepresented in the assassin-for-hire market.

Wilma and I each have our roles. I'm the public face of our little enterprise. I meet with clients to discuss their needs and pick up payment when we've done the deed. I also meet with our suppliers, such as Del. While he may suspect I don't work alone, Del was never tempted to stick his hand into the tiger's cage, which is a good thing given Wilma's strong preference for pain and power tools.

In her spare time, she does wonderful needlepoint and is a better chef than Hannibal Lector, not surprising considering her skill with a butcher knife. But beyond cuisine and needlepoint, Wilma has few passions in life.

Occasionally we find ourselves in bed together. Sex with Wilma is a little like playing chess — always five moves ahead. While I'm on the crest of orgasmic fury, in her head she's already showered and is eating breakfast.

It's unnerving.

Few people have met Wilma face-to-face in a business situation. Those who have didn't last very long.

You probably have the impression Wilma is cold and cruel. She is. But no more so than a Verizon customer service rep.

The bottom line is that Wilma is the best person to have covering my back.

~

"Well this makes about as much sense as everything else," Wilma said after reading Yamahaha's rap sheet. "Any insight on how this schmuck got so unlucky?"

Wilma honed the blade of the four-inch flick knife she keeps tucked in her bra. She says it's her good luck charm.

I shrugged. "He apparently knew too much and somebody wanted to keep him on ice."

"They should've just killed him."

"Not everyone thinks the same way you do."

This earned me a sour look.

"We need to have a talk with him."

"How are we going to do that? We're allergic to prisons."

Neither of us had ever seen the inside of a jail. We're too good at covering our tracks. The police have no idea who we are or what we do. If they did, it would upset them.

Prison does feature prominently in many of my dreams. Jung believed all aspects of a dream are you. If this is true, and I hope it isn't, then I'm already a prisoner.

"There is a way to get to Yamahaha," she said.

I knew I was not going to like Wilma's solution.

~

"Wow!" Promod exclaimed after Wilma explained what we wanted. His eyes flicked from Wilma to me and then back to Wilma.

I squirmed uncomfortably and felt like a worm waiting to be put on a hook, except I don't think worms have much comprehension of fishing and their role in the sport. At least not until they see the open mouth of a bass.

The problem was that I still didn't entirely trust Promod after our last experience. I assumed he'd learned his lesson, but I was literally putting my life in his hands, and in his hacking skills.

"If it were a federal prison, it would be difficult. But the good news is that Sawmill Grove is a privately-owned facility contracted out to the state."

Good news indeed.

But not for me.

Not when Wilma's plan called for me to be the inside man on this little caper.

"Because it's part of a company, I should have no problem hacking into their system. I need a few days to nose around in there and get to know the lay of the land so to speak."

~

Sawmill Grove Maximum Security Facility is located in central Michigan and houses the most violent offenders in the Midwest. It was built ten years ago and in all that time no one had ever escaped.

The prison was located on top of a hill with a single road leading in. The surrounding land had been cleared for a quarter mile. The skies above were patrolled day and night by drone aircraft with heat-sensitive and infrared camera systems. The double walls went ten feet down into the ground, making it impossible to tunnel under them.

Every inmate had a tracking chip implanted under his skin. This practice was currently being challenged in the Supreme Court by the ACLU, who considered it "intrusive". Intrusive or not, it meant the corporation could account for every one of the 1,100 inmates at any given time. Each chip was tied to the individual convict's profile and broadcast vital information such as weight, height, and general physical condition. That data allowed the company to tailor meals and other necessities with precision.

"I don't want something planted under my skin."

My complaint fell on deaf ears.

Promod was completely absorbed in testing their security and cracking the corporate firewall.

Wilma just ignored me.

We needed to speak with Yamahaha face-to-face and getting me inside Sawmill Grove was the only way to do it.

THE CALENDAR SHOP

The Big House.

The Hoosegow.
Mainline Joint.
Stony Lonesome.
Con College.
Glass House.
The Bucket.
Crowbar Hotel.
The Slammer.
The Calaboose.
The Cooler.
The Hole.
The Joint.
The Jug.
The Pen.
Pokey.
The Sneezer.
The Clink.
Stir.
Chill Factory.
Calendar Shop.
Ice House.
Up the River.

The idea of going to prison was never on my bucket list. I'd considered the possibility from time to time. In our line of work, it's an occupational hazard, like being cut down in a hail of bullets. I have thought about it but I never actually *believed* I would end up in a place like Sawmill Grove. And I certainly didn't anticipate having to go there on a voluntary basis.

While Promod was hacking into the prison's system to set up my visit, Wilma and I headed for Fort Knox Secure Storage, the self-storage complex we own. Although it's a combination Batcave and Fortress of Solitude, from the street it looks like something you'd see on any episode of *Storage Wars*. Having a place like this gives us a great spot to stash weapons, vehicles, high-tech gadgets, and other knick-knacks of our trade.

With the latest in surveillance technology, Fort Knox was as safe as a castle. We also have a virgin computer server which is not connected to the real world. Other features are a state-of-the-art alarm system, shooting range, vehicles of every description, and luxury apartments for Wilma and me. We have enough food and supplies to hunker down for at least a year.

Wilma latest project in her on-going quest to improve her skills was a helicopter simulator. I hoped this would be more successful than the unpleasantness which happened when she took up flower arranging.

~

I needed to mentally prepare for life on the inside. Meditation, I decided, would help me cope with the stress of being in a maximum security facility. So I borrowed Wilma's yoga mat.

Another phase she went through.

Sitting cross-legged on the floor, I tried to clear my mind. I focused on every breath, inhaling deeply, holding it and then exhaling, feeling every molecule of oxygen, becoming one with myself, finding …

"What the fuck are you doing, you asshole!"

I opened my eyes to a flashing red light and Wilma glaring down at me.

"Something's triggered the alarm and you're blissed out."

I stood up and grabbed my gun.

We spun around at the sound of a throat being cleared.

"Hi, guys," Promod said cheerfully.

He froze at the sight our pistols pointed at his nose and held up his hands in mock surrender.

"Don't be upset," he said with a smile. "Next time I'll disable the alarm."

It drove us crazy that in spite of all our security, Promod showed up whenever he pleased.

Our hideaway has several escape tunnels. One leads to the Target next door. The entrance is behind a sliding wall at the back of one of the change rooms. I'd put a pinhole camera in the wall so we could be sure it was empty if we needed to beat a hasty retreat.

While the secret exit was supposed to be only for emergencies, Wilma goes back and forth all the time to shop.

Sometimes when I'm bored, I used the camera to scope out women changing. Add *Peeping Tom* to my list of foibles. To be quite honest, most of the women who shop at this Target aren't all that attractive. Some are downright horrifying.

But, like a motorist passing an accident scene, I can't look away.

I'm just glad it isn't Walmart.

~

Promod sipped bubble tea. "For such a large company, they have lousy security. There are lots of vulnerabilities in the system."

"Who? Target?" I thought we were still talking about our emergency exit. I didn't realize he'd moved on to the prison corporation.

Promod glared at me. He didn't like to be interrupted when he was on a roll.

"Their biggest vulnerability is the way records are transferred from the State Corrections Department to their prison management database. They don't even use a secure FTP. It'll be a piece of cake to dummy up a file for you and slip it into their computer.

"Same thing goes for Wilma. I can create a credible personnel file for her as a correctional officer transferring from another one of their facilities."

Wilma looked at him skeptically. While this whole scheme was her idea, she didn't like putting herself inside any more than I did. Again, it came down to trust. And specifically, whether or not we could depend on Promod to hack the system. The other, darker possibility was that he would get us inside and slam the door. Then he would be free to work his magic on our off-shore bank accounts and disappear into the ether, leaving us in the clutches of a very confused prison corporation with a shitload of uncomfortable questions to pester us with.

Promod looked at us nervously, anticipating what we were thinking.

"It'll work," he said. "I pledge my life and the lives of my family. Give me a chance to make amends."

The memory set my teeth on edge.

He did seem sincere. But he was also a master of social manipulation. It was what made him so good at computer hacking. He could charm his way into any system if he found just the right gullible sucker.

My anxiety levels rose another notch.

Promod smiled confidently and continued. "I think the best thing is to make you some kind of a white collar criminal. You know, a Wall Street type, maybe a stock trader who got caught using insider information. That way we don't have to concoct an entire criminal background. You're just a poor sap who made a mistake and has to pay for it. It's all good, I promise."

Promod rested his hand on the kitchen counter.

Wilma slammed down a meat cleaver. The blade quivered a scant quarter inch from his fingers. He jerked back his hand in horror.

Wilma held up the cleaver. "Promod, you fuck this up and I'll track you down and start taking souvenirs." Her voice was as cold as Edmond Hillary's nose hair. "Now get out of my kitchen. I'm making dinner."

"Thanks for the invite, but I've got my daughter's soccer game tonight."

Promod passed me a boxed set of *Oz Season One* on Blu-ray.

I looked down at the cover art, a pair of gritty hands gripped the bars of a prison cell.

~

"So do you think we should trust him?" Wilma asked between bites of a delicious lamb curry.

She was a superb cook and, even though I don't like lamb all that much, I ate it with enthusiasm. As I tore off pieces of Naan bread and dipped them into my curry, I kept thinking of that meat cleaver and how close it had come to taking off Promod's fingers.

"What choice do we have? We can't just stroll in there on visiting day and ask to see Yamahaha."

She nodded thoughtfully. "He could be playing us."

"Who? Yamahaha?"

"No, asshole. Promod. Maybe he set the entire thing up just to lure us into prison and keep us locked up."

"It had occurred to me." That was putting it mildly.

This was the kind of devious scheme Promod was capable of.

Use Laura as a honey trap and then get us into something we can't get out of.

"Maybe he resents the money," Wilma said.

Money would certainly be a big motivation for him.

Our last caper had netted us over five million. In the end, it was Promod's talents that made it possible to score big. And even though he'd betrayed us, he still felt entitled to an even share.

We thought we were generous just by leaving him alive.

"Should we walk away then? Tell him the whole thing is off?"

We let this option hang in the air like a SpongeBob piñata.

My mango ice cream seemed to mock me.

Damned if you do, damned if you don't!

I ate the cheeky little bugger.

PACK A GOOD ANAL LUBE

Life, as I've discovered, all comes down to faith.

Faith that your pilot on this morning's flight hasn't been out boozing all night with Denzel Washington.

Faith the pipefitter who installed the boiler on your furnace knew what he was doing.

Faith the other guy is going to stop at the red light at that intersection you're approaching.

Faith that our leaders in Washington have our best interests at heart.

Well, the last one might be going a little *too* far.

In the end, we decided to put our faith in Promod.

Decision made, I spent the rest of the evening acquainting myself with the horrors behind bars as depicted in *Oz*. I had to turn away during the rape scenes. I wondered if that actually happened in prison.

Stupid question.

Of course, it did, especially when you're young and handsome like me. Being butt-holed by some burly tattooed ape from the Aryan Nation wasn't high on my list of fantasies. I decided I needed to take precautions.

I spoke to Wilma about it at breakfast the following morning.

She smiled reassuringly. "Don't worry, I've got your back."

"But what about when I'm in the shower?" I squeaked.

"Well," she said, "I'd pack a good anal lube if I were you."

She laughed in a way that told me she might not be joking.

I lost my appetite even though she'd cooked a fantastic corned beef hash. I pushed my food away and her eyes narrowed.

"Better eat while you can. Prison food isn't all that good. Anyway, you'll need your strength if you're going to survive all the raping," she chuckled.

I began to have second thoughts ... and third ... and fourth ... and ...

~

Promod dropped by later in the day to go over our profiles.

I'd be Sheldon Hofsteader, a fund manager convicted of insider trading and given a stiff sentence as an example to any Wall Streeters who might be tempted to stray.

The fingerprints on the file were lifted from handrails and tables at the Troy mall. Promod created a mug shot from a photo of me smirking at the camera. When he was finished, the counterfeit ID was perfect. But I was still troubled by the fact my picture was going to reside in the prison's database and that I would be captured in their video surveillance system.

"Everything feeds into the same mainframe," Promod said. "Once you give me the word, I'll erase it all. You'll just disappear as if you'd never existed."

A cold hand clutched my balls.

Wilma's role was easier. She'd become Wanda Miller, a correctional officer with nine years of experience in one of the corporation's Arizona facilities.

"I checked the guard and administration personnel records carefully to make sure no one at Sawmill Grove had ever worked in the prison out there. You're clean. And with the profile I put together you'll have seniority, which means you can move around freely."

Wilma tapped the tabletop nervously with her meat cleaver. "And you make me disappear too?"

"Of course," he said lightheartedly, "just don't make too many friends in there."

What we didn't tell Promod was that Steve Carlson had rigged a new set of concealed LEDs that would really fuck with the prison's CCTV coverage. Once Wilma had them in place, they'd cause intermittent digital breakup and interference with the signals. This would be a great distraction while we went about our business.

~

I'd dropped by to see Steve that morning. After my disturbing *Oz* marathon, I wanted to see if he had anything I could smuggle into Sawmill Grove to defend myself.

"Difficult, but not impossible. I have a small gun that's in pieces and would be perfect to carry into a prison. The entire thing, plus ammunition, fits in a little plastic tube."

"Sounds good. Where do I put it?"

"How tight can you clench your ass?" He laughed and I knew he was joking about the ass gun. "Just sharpen a toothbrush handle. It makes an excellent weapon."

"And then my dental hygiene will go all to hell."

"Well, I guess you have to weigh that against having your fudge packed."

I had another vision of a hairy Aryan and decided my best option was to throw the *Oz* discs in the garbage.

"I do have something that might come in handy, though."

Steve led me to a workbench where a pinkish mass sat in a Petrie dish.

"I designed it to look like a scar."

He flipped it over and revealed a series of tiny parts embedded in the underside.

Baffled, I picked it up and examined it carefully.

"It's a miniature drone. I got a contract to make them for an agency best left nameless. The parts snap together into a tiny flying machine no bigger than a house fly and it broadcasts high definition video. It's just a prototype, but I sure would like someone to field test it."

Then he opened a drawer, took out an iPod, and handed it to me. "You control it with this."

Steve turned and picked up the fake scar.

"I'll give you a special adhesive so you can put it on your arm. When you need to use the drone, just rub on some Sprite. The citric acid will dissolve the glue."

He put the whole kit in a bag along with the iPod and handed it over. "No charge."

I wasn't sure how I'd put it to use, but I took it anyway.

~

In our world of subterfuge, identities get lost. We're always becoming different people. When you switch identities as much as we have, eventually you lose sight of who you are.

It had so been a long since anyone had called me by my birth name, I'd practically forgotten it. As for Wilma, she never even told me her real name.

It doesn't really matter.

The only name that counts is the one your tombstone. That one should be false as well, just in case you have to come back from the dead.

It happened to me once, but that's another story.

~

Promod had put together files that would help us familiarize ourselves with our prison identities. We needed to make certain we had every detail right. If either of us fucked up, it would be very, very bad.

We spent a few minutes getting into character and then quizzed each other. At first, I played Sheldon as wimpy and unassuming. Wilma, however, gave me some feedback. This guy was a high-powered trader and would be really arrogant and aggressive. I adjusted my acting accordingly until we both felt I'd hit the right note. It was not quite a Tony Award-winning performance, but good enough to snag a Golden Globe.

Wilma came out of the gate as Wanda. She played it with just the right mix of authority and a subtle undercurrent of compassion. She was a natural actress and had honed her skills as Yum-Yum in the University of Michigan Gilbert and Sullivan Society's production of the *Mikado*.

Recalling Wilma singing *Three Little Maids From School Are We* made Little Rip's sunrise.

"Grant a condemned man one last wish?"

She smiled wickedly.

After a few hours of passionate but discorporate *coitus gigantus*, I was spent and lay with my tongue idly circling her navel.

Wilma purred contentedly.

"That was fulfilling," she whispered. "When you're ready again, I'll get out one of my dildos and help you prepare for the prison experience."

SAWMILL GROVE

The journey to Sawmill Grove Correctional Facility was one trip where I wasn't in a hurry to arrive at my destination.

Promod had prepared the proper Voluntary Surrender documents and had moved my false file into the prison's mainframe. They would be waiting for me with open arms and welcoming smiles.

Wilma had rented a car at the airport using a phony credit card. At the prison's Intake Unit, she played a distraught wife to the hilt. Well, maybe overplayed it a bit. Her acting skills did not extend to drama; musical comedy was more her forte.

I passed through a series of gates and solid doors. As one closed behind me, another one opened up.

"I get to keep the iPod, right?" I asked the guard who bagged my clothes and was now putting my valuables into a large manila envelope.

"Sure, we just have to check it over first. You'll get it back in a couple of days. Think you can live without your Lady Gaga that long?"

I resisted the urge to point out that Lady Gaga was not my cup of meat.

He stared at me defiantly, challenging me to become indignant. I only nodded, giving him back nothing. As far as I was concerned, he was just the concierge at this little resort.

According to his ID badge, the guard's name was Scuggins. I made a mental note to have Wilma put the super laxative she'd been experimenting with into his coffee. That would teach him the real meaning of the word *asshole*.

I changed into the white jumpsuit Scuggins handed me. *SGCF* was stenciled across the front and back. He pointed to a stack of blankets, underwear, socks, a pair of canvas shoes, a tube of toothpaste, a toothbrush, and deodorant. Scuggins ordered me to pick them up and follow him.

I'm in the jailhouse now, resonated in my head as he took me along a corridor and into a cell block.

A final metallic clang echoed behind me.

I was well and truly locked up.

~

The state of Michigan spends nearly $2 billion a year on its correctional system. We pay more for prisons than we do for colleges. A lot of this has to do with the war on drugs and mandatory sentencing guidelines which choke our jails and have created a growth industry in private incarceration facilities.

I suspect some of the same corporations who run these places also lobbied hard to get tougher sentencing in the first place. There are even a few well-documented cases of judges colluding with private prisons to send business their way. In one instance, the judge actually owned a piece of the action.

Gotta love America.

You can buy anything here, including injustice.

~

Correctional Officer Scuggins led me into a common area and made me stand at attention while holding my stuff.

"Wait here."

Scuggins strode over to an office and knocked on the door.

A middle-aged guy poked his head out, saw me, and retreated back inside. I had the fleeting impression of a bald dome and bad skin. He emerged and accompanied Scuggins to where I stood.

Baldy swayed slightly even though there was no breeze. Shaking hands and bad hygiene marked him as a heavy drinker. But most of all, I was fascinated by his nose, a yellow squash covered in genital warts.

"Unzip your jumpsuit." The smell of a fermented outhouse wafted from his mouth.

I looked around for somewhere to put the stuff I was holding. Scuggins stepped up to me and slapped the blankets and toiletries out of my hands. I stared at them dumbly.

"You heard the doc."

I unzipped my jumpsuit and the doctor pulled it off my shoulder. He swabbed me with an alcohol pad and held up a massive hypodermic needle with a tip shaped like a spade. It was razor-sharp.

"This might sting a little," Doc said as he jabbed it under the skin below my collar bone.

I screamed.

It didn't sting. It fucking hurt, like a white-hot poker had been rammed into my shoulder.

"Now that didn't hurt a bit," he said.

I looked at the smug expression on Doc's face and then at the hypo. I was barely able to restrain my overwhelming desire to rip it out of his hands and jam it up his nose.

Scuggins stepped forward with a scanner and waved it across the wound. It beeped and he studied the display for a moment.

"Workin' good, Doc."

Doc grunted and slapped a bandage over the injection site. I felt a little sick from the pain.

"What would happen if it didn't work?" I asked.

"Well then," Scuggins smiled, "the doc takes it out and we put in another one. We keep trying until we get one that works. Once we had to do a guy four times before we got one that worked."

I resisted pointing out that it would be less painful if they tested them *before* putting them in. But I think they'd already considered that and ruled it out.

After all, why spoil the fun?

"What is this thing?" I asked as I rubbed my shoulder.

"It's how we keep an eye on you," Scuggins replied. "So leave it alone."

"Isn't that a blatant violation of my civil rights?"

They both laughed. Scuggins pointed at my stuff on the floor. I picked it up and followed him. He continued laughing as he led me to a cell.

~

Marty Borman sat on the upper bunk dangling his feet. When the cell door opened, he jumped down and stood at attention with an enormous shit-eating grin on his face.

"You got company, Borman," Scuggins told him as he ushered me into the cell.

Borman stared at me the way a dingo eyes a toddler.

70

His bulging eyes and fleshy blue lips gave me the creeps. He was a little over 5'6" and weighed at least 270. Most of the excess weight circled his equator. Although he was a heavy little dude, I figured one punch to the throat would turn him into custard.

"You two get acquainted now," Scuggins said lightly and shut the door.

The electronic bolt slammed home.

I ignored Borman and looked around my new digs. It was a four by nine space filled with one bunk bed, a small metal desk bolted securely to the wall and a stainless steel toilet with a small sink beside it.

Since Borman already had the upper bunk, I put my things on the lower one. I sat down and put my head in my hands and sighed.

"So what are you in for?" His voice gave whiny a new dimension.

Asking me this was a clear violation of prison etiquette. You should never ask another prisoner what he was in for. It was a sign of disrespect. In Borman's case, I chalked it up to stupidity.

"Wanna know what I did?" he asked.

I continued to ignore him. A headache coming on and I was certain there would be no aspirin among the things they'd given me.

"I'm a molester," he said with pride.

That icy hand clutched my balls again.

He leaned over and looked down at me.

"So, are we gonna be friends or what?"

The *or what* sounded like the best option, so I kept up the silent treatment. I just lay back and pretended he didn't exist.

That none of this existed.

He finally got the point and shut up.

Marty Borman?

What kind of sick parent would name their kid that? They must've been white supremacists.

I decided it would be a good idea to draw a line between us.

"Borman, you come down out of that bunk for any reason after lights out and I'll make earrings out of your balls. Understand?"

"But what if I have to pee?"

"Piss in your mouth for all I care. Just don't come down here."

"But I thought we could be *friends.*"

His emphasis on that last word made it crystal cathedral clear what he considered friendship to be.

"This isn't summer camp, asshole. You just stay up there if you know what's good for you."

"Oh yeah, well I got friends in here and they're gonna love you. They like all the new fish."

"And stop talking like James Cagney."

"What's he in for?"

Just my luck to get stuck with a cultural illiterate.

Molesters I can kind of understand. They're compulsive and can't control themselves. I've even killed a few when hired by parents who felt the courts had let them down. But not having even a basic grasp of popular culture was an unforgivable sin, especially in the age of Turner Classic Movies and Netflix.

I needed a distraction so I began to think about what Wilma might be up to. She wasn't scheduled to arrive until tomorrow morning. Right now she was probably cooking something delectable. Then she would get undressed and climb into that large bed of hers and ...

Raspy breathing from above pre-empted my fantasy.

This is gonna be hell.

I prayed that Promod would quickly locate Randy Yamahaha's tracking chip. Then he could let Wilma know and she'd relay the information to me.

Yamahaha likely had a very low pain threshold. It wouldn't take much persuading to convince him to give me the name of the person who'd hired him to be the go-between.

I heard the disturbing sounds of Borman's nightly constitutional coming from above. From the all the moaning and groaning, he must've been fantasizing about frolicking at a Boy Scout jamboree. It made me sick to even think about it.

Instead, I focused on my southern belle Mandy Shugar. I let her swelling breasts block Borman's frenzied moans. I teased her nipples and felt them getting hard under my tongue. Her hand slid along my naked flesh and traced a path across my belly ...

"Hey, Fish, stop playing with yourself!"

Scuggins shone his flashlight at Borman.

"Just coming, boss," he squealed.

"Let go of it, Borman, or it's the cooler."

The light hit me in the face and I covered my eyes.

"And you settle down too, Hofsteader."

The light went out and he walked away. Borman quieted down and went to sleep.

After a few minutes, I drifted off to the gentle lullaby of a thousand convicts snoring.

ANOTHER BEAUTIFUL DAY IN STIR

Morning came early at the Greybar Hotel.

At 6:00 an alarm bell sounded through the cell block. Just like in the movies, guards walked down the rows of cells banging the bars loudly with their batons.

"Morning, Sunshine."

"Up and at 'em."

"Another beautiful day in stir."

"Haul your lazy ass out of bed."

When I opened my eyes, Borman was already dressed and standing at attention next to the cell door. I was going to point out this was a blatant violation of our roommate agreement when I saw the guard standing there looking at us.

"Get the fuck out of bed, Fish," the guard screamed.

I leaped up and pulled on my jumpsuit. The mean guard was joined by a second one.

"You almost missed your breakfast," she said.

It was Wilma to my rescue. I felt better now that I knew she had my back.

Borman rubbed his crotch. "I got breakfast for you right here, Baby.

Wilma frowned. "I'm not on *that* much of a diet."

I suppressed a smile at the sight of Wilma in her guard uniform. She looked every inch the model of a perfect correctional officer. I gazed at Borman and hoped to God she had brought me a Taser.

~

The breakfast portions were perfectly rationed to each prisoner's size and weight. The emaciated guy standing in line in front of Borman got three pancakes and two sausage patties. Borman got one of each. To my alarm, I also got one of each. Maybe Wilma was right, and I did need to lose a bit of weight. This sure seemed to be the place to do it.

Here at Sawmill Grove, they took the expression *'prison diet'* literally. It made sense, though. Get each prisoner to an average BMI and it cut down on health care costs. Fat guys had a whole menu of ailments to choose from. Skinny guys were also susceptible to all kinds of illnesses.

I took my skimpy breakfast without complaining.

What did Emily Post say about prison mealtime etiquette?

This is the perfect occasion to meet some interesting and stimulating people and engage in lively conversation.

However, there didn't seem to be much chance of that happening here. The entire mess hall was filled with a thousand dim bulbs grimly hunched over their breakfasts.

My attention was drawn to a table near the center of the room where several guys were joking and laughing loudly. I walked over and sat down.

"Morning," I said lightly.

Three heads swiveled my way. The one in the middle smiled.

"Have a seat," he said.

It wasn't meant as an invitation. I detected the menace underneath but just grinned back at him.

"Thanks, I already have." I looked from face to face. "So guys, what's on for today?"

For a big guy well out of his BMI target range, the stack of five pancakes and six sausages on his plate said he had special privileges. His buddies each topped in at over three hundred pounds. The cooks hadn't even bothered to give them plates. The food had just been piled on their trays.

I pointed to the tray of the guy closest to me.

"You going to eat that?" I reached over and stabbed a pancake.

He started to lunge forward, but the man in the middle put a restraining hand on him.

"Owl here gets upset when you interrupt his feeding time."

Owl's arm hovered in the air.

Ignoring them, I carved up my breakfast. While everyone else had been given a small packet of what might pass as jam, they had a whole bottle of Grade A maple syrup.

I picked it up and poured half of it on my pancakes.

He watched me warily. A circle of swastikas ringed his neck. Both his minions had similar tattoos. I pointed at them.

"You guys look like a Panzer division."

The henchman to his left jumped up. Again he held him back.

"So you're a tough guy, are you?" he said calmly. I liked his voice. He sounded like a tax accountant explaining my allowable deductions.

"Not really. Just hungry and you guys seem to have more than your fair share." I waved my fork toward the tall stack of pancakes on his plate.

His buddy sat down with a thud and began to eat his breakfast. Every so often he looked up at me and glared.

"I'm Sheldon, by the way. Sheldon Hofsteader."

"Like that brainiac on TV." It wasn't a question.

Oh, great. Someone well versed in popular culture.

"That's right. You wouldn't believe how many comments I get about my name."

"You got balls, I'll give you that." He smiled and extended a hand. "I'm Bob Neill."

"I know. You're the head guy when it comes to keeping white power alive and well around here."

Neill nodded. "I don't figure you for the brotherhood. You ain't got any ink."

I shook my head and swallowed a piece of sausage. The unpleasant aftertaste made me think they hadn't used real pork or beef. I didn't want to think of what *really* might be in there.

Turtle perhaps?

Even though they were thick and mealy, I decided to eat the pancakes anyway.

"Allergies. Tattoos make my skin crawl."

"So why exactly are we talking?"

I *did* like the sound of his voice, it was relaxing. I wondered if I would have the same reaction if he were kicking the shit out of me in the shower.

"I need some information, and I figure you're the guy who's plugged in around here."

"And why would I want to help you?"

"Because I can get you a great deal on Herman Goring's staff car."

He chuckled with amusement, then leaned over and wrapped a beefy paw around the back of my neck, pulling my face close to his. "I like your sense of humor. If I didn't, you'd be pulling that tray out your ass right now."

"Glad I made a good first impression then."

He released me and sat back.

"Luke Gabriel," I said.

He hesitated, and I knew I'd gotten his attention.

Once upon a time, the Michigan Militia had been the top guys when it came to white Aryan superiority, but Timothy McVey kind of ruined things for them when he blew up that building in Oklahoma.

In the racist vacuum that ensued, a couple of other self-styled Nazi wannabe groups had emerged from under the rocks. The two most prominent were Keep Michigan White and the White Michigan Brotherhood. As with most groups who have similar goals and objectives, they hated each other.

Keep Michigan White was led by a pencil-necked geek by the name of Luke Gabriel. He always reminded me of Beetlejuice whenever I saw him on TV. The White Michigan Brotherhood was headed up by my new friend Bob Neill, who, along with several of his lieutenants, was serving five to seven for armed robbery. Apparently they had been trying to finance a race war by sticking up Brink's trucks.

Not wanting to come in here completely blind, I'd had Promod scan all the prisoner records and compile dossiers on the ones who might come in handy. Pseudo Führer Bob Neill was at the top of the list. According to our intelligence, he ran things inside Sawmill Grove.

The other interesting fact our research told us was that Randy Yamahaha didn't seem to exist within the walls of this facility.

"Maybe he ratted someone out and they've got him under another identity." Wilma had suggested.

This was a distinct possibility. From every account, Yamahaha was a Class A weasel, and I'm sure he had *snitching* on his resume.

Getting back to the politics of white racism …

While Bob Neill and his men were inside, Luke Gabriel was making moves to take over and merge the two groups. Once he accomplished this, he'd vowed to send in someone to put good old Bob in the morgue. While Neill had some power in here, it didn't stretch beyond the razor wire.

And that's where I could help him.

Quid pro quo.

"What about Gabriel?" he asked, his eyes becoming slits like the gun-ports in a pillbox.

"You help me and, by this time next week, Luke Gabriel will be an unpleasant memory."

They say if you look long and hard enough you can see into a man's soul. Bob Neill looked long and hard at me, and I think he saw what was underneath.

It was a cold dark place, with no soul in residence.

"All right. So what do you want from me?"

I noticed his voice had taken on a slightly nervous tone.

"Randy Yamahaha."

"Sounds like a chink," one of his minions chuckled.

Neill shot him a *'shut the fuck up'* glance and asked, "What do you want with that little scumbag?"

"I want to know what he uses to get his teeth so white," I replied.

In other words, 'don't ask'.

And a loud alarm signaled the end of breakfast. We rose from the table and joined the other convicts carrying their trays to the racks by the mess hall doors. We hadn't finished our conversation, but that's prison for you.

A lot of things go unfinished here.

~

They put me to work in the prison wood shop cutting uprights for highway signs.

I'd been thinking about retirement since we came into all that money. Some sort of hobby seemed in order, but woodworking wasn't it. I was intimidated by all those sharp blades. Maybe it was years of watching Wilma at work with her power tools.

Of course, she wasn't into woodworking.

I'd developed great respect for a circular saw blade, and how quickly it cut through flesh and bone. When I had to take shop in high school, they'd shown a safety film which depicted gory accidents in graphic detail. It was quite a spectacle of dismemberment and bloody lacerations. The highlight was when a piece of doweling broke loose from a lathe and impaled the operator. I remember wishing they'd shot that scene in 3-D.

I spent an enjoyable time cutting four-by-fours while constantly counting my digits. By the end of the day, I was exhausted and relieved that

I was just visiting. I couldn't imagine what five to ten years of this day after day would be like.

Probably a lot like working on an assembly line at Ford.

~

As I sat by myself at dinner that night, I wondered how Wilma was getting along. Maybe she'd had more luck in tracking down Yamahaha. We figured it was better for her to be assigned to the night shift when it was easier to move around. I knew she'd play it cool and only get in touch with me when she needed to.

Across the mess hall, I saw Neill and his little Nazi companions watching me. He was still sizing me up, probably trying to figure out if I could deliver what I'd promised.

Dinner was some sort of meat served with alleged vegetables. It swam in a gray cream sauce that reminded me of a backed-up sink. I ate about half of it before giving up in disgust.

My weight loss program was made a whole lot easier.

~

When I finally got back to my cell, I found Borman rolling around on the floor in the grip of some kind of seizure. I tried to get Scoggins' attention when he walked by. He looked casually at Borman, who was now foaming at the mouth. Scuggins shook his head.

"Don't know and don't care," he said and walked away.

Maybe this was what happened if you masturbated all the time. I thought about helping the poor guy up before he aspirated on his own vomit. But as he continued to flail, I found it rather relaxing.

There were tell-tale red marks of a Taser on the back of his neck. I stepped over his gyrating body and sat on my bunk. A brown craft envelope with my name on it had been torn open, and the iPod had spilled out.

Wilma has a fondness for electrical engineering.

Borman had apparently been trying to steal my stuff when she sneaked up behind him and zapped him good. I turned on the player, plugged in my headphones, and lay back to watch the latest *Star Wars* movie on the tiny screen.

Later, when he regained control of his motor functions, Borman slunk back into his bunk and ignored me. I drifted off to sleep after my first full day in prison to the pleasant sight of Jedi Knights disemboweling Jar Jar Binks with light sabers.

Bob Neill sat down across from me the next morning at breakfast. I was preoccupied with trying to figure out which end of the chicken the slime on my plate had come out of. I noticed he had French toast. It had even been dusted with powdered sugar. He took a slice from his plate and put it on mine.

"I thought about it and, if you can do what you say you can, we got a deal," he said. "One condition, though."

I ate the French toast. It was delicious.

"Oh yeah? What's that?" I said between bites.

"I want you to nail Gabriel to a flaming cross."

He smiled at the image in his head. I wanted to point out the symbolic subtext of this but held my tongue. I just hoped Luke Gabriel wouldn't rise from the dead three days later. That might fuck up my atheist beliefs.

"No problem," I told him and we shook hands. I noticed his fingers were tattooed with N A Z I R U L E across the knuckles. That would probably limit his chances of getting a membership in the *B'nai B'rith*.

"He's been in the cooler since he got here last year. As far as I know, he hasn't seen anyone in that whole time."

I momentarily had a hard time swallowing.

Jesus! A year in solitary …

Yamahaha would be a basket case.

BEING RUPERT WHIPPLE

Wilma dropped by to see me that evening after lights out.

Borman cowered in his bunk at the sight of her. She slipped me her Taser, and I zapped him on the ankle. Once again he went into a conniption fit. While he thrashed around, we could have an undisturbed conversation.

"He's been in isolation for the past year," I told her. "Under the name of Rupert Whipple."

"Are you making that up?"

"No. They enjoy joke names around here."

"After a year in the cooler, he won't know which way is up," Wilma said.

I nodded in agreement.

I saw Scuggins approaching and tried to pass back the Taser.

She shook her head. "Keep it, I've got plenty."

"Everything okay here, Miller?" Scuggins asked.

"Yes, sir. The prisoner seems to be in distress, sir."

Scuggins looked at the still writhing Borman and smiled. "Maybe he's upset."

"No, sir, he appears to be having a fit, sir."

She did an excellent impression of a subordinate, but I could tell she hated it and was fighting the urge to feed Scuggins his own genitalia.

"Would you like me to report it then, Miller?"

I returned to my bunk and slipped the Taser under my pillow.

It was fun to watch her barely contain her rage as Scuggins baited her. I could clearly see his name at the top of Wilma's shit list. Scuggins didn't know it yet, but he was going to come to a dreadful end.

81

"No, sir."

She lowered her eyes submissively, and I swore I could see visions of surgical instruments dancing in them. When it came time for Wilma to deal with Scuggins I took comfort in the knowledge he would never even see it coming.

She watched Borman shake, rattle, and roll for a few more moments and then turned away. Wilma followed Scuggins out of the cell block, and the lights went out for the night.

I watched a double feature of the original versions of *Texas Chain Saw Massacre* and *Last House on the Left* on my iPod.

The classics can't be beaten.

~

Promod had hacked my iPod into the prison's internet so I could send and receive email. A note from Wilma was waiting for me the next morning.

~

Bob Neill looked up from his Eggs Benedict and lifted his eyebrows.

"Something on your mind, Cooper?"

I hadn't touched my breakfast. It was some kind of cereal that looked and tasted like warm plaster.

Ever since my public embrace of Neill and his little Nazi buddies, I noticed most of the other prisoners kept away from me. Normally I get along with pretty well everyone. Even some our targets had warmed to my natural charm. But since most of the other cons figured I was now part of Neill's Reich, they kept their distance. They averted their eyes when I passed and stared at my back in fear or hostility.

I wanted to declare to all within earshot that I felt the same way as they did about these goons; sucking up to them was only a means to an end. But we all have our parts to play in life and this was mine — pretending I was a fledgling storm trooper in Neill's twisted vision of white supremacy.

"I need to get into solitary," I told Neill.

"I'm not even going to ask why you'd want to do that," Neill said, "but I think I can help you out."

He looked around the mess hall at the other prisoners who were hunched over their breakfasts, protecting their gruel.

Neill leaned in close. "See that nigger over there?" He nodded at a young black guy at the next table.

"Why don't you dump your cereal all over his nappy head. Maybe that'll straighten his hair for him."

I frowned and then rose, carrying my bowl in front of me like a character out of Dickens. Without a word I stood behind the man and tipped the contents onto his head. I hoped there wasn't anything in this crap that might cause permanent hair loss.

To say my victim got upset would be putting it mildly. He jumped up with a scream of rage and proceeded to beat on me, venting all the anger and desperation that had been building up ever since he'd been tossed into this joint. Luckily I could roll with his punches and kicks, an occupational skill, and was able to avoid any kind of lasting damage to my vital organs and bones.

Guards rushed up and dragged us apart.

Voila! I had a new home.

CHEW TEN TIMES

It was cold in the cooler.

I guess that's so the residents can chill out. Since I was going to be stuck in solitary for six days and seven nights, I was going to have a lot of time for chilling.

A narrow bunk filled my tiny cell. The remaining space was taken up with a metal toilet and sink. There was no window, no bars, and no distractions, except for the smell of the toilet. The only connection to the outside was a narrow slot near the bottom of the door where they pushed my meals through twice a day.

Whereas the food in the mess hall was dismal and tasteless, the food here was downright gruesome.

Oh well, I'll while away the hours watching my body fat dissolve.

These cells were designed to painfully magnify sound to discourage any screaming, as my friend from the cafeteria quickly found out to his dismay.

When he quieted down, I crouched by the food slot.

"Sorry for dumping on you," I told him. "I didn't mean for you to get locked up in here."

I hoped his resulting barrage of shrieked obscenity was somehow cathartic. After he'd finished, he stayed silent for the rest of the day.

So much for apologies.

It's so much easier to get work done when you're the center of your own universe and not worrying about apologizing every time you stab someone.

I guess that's why I love *Curb Your Enthusiasm.*

~

The cooler was designed to allow you to reflect on the error of your ways. Deprived of any outside stimuli, I found myself turning inward. I put my reflection time to good use by recalling some of our most memorable hits.

Normally our job is pretty mundane — bullets and blades with the occasional explosive thrown in for variety or effect. But occasionally a target stands out.

Pops Mayhew, the beloved children's author, is on the top of my list.

~

We recalled with great fondness Pop's classics from our childhood like *Chew Ten Times* and *Alphabet Soap*. Wilma had a particularly soft spot for *My Friend the Wind*, which penetrated her shell and made her cry. Tears from Wilma, however, are probably as toxic as cyanide.

You might wonder why anyone would want to kill a cherished children's author.

One look at the man who hired me to do the deed explained it all. He was a little ferret of a man who used Eddie Haskell as his nickname. It suited him.

Eddie turned out to be Shay Lissard, Pop's literary agent, which I learned when he passed me a business card. He suggested my adventures might make an excellent book and he would be happy to represent me.

I was going to remind him what *discretion* means, but he was an agent so I cut him some slack.

Lissard had just negotiated a huge contract for all Pop's work. Pops Mayhew, however, had begun to espouse some rather bizarre notions, including his belief in a conspiracy where FDR and the British Royal Family had started World War II as part of their bigger plot of global domination. According to Pops, Hitler was just a poor patsy they duped into becoming their fall guy.

Interviews with Pops were now focusing solely on his conspiracy theory instead of his children's stories. This added what newspaper editors liked to call *dimension*.

Already this strange obsession was killing his book sales. The British publisher, offended by Pop's views of the Royal Family, had canceled reprints of his books and was demanding the return of a hefty advance.

Something had to be done, and quickly before Pops completely destroyed his legacy.

And that had brought Lissard, a.k.a. Eddie Haskell, to me.

While it made me uneasy to dispose of a revered icon like Pops Mayhew, it did appeal to me on another level because we charge a premium for killing a celebrity. Whacking a household name means an extra 15%.

"It needs to look like some kind of brain thing to explain his weird beliefs," Lissard told me.

Lissard was really starting to get on my nerves. He was constantly checking for text messages while we talked.

"A stroke, or something like that," he continued not taking his eyes off the screen. "And it has to be done now before he ultimately destroys all the value of his work. What kind of parent is going to buy their kid a book from a guy who likes Hitler?"

I could probably name a few but remained silent while he continued.

"I got an agency lined up to position the idea that Mayhew was delusional because of brain damage." He touched the side of his head.

Agents! And I thought we were cold-blooded.

Lissard ended our meeting by getting up and slapping down a thick envelope of cash. Luckily we were having lunch in a restaurant where Detroit politicians liked to dine. The sight of an envelope full of cash on the table didn't even raise an eyebrow.

The ignorant prick walked off without saying goodbye. I shook my head in disbelief and pocketed the money.

~

I couldn't decide if Steve Carlson was completely off the rails or just enthusiastic.

"I put together something that can cook a brain, or any other body part for that matter," Steve told me several days later. "It works like a microwave. Only instead of cooking Orville Redenbacher's, it pops brains. Five minutes wearing this and he'll have a tumor the size of Toledo."

He passed me a strange looking device that resembled what a demented kid might put together for a science fair project. It was a Tiger's baseball cap with a whole bunch of thick wires leading to a box the size of a toaster. The box had a single dial on it.

"Set it at five or above and have him wear it for ten minutes. Then it's lesion city. He'll be dead in about three days."

"How much is it?"

"Do you want to rent or buy?"

We agreed on a price to rent it for a week and he packed it up.

"Oh, and after you turn it on, move as far away as possible to avoid any side effects."

"What sort of *side effects* we talking about?"

He smiled. "Let's just say that having two dicks isn't all it's cracked up to be."

I decided to let Wilma handle the brain cooker.

Doubling her genitalia would be an added bonus.

~

Pops Mayhew had a lovely place outside Traverse City, a two story log home with a wrap-around porch. A couple of hundred feet away was a matching cabin he used as his studio. Pops liked to work there at night, which is where we found him when we dropped by.

Mayhew was bewildered, not only by our presence but by the alien masks we wore. He probably thought we were part of *the conspiracy*.

Before he could move, I pinned his arms to his sides and Wilma wound Cling Wrap around his body. It's a neat trick to immobilize a victim and leave no marks.

I glanced over at Pops' work table while fixing the baseball cap to his head. I was curious to see what he was working on. Instead of a whimsical sketch of a laughing train or a crying whale, there was a drawing showing FDR using Hitler as a hand puppet.

I tried to imagine what delightful tale this would illustrate.

"Ready?" Wilma said as I stepped way back.

I went outside while the cooker hummed and crackled. I counted off five minutes on my Timex. When Pops was done, I signaled Wilma. She shut off the machine and he slumped forward in his chair, drooling and insensible. Whoever found him would think he'd collapsed over his drawing table.

~

When Pops didn't come in for his bedtime Ovaltine, his housekeeper went out to the studio and found him babbling about the aliens Prince Charles had sent to abduct him.

He died three days later. By then the PR machinery had framed his unusual obsessions as the result of his illness. They worked their magic and turned revulsion into respect.

Pops was even forgiven by the Royal Family and, from personal experience, I know they don't forgive easily.

After Lissard had paid the balance, I held up his card and told him I might drop by to see him some evening. He may have been annoying, but he was smart enough to get my inference.

Keep your fucking mouth shut.

I knew with a douche like Lissard this should be enough, but I held onto his card anyway.

Hell, you never know when a good agent might come in handy.

A SAFE LANDING

The clang of my evening meal arriving interrupted my trip down memory lane.

Expecting another disgusting culinary perversion, I was surprised to see a McDonald's Happy Meal. My iPod sat beside it along with several cans of Sprite and a Butterfinger candy bar.

Wilma is in the house.

I gobbled down the burger and fries and chugged a can of the soda. I saved the Butterfinger for tonight's movie. I hoped Wilma had put something good on the iPod.

When I pushed the tray back through the slot, she bent down and spoke quietly. "He's in cell six."

"Thanks for the Happy Meal. It was wonderful."

There was no response. Wilma wouldn't have seen giving me a great meal like that as *wonderful.* For her, it would just be practical, a way to keep my strength up for the job at hand.

I sat on my bunk and used some drops of Sprite to dissolve the glue on my fake scar. After a few minutes of rubbing and some painful skin tearing, it came free.

I assembled the housefly-sized drone.

~

The drone was a marvel. Steve was brilliant.

Although I admired the technology, I also felt uneasy. Virtually noiseless, the drone would be almost undetectable. The possibilities for eavesdropping were endless. I imagined a drone as a literal fly on the wall, spying on Wilma and me as we plotted our nastiness.

While this thought was unsettling, there wasn't anything I could do about it, so instead I got to work mastering how to fly the little sucker. It was tricky but I finally got the hang of it. I practiced until I could land the drone on a dime.

~

It was almost 2:30 when the door to the solitary confinement unit closed with a loud bang. Heavy footsteps approached the cellblock and stopped.

A loud shriek rattled my teeth.

I piloted the drone under the door of Yamahaha's cell. He was on his bunk with a guard punching the shit out of him. The beating was sadistic even by my standards, but Yamahaha just lay there and took it. The guard finally dropped his fists and turned to leave. Scuggins arrogant face filled the screen.

"Any day now they're finally going to tell me to kill you. Maybe even the next time I come to visit," Scuggins said over his shoulder. "That should give you something to look forward to."

Now that's just cruel.

It's one thing to kill a person, but it's quite another to keep them in suspense about *when* it's going to happen.

Yamahaha was curled up on his bunk. He looked like the loser of a prize fight — nose smashed flat, right eye swollen shut, front teeth knocked out, and a lot of blood was running from his left ear.

What the fuck had he done to deserve this?

It doesn't really matter. The only thing I cared about was the name of the person who'd hired us to kill the Judge. Nothing else mattered.

~

Once Scuggins was gone, Yamahaha gripped his ankles and rocked back and forth on his bunk sobbing quietly. I piloted the drone out of his cell and parked it on my ceiling next to the light bulb to recharge its solar battery.

I lay back and thought about what I'd seen and heard.

All the lights were kept blazing 24/7. The constant illumination was disorienting. In the short time I'd been here, I'd already lost track of whether it was day or night. After a year in isolation, I figured Yamahaha was royally fucked up.

~

I sent an email to Wilma and explained what had happened. We needed to do something soon before Scuggins made good on his threat to kill Yamahaha. If the poor bastard died, so did any chance of finding out who was pulling his strings.

I put on the sleeping mask Wilma included in my Happy Meal and drifted off to more pleasant memories of our past hits.

It was better than counting sheep.

I filtered out the kicking, screaming, and begging and only concentrated on those final delicious moments when it dawned on the victim that he was about to die.

~

My cell door opened and Wilma walked in. She wrinkled her nose at the reek of my body odor and looked disapprovingly at the empty fast food containers I'd thrown on the floor.

"Sorry, the maid hasn't been by to freshen up the room," I said sarcastically as I sat up. "What time is it?"

"Just after 5:00."

"In the morning?" I groaned. "I hope you brought donuts and coffee."

She pointed to my waist. "You're looking a little thinner already."

"Yeah, my prison diet does seem to be working."

I changed the topic. "Did Promod mess with the cameras?"

"I hope so. For his sake."

Promod was probably drinking coffee and eating a donut as he manipulated the prison's internal CCTV system from the comfort of his office.

I was still nervous that he held our freedom in his hands and could drop us in a vat of shit with only a few clicks.

If we managed to pull this off and he erased our trail, we ought to send him a nice thank you gift.

Wilma picked up my last can of Sprite.

"Come on. We don't have much time. I'm supposed to check in at twenty after."

SP-117

Wilma unlocked the cell door.

When we went in, Yamahaha didn't react, he just sat staring blankly at the wall.

"He's in lollypop land," I whispered.

"Then let's give him a taste of reality."

Wilma took out a small vial of colorless liquid and popped open the can of Sprite she'd taken from my cell. She squirted a few drops of the liquid into the can using an eyedropper.

Let me digress for a moment.

One of the more interesting side effects of the fall of the Soviet Union was the number of exciting new products that came into the marketplace. These included everything from AKs to small tactical nuclear weapons.

A group of former Soviet espionage operatives set themselves up as a kind of black market for surplus spy stuff. SP-117 had been developed as the perfect truth serum by the chemists in Department 12 of the KGB. Tasteless, colorless, and odorless, it could be slipped into a drink and would loosen the tongue within seconds. Best of all, the subject wouldn't remember saying anything afterward.

These ex-intelligence types were positioning it as the ideal love potion. From what I understand, Bill Cosby is their best client. He puts it in all his Jello.

Wilma and I found more imaginative uses for it.

She handed the Sprite to Yamahaha. He held it limply and continued to stare.

"Have a little drink, Randy," she urged. "You'll feel better."

He nodded slowly and took a sip. Yamahaha opened his eyes a tad as he tasted the soda. It was likely the most flavor he'd experienced in months. Then he chugged the entire can and then crushed it with a satisfied burp. A few seconds later, he let it tumbled to the floor. I scooped it up and leaned in close so he could get a good look at my face.

"Hello, Randy. Remember me?"

He thought about it for several minutes and then finally the light came on. He smiled up at me blissfully. "I do remember you." His gaze drifted toward the ceiling and his smile broadened.

I snapped my fingers to get his attention.

"What do you remember?"

"They paid me a thousand bucks to hire you."

"Hire me for what?"

"To kill that judge. They didn't like him very much. Maybe he wasn't very good at judging." Yamahaha giggled as if this was the funniest thing he'd ever heard.

"Randy … Randy … Focus. Who paid you?"

"I don't know his name …" He was drifting off again.

"What did he look like?"

"I don't remember. Everything's all fuzzy."

I tried to remain patient but knew the clock was running out. The effect of SP-117 only lasted about ten minutes. Wilma having to check in at the guard desk in less than five minutes added to the tension. Sending a search party after her was the last thing we needed.

"Where did you meet him?"

"In Beefalo. We shuffled off to Beefalo."

He began to laugh again and I felt like plucking out one of his eyeballs.

"Where in Beef … Buffalo?"

"Oh, I don't know … A diner I think … One of those really cool places that looks like an old-fashioned trailer … The Lakeside or Lakeview or something … They smoke their own bacon … It was marvelous."

"Do you remember anything about the man who hired you?"

"He was white, I think. Oh, wait. His face was all covered in scars like he'd been necking with razor wire."

"Time to go." Wilma grabbed my arm.

I took a final desperate look at Yamahaha. After everything I'd endured over the past week, this was all I had to show for it — a diner somewhere in Buffalo and a scar-faced man.

The radio on Wilma's belt crackled. She ripped it off and answered it. "Four one check."

"Hey, coffee's ready," a disembodied voice replied. "Matheson's wife baked some more of those carrot muffins,"

"On my way," she said and put the radio back on her belt.

~

Wilma relocked Yamahaha's cell and walked me back to mine.

"It's time to go now. We got everything we can from him."

I shook my head. I couldn't believe what I was about say.

"I have to stay awhile longer. There's one thing I still need to do."

She considered this for a few seconds. When it dawned on her what it was, she broke into her patented evil grin and shut the door.

"Bring me one of those muffins," I yelled after her.

~

I plugged the iPod into the small power supply Wilma had smuggled in. It would give me an additional eight hours of viewing time. She'd loaded on a bunch of Three Stooges shorts to keep me entertained. The *Shawshank Redemption*, one of my all-time favorites, was also on my playlist along with *Escape From Alcatraz* and the *Green Mile*.

Wilma was a very cruel woman.

Before commencing my own Canned Film Festival, I flew the micro drone to Yamahaha's cell and parked it on his ceiling. It would go to sleep until its motion sensor was activated. Then it would automatically override whatever I was watching.

At least I hoped I would be able to watch the Stooges without being disturbed.

~

I was almost through the fourth Stooges epic when it was interrupted by a live image from Yamahaha's cell.

Scuggins was back. I watched as he picked up the smaller man.

"Well, Randy, it's time to go now," Scuggins said as he pushed Yamahaha against the wall.

Then he ripped a four-foot length of cloth off the mattress and knotted it around Yamahaha's neck. He didn't resist as Scuggins lifted him off the ground and wrapped the other end of the cloth around the light fixture. Scuggins released Yamahaha and the poor sap dangled helplessly.

The light went off and the micro drone cycled over to night-vision mode. The picture was green and less distinct. I didn't see Scuggins.

My cell door flew open with a bang.

The bastard found me out!

I braced myself for the kind of beating Scuggins had given Yamahaha.

A figure towered in the doorway.

It was Wilma.

"Come on," she called and disappeared.

ALL THE APPEAL OF A
KIM KARDASHIAN PAP SMEAR

I ran to Yamahaha's cell.

A dead Yamahaha was still dangling from the light fixture, his tongue protruding between blue lips.

I moved toward him.

"Leave him," Wilma snapped. "Help me over here."

I looked down. Wilma was struggling to keep Scuggins pinned to the floor. I grabbed her Taser and squeezed the trigger. With a soft crackle, he went limp.

Together we got Scuggins to his feet and dragged him to the bunk.

Wilma stuck a syringe into his neck and we waited for the serum to take effect.

"Can Promod do it?"

"He says he can."

Wilma patted the spot on my shoulder where the tracking chip had been planted. She took a scalpel from her pocket and yanked the protective cover off the blade.

"Hold still. This is going to hurt."

Wilma pulled my jumpsuit away from my shoulder and deftly carved out the tracking chip. She handed me a large piece of gauze to hold over the wound.

"Put some pressure on it," she said as she wiped my blood off the chip.

"Open your mouth," she ordered Scuggins.

Under the spell of the SP-117 Scuggins obediently opened his mouth. Wilma dropped the tracking chip in and pushed his jaw shut.

"Swallow."

He gulped and smiled lazily.

"I'd really like to fuck you," Scuggins said in a drunken drawl. He gazed at Wilma with lust filled eyes.

Wilma's expression said it all — Scuggins had the sex appeal of a Kim Kardashian pap smear.

"What do you want to do with him?"

"Leave him. It'll wear off in a few minutes and he won't remember a thing."

I took one last look at the late Randy Yamahaha and wondered how he'd gotten in so far over his head. Whoever was behind this had friends everywhere.

Back in my cell, Wilma quickly stripped out of her guard's uniform revealing an identical one under it.

"This should fit," she said handing me the one she took off.

It was almost 6:00 and the shift change was coming up at 6:30.

Promod was already erasing Sheldon Hofsteader's digital existence from the Sawmill Grove databases.

I strolled out of the solitary confinement unit with Wilma and through the central cell block. We looked like any other pair of guards on their rounds.

"You got any of that SP-117 left?"

"Yeah, there's still a little in the needle," she replied. "Why?"

I could tell she didn't really wanted to hear my answer.

I walked to Bob Neill's cell and unlocked the door. He and his two stormtroopers were snoring loudly.

Without ceremony, I stuck the needle into his arm and pumped in a little truth juice.

~

I walked Neill over to my old cell and whispered something in his ear. Opening the door, I pushed Neill in. Marty Borman looked up in surprise and then abject terror as Neill walked over to his bunk. I locked the door behind him.

"Tell him," I ordered.

Neill smiled drunkenly at Borman. "I wanna be your bitch."

Borman flashed a huge smile and took Neill's hand.

Things might be a little bit awkward between them in the morning.

~

I grabbed a muffin off the plate in the guard room as we sauntered out the door and into the parking lot. Five minutes and three gates later, I was a free man.

Thanks to Promod, all traces of our visit had been carefully scrubbed from the bureaucratic mess that is Sawmill Grove Correctional Facility.

SHUFFLE OFF TO BEEFALO

On the way back to town, I made Wilma stop at Denny's for a *Grand Slam* breakfast.

"Take it easy on the calories."

Wilma was sipping black coffee and nibbling the crust off a piece of dry toast.

"Stop nagging me about gaining a few extra pounds," I snapped.

I was sensitive about my weight and her constant fixation about it.

"I need a partner who's fast on his feet, not huffing and puffing because he's dragging along sixty extra pounds."

Wilma did have a point. The extra weight had been slowing me down a bit. And Little Rip didn't have his usual zing.

My *Grand Slam* breakfast suddenly tasted like toasted particle board. I set my fork down and wondered what our old friend Scuggins was up to.

I called Promod and he assured me the tracking chip was working just fine. He'd reprogrammed it so we could use it to keep tabs on Scuggins.

"We need to get Promod a lovely gift," I told Wilma after I hung up.

"Costco's got a three for one special on paper shredders this week."

"That's kind of impersonal."

"How about one of those Dyson bladeless fans then."

Yeah, that's much more personal.

~

Back on the road, we tossed around gift ideas to pass the time while I followed the little blip that was Scuggins on my Android. He drove south, apparently not returning to the prison. I wondered if he even worked there.

Suddenly it occurred to me there might actually be more fake guards than real ones at Sawmill Creek.

"He's heading for Detroit," Wilma said.

~

I was looking forward to being home for a while. Shaking off the dust of the big house would be nice. My brief stay in solitary was bound to cause some grief during the coming nights. I felt a fleeting desire for the late Dr. Vessier to help me cope with the trauma.

Did she have a nice funeral?

Alas, my dreams of rest and recuperation were not to be. Scuggins didn't stop in the Motor City. He continued south toward Toledo.

Before reaching Toledo, Scuggins turned onto 280 and continued south to I-90 eastbound. This opened up a range of possible destinations: Cleveland, Columbus, Erie, Pittsburgh. But there was one that stood out like a shining beacon on the horizon, the one that Randy Yamahaha mentioned to me just before he dangled.

Fucking Beefalo ... Buffalo, New York.

~

They call it the Queen City, although I'm not sure why. I don't think it's a hot honeymoon destination for gay couples. Somehow I doubted gays would find Buffalo as stimulating as Key West or San Francisco, but I might be missing something. I'd never been there myself, so who was I to judge.

Wilma had. She referred to it as a *shithole*. I asked her to define *shithole* for me using Detroit as a baseline.

"There's nothing to see, the shopping's horrible, the food's greasy, and the weather's lousy. Stuffed peppers, Genesee Beer, and hot wings are the only culture they have."

I hate to contradict Wilma. It can be extremely dangerous.

A quick Google search showed there was lots of culture in Buffalo. They had a vibrant PBS affiliate, a philharmonic orchestra, live theater, an excellent art gallery, and plenty of good restaurants. They also had NFL and NHL franchises.

Like Detroit, Buffalo had once been a great city, thriving in the 19th century as the largest port on the Great Lakes and gateway to the west. But alas, the transcontinental railroad had put a pin in their prosperity balloon and it was downhill ever since. The steel mills closed and manufacturing jobs went to sweatshops in the Third World. Buffalo, like a lot of other Rust Belt cities, fell into despair.

But the folks of Buffalo never seemed to give up. It was like Detroit in that respect. The Queen City's proud citizens cling to hope like that dangling kitty in the poster.

While it might once have been a great place to live, today Buffalo is known for one thing and one thing only — blizzards. Cold winter winds howl across the surface of Lake Erie and funnel down at the east end where they slam into the city.

These winter storms hit over and over but don't get the residents down. They just shovel out and then make their way to their local drinking establishment to quaff ice-cold Genesee and eat lava-hot wings.

Buffalonians are a hearty bunch.

~

The local radio station was warning of a monster winter storm poised to strike Buffalo later in the day.

"Did you pack our winter stuff?" I asked Wilma.

"We can stop and pick up what we need.

Since we never know where work is going to take us, we find it prudent to keep a few changes of clothes and toiletries in the trunk. Being prepared also makes checking into hotels so much easier.

Weapons are never a problem either. We keep a supply close at hand in various hidey holes strategically cut into the framework of the car. After all, it's hard to do a job properly without easy access to the right tools.

We have our preferences when it comes to work. I like good old-fashioned firearms. They're concealable, simple to use, and, thanks to the tireless efforts of the National Rifle Association, absurdly easy to obtain.

Our source of supply is southern gun shows where cash is king and real identities are for morons. Recent rumblings say the government might actually enact legislation when it comes to gun shows, but so far the NRA has successfully kept this off the table. Every year I write them a big check so they can carry on their good work.

Realistically, however, we're probably only one or two school massacres away from tighter gun control. I can see a day when not even the NRA will be able to hold back the tide.

Not to worry, though, Steve assures me he is working on a 3-D printer that will produce as many untraceable high-caliber weapons as we can possibly use.

Isn't technology grand?

Wilma uses guns if she has to, but she really *loves* bladed weapons and power tools. Nothing satisfies her more than donning coveralls and a face shield and going to work.

The gleam in her eyes is touching when she's presented with the opportunity to use her cordless saws-all.

Of course, most people who see that glimmer have a slightly different response.

~

While we packed for all eventualities, we hadn't considered blizzards. The winter gear we had with us would be inadequate for raging winter storms, so we stopped at an outlet mall outside Cleveland to get blizzard-proof clothing.

All I could do was laugh when I saw Wilma. She was puffy and shapeless in her down-filled parka.

Keeping it stylish is not easy when shopping for winter clothes. I lucked out, however, and found a ski jacket and boots from an Italian designer who likely has never seen ice outside of a drink.

I did a pirouette in the parking lot to show off my new ensemble.

Wilma hooted. "That won't even stop a warm summer breeze."

I resisted pointing out that her jacket made her look like the Michelin Man.

My nuts were important to me.

THE LAKE EFFECT

The first flakes found us east of Erie, Pennsylvania, and I sure was glad we didn't have much farther to go.

"Looks like he stopped somewhere downtown." Wilma was looking at a map of Buffalo. "On Main Street, at a place called the Lake Effect Diner."

I flashed back to Yamahaha in solitary confinement, stoned to the eyeballs on my magic truth serum. He'd mentioned where he'd met his contact.

"A diner I think ... One of those really cool places that looks like an old-fashioned trailer ... The Lakeside or Lakeview or something ... They smoke their own bacon ..."

~

A foot of drifting snow was the only thing filling the parking lot of the Lake Effect Diner. Well, that and Scuggins's car. He was sitting at a table by the window staring out at the raging storm. He didn't appear fazed by it at all.

We'd parked on Main Street and waited patiently. The Lake Effect was one of those aluminum eateries that use to dot the landscape back in the good old days. It looked very cool and retro. A quick scan of reviews on Yelp told me the food was delicious, especially their double-smoked bacon and sourdough toast. Although it was only mid-afternoon, like any good Hobbit, I felt like having second breakfast.

Scuggins finished his meal and left. He leaned into the icy wind, walked to his car, and drove off. The diner was now empty and, without asking Wilma, I pulled into the parking lot.

"What?" She looked down Main Street where Scuggins was disappearing into a wall of snow and shook her head.

"Come on, this place was on *Diners, Drive-Ins, and Dives.*"

Forget your Michelin guide, the *Triple D* seal of approval meant thousands of empty calories, just the thing to help me weather the storm.

Wilma hated that show. She'd once expressed the desire to force the host to bob for French fries in a deep fat fryer.

~

"It's going to be a raw one," our server said by way of greeting. She was a perky young thing who I suspected was a student at the University of Buffalo a couple of blocks away.

Outside the window, snow was blowing horizontally. Our car was rapidly disappearing in a massive drift.

"Lucky you're in here."

"Yeah, it's pretty wild out there," I replied.

The waitress sighed. "And it isn't even Halloween yet. Usually, we don't get snow like this until at least Thanksgiving."

She poured us each a cup of coffee and walked off to bring our orders to the cook.

Wilma was in a funk. Neither of us had slept in over a day and any adrenaline from our recent prison escapade had long since dissipated. The only thing that might lift her spirits would be crushing someone in an industrial press. To distract herself, Wilma hunched over her cell phone screen to see where Scuggins was going.

The tracking device she'd shoved down his throat back at the prison was working correctly. Before she fed it to him, Wilma sealed the device inside a tiny capsule with another surprise, a small lump of plastic explosive about the size of a low dose aspirin. If things got out of hand, she could send a command from her cell phone and Scuggins would have one hell of a stomach ache.

Scuggins's shit-eating grin and biting sarcasm flashed in my head and I relished the idea of making his colon go boom.

Wilma looked up from the screen. "Let's go to the Falls."

I'd never been to Niagara Falls. What a great idea. "It's the honeymoon capital of the world. We can get a suite with a heart-shaped tub."

Wilma held up the phone.

Scuggins was in Niagara Falls.

"Maybe he got stuck and had to stop for the night," I said. "I wonder which hotel he checked into and if he has a heart-shaped tub."

"This map's too small." Wilma ignored me. "When we're back in the car, I'll bring it up on the tablet and we can see where he's landed."

Our food arrived and was every bit as delicious as the Yelp reviews said it would be. The hand-cut bacon had a distinctive flavor of hickory and was cooked just the way I liked, with texture and not too crispy. The organic eggs were fresh and the sourdough toast was sharp and sweet.

This was a meal I wanted to linger over. My Denny's breakfast became a distant memory.

Alas, it was not to be.

The manager approached and set our check on the table. "Sorry, folks, we're closing up for the day. The roads out there are getting more dangerous. They're even going to close the Interstate. You should find a hotel for the night."

Wilma looked up from her smoked ham.

The manager stepped back and gulped.

I smiled and assured him we would be on our way shortly.

I laid a $100 bill on the check. "Keep the change."

He scooped them up and disappeared into the kitchen.

~

We crept along the highway toward Niagara Falls. There was no other traffic on the road. After all, who would be insane enough to drive in this?

Occasionally the curtain of blowing snow parted, revealing the road ahead. During one of these intervals, I saw a tall bridge. My stomach gave a familiar lurch and I gripped the wheel.

"Bridge," I chirped, my mouth gone dry.

Wilma looked up but the bridge had disappeared in the snow.

"Good, that's the first of the Grand Island bridges. We're going the right way."

I caught a glimpse of the raging river far below. It was a long way down.

At the highest part of the bridge, the tires slipped. The car slid sideways towards the fragile-looking guardrail. Gripping the wheel so tightly my knuckles turned white, I eased the car back into the lane, fighting an overwhelming desire to close my eyes and scream.

Wilma was oblivious to my terror. She stared intently at her phone.

"According to Trivago, the only decent place in the Falls is the casino. I've booked us a suite."

Even though we were on the downhill side of the bridge, my heart was still trying to bid adieu to my chest.

"Sounds good," I squeaked. "Does it have a heart-shaped tub?"

"Yes," Wilma sighed.

I felt better until I remembered what she'd said.

"The first of the bridges ..."

~

You folks just made it," the valet said as he took the car keys. "I heard an eighteen wheeler just slid off the Grand Island Bridge. If you hurry down to the Falls, you might see it go over."

Wilma smiled and for a second, I thought she was seriously contemplating it.

I chased the horrifying vision from my head with happy thoughts of a warm, heart-shaped tub and a massive room service meal with plenty of champagne.

~

There is nothing more poignant than the sight of an empty casino. All those slot machines standing around desperately hoping someone will come by and pull their levers while the croupiers and dealers wait idly by their tables drinking sodas and praying for their shifts to end.

The staff stirred with anticipation as we strolled through the gaming hall and didn't hide their disappointment when we didn't pause to gamble.

Wilma and I take a lot of chances in life, it comes with the territory. But the thought of wasting our hard-earned cash in a place where the odds are horribly stacked against us is just repulsive.

The staff, however, viewed us as parasites. We ate in their restaurant where massive portions cost next to nothing, booked a luxury suite at the same rate as a Motel Six room, and enjoyed live entertainment at a bargain-basement price.

On a typical day, when the casino was bursting with jerks throwing away their mortgage money, we wouldn't have been given a passing glare. But in this deserted environment, the employees' resentment toward us was palpable.

This was a problem.

We stood out.

The staff would remember us and that would not be good if things went bad.

Wilma lowered her head and stared at the floor feigning embarrassment. I followed her lead and we made our way to the elevators as quickly as possible keenly aware of all the eyes upon us.

If I was capable of it, I might have even felt sorry for the staff stuck here in the middle of a blizzard with no one to fleece.

Oh well, it could have been worse. I thought of that eighteen wheeler going over the falls.

And there was always a slim chance that a busload of seniors flush with their Social Security checks would come by and cheer everybody up.

~

The bed was the size of a tennis court and the heart-shaped Jacuzzi would be an excellent way to wash off the stink of the big house. I stripped down and jumped in. Little Rip loved the liberating effect of the water jets.

I looked hopefully at Wilma, who just sighed and got naked. For such a lethal woman, she has a fantastic body. Not fashion model spectacular, but well-toned and evenly portioned.

I got busy and scrubbed her back. Her muscles were as tight as an evangelist's asshole. After a few minutes under my magic fingers, they began to loosen up. She leaned against me and started to nibble on my ear. Little Rip always enjoyed his visits with Wilma and after the lonely nights in prison, he was up and raring to go.

While heart-shaped tubs might be an attraction in hotel marketing brochures, in reality, they're a bit of a nightmare when it comes to lust-making. It's almost impossible to get a good grip, and there's a real danger of accidentally drowning your partner.

We climbed out of the tub and threw ourselves dripping wet onto the bed. I licked Wilma dry and she returned the favor. Like a groundhog stirring from his winter slumber, Little Rip rose up to see his shadow.

From the urgency of her grasp when she pulled me on top of her, I knew she wasn't interested in a lot of foreplay. When I entered her, she wrapped her legs around my butt, forcing me in deeper. I pinned her hands together and slammed into her with wild abandon. She bit my right earlobe so hard she drew blood.

I knew it wasn't going to take her long but I was worried that all my pent up prison energy would make me come first. I tried to think un-erotic thoughts but I kept circling back to that heart-shaped tub. Finally, I visualized plunging into the Niagara River from atop the Grand Island Bridge and that did the trick.

Wilma arched her back with a loud scream and deflated under me.

I thought of the heart-shaped tub once again and a few seconds later I joined her in ecstasyville.

Sex with Wilma was always fantastic, unless, of course, she was going to kill you afterward.

Describing our sexual relationship is difficult. There's no emotional connection, thank God. That's far too messy and really fucks things up. It's also not like being friends with benefits because I wouldn't exactly describe us as friends.

When it comes to sex, we have a mutual arrangement. We just feel when we're in heat and then go for it.

While we're doing it, it's as if we're in two separate places with a single intense connection that's a pipeline for our lust. We usually come together producing what I consider some of the most satisfying orgasms I've ever experienced and then in the next instant retreat back to each of our personal spaces.

I like to think this is the most perfect of all sexual partnerships — physical, unemotional, exciting, intense, and uninvolved.

I imagine most marriages are like that.

SPARKY FLETCHER

Wilma pulled on a robe and went to the laptop to check on dear Mr. Scuggins.

"Look at this," she said over her shoulder.

Still naked, I walked over and stood behind her. The now stationary red blip was blinking merrily. Wilma brought up a Google satellite image of the area and zoomed in on his position. Scuggins was in a large compound a few miles north along the Niagara Gorge.

The complex covered twenty acres beside the river. A large house perched on the edge of the gorge. Several other buildings were scattered around the property. Fences were clearly visible when Wilma zoomed in.

It was the perfect villain's lair, secluded with a spectacular view, the kind of place where Blofeld and Goldfinger could put their feet up and relax. I was jealous and wished we had a place where we could laze around and plot our evil deeds.

One thing that gave me uneasy was a long building which I suspected was a kennel. They probably had doggies roaming around at night. I pointed it out to Wilma, who hated dogs more than I did.

She nodded.

"What are we going to do about the pooches?"

Ignoring my question, she tapped the screen. "It's about five miles away. From the look of the access roads, we'll never make it in this storm."

Wilma was right. Even if we could miraculously get the car down there, we'd stand out like a severed ear.

I looked out the window and saw nothing but snow whirling past.

Not a fit night for man or beast to be out.

And the perfect occasion to go calling on Mr. Scuggins and his puppet master.

"I have an idea."

"Oh?" Wilma sounded dubious yet she hadn't even heard my brilliant idea. From long experience, however, she knew something insane was coming.

And it was.

"Let's give Promod a call."

~

Promod spent a couple of minutes complaining about the sore back he'd gotten from shoveling snow the night before when the blizzard had passed through Detroit.

"You should hook a plow to the front of your Bentley," I suggested helpfully.

This did not improve his grouchiness and he didn't even bother to ask what I was calling about.

I ignored his sullenness and cheerfully explained what we wanted.

He groaned. "I thought after the prison thing we were even."

"Yes, and thanks for that, but it was really more of a test to see if we could trust you again."

"And?"

"I'm happy to say you passed. But we need another favor."

There was a long pause and I was worried he might have hung up on me.

"Do I get paid for this favor?"

I was beginning to reconsider buying him that gift. His hostility was putting a barrier between us, but I managed to keep my tone warm and friendly. "Sure, how's a thousand bucks sound?"

"I make that every fifteen seconds with this new banking thing I'm doing."

Wilma took the phone. "I'll sweeten the offer. How about I sauté your spleen and serve it to you on a bed of zucchini flowers."

There was another long silence.

"Sorry, Promod, I forgot you were a vegetarian," Wilma said with just the right hint of spite.

She was not in a forgiving mood. In her eyes, Promod had committed an unpardonable sin when he betrayed us. Wilma would never trust him again. He was really lucky that I'd intervened at the time or she would've turned him into dog food.

The sword hanging over Promod's head was dangling by a thin thread and Wilma felt the need to remind him of his sins from time to time, especially when he got cocky. Of course, her attitude made my job of relationship management more difficult. I wanted Promod happy and willing but I needed to make certain my partner was confident he wouldn't pull a fast one again.

I took the phone back from Wilma.

"Promod, don't worry. We'll treat you well. Wilma still has some anxiety about your momentary lapse in good judgment. You're on your way to getting out of our lives forever."

That was a little white lie. Promod was far too valuable a resource to escape our icy grip and he knew it. I knew he harbored a secret desire to put us under and would probably turn a profit doing it. I took his unwillingness to help as a good sign, a sign that he wasn't hatching a scheme against us.

Understanding the motivations and agendas of people is an absolute necessity in my world. In a world founded on subterfuge and deception, the ability to be the most distrustful is paramount.

Promod sighed. "What do you need?"

"We need to know who owns this compound."

"I can do a title search and email you the results within a few minutes. The rest I'll get to in the morning."

That wasn't good enough.

"We're going in tonight. We need a way in and we need a way out."

Promod started to object but I cut him off. "And if we don't get in there tonight, we're coming after you."

More silence. "Give me a few hours," he said and hung up.

~

We went downstairs to get something to eat. It was nearly 9:00 and we had plenty of time before our nocturnal activities.

"Hey look!" I pointed to a poster outside the casino's ballroom. "Sparky Fletcher!"

Sparky was a Motown legend, one of the original stars along with the Supremes, Stevie Wonder, The Miracles, Gladys Knight and the Pips, and Marvin Gaye. I had a soft spot for all Motown artists and Sparky in particular.

His next performance was at 10:00.

"Let's catch the show."

"Sure. It'll kill some time." Wilma was less than enthusiastic about taking a trip down Motown Memory Lane.

~

The Casino Ballroom was as gloomy as the rest of the place. I half expected Sparky's show to be canceled, but the maitre d' assured us it wouldn't be.

I asked for a good table near the stage.

He waved his hand at the nearly empty theater. "Take your pick."

I chose one right down in front.

A waiter handed us menus. The signature dish was a hamburger the size of a landmine. I was about to order one when I caught the disapproving glare Wilma shot me. She knows me so well.

I opted for a quarter roasted chicken and side salad instead.

After our meal, we settled in for an evening of classic rhythm and blues.

I remembered the first time I saw Sparky. It was in the mid-1990s and he was headlining a Motown revival show backed by a fifteen-piece band and eighteen dancers.

It was a powerhouse performance by an artist at the peak of his career.

So fast forward twenty years and imagine my surprise when the very same Sparky Fletcher, using the code name Rowdy Yates, was sitting on a park bench next to me whining about how his parasitic manager was bleeding him dry. Not only that, he was down to his last million and the IRS was circling like a bunch of ravenous hammerheads.

Sparky had invested $50,000 in our business solution and was delighted when his manager met a horrible fate a few weeks later.

I had hoped for his sake this would mark the beginning of a career upturn but unfortunately, it looked like that hadn't happened.

Sparky burst onto the stage shedding sequins from his ratty suit. He propelled his seventy-year-old body around with gusto. Too bad his anemic backup band couldn't match his electrifying performance.

The only hiccup in an otherwise perfect act was when he recognized me in the audience. Sparky stumbled over a line but, to his credit, took only a couple of beats to recover.

The audience jumped up and cheered at the end of the set.

Sparky wore a smile that lit up the room. He bowed deeply and left the stage with a theatrical flourish.

~

Imagine our surprise when a waiter arrived at our table and presented us with an expensive bottle of wine.

"Compliments of Mr. Fletcher," he said.

The star himself arrived a few minutes later and sat down without waiting for an invitation.

Wilma shrank into the shadows. He didn't pay any attention to her but eyed me suspiciously. I knew what he was afraid of.

I held up my hands. "Great show, Rowdy."

He balked at hearing the name he'd used during our last meeting.

"Don't worry, this is purely accidental. I'm just visiting the Falls to take in the sights.

"Well, it's Kismet then, our meeting like this."

"Exactly."

I wasn't sure what *Kismet* was. It sounded like a hemorrhoid treatment.

"I was thinking about you just the other day," he continued.

"Really? Nice thoughts I hope."

He nodded enthusiastically. "About how you handled that little issue with Ralph Fisher for me."

Fisher was his former manager, the one we stuck head-first into the record pressing machine.

"Yes," I said, "he was a groovy guy."

He sure was after the machine had finished with him.

"I have another little problem that I was hoping you could help me with."

"Sorry, Sparky, I don't do return engagements."

He reached over and grabbed my arm. "She's bleeding me dry ..."

"I assume you're referring to your significant other."

"My current wife."

"Shopping or lover?"

The two most common causes of marital discord.

"Cats," he spat. "She has dozens and dozens. The house reeks like a litter box and she's spending all my retirement savings on really expensive cat food. The damn animals eat better than I do."

"Why don't you divorce her then?"

"I can't afford any more alimony. I already have six ex-wives on the payroll. That's why I have to play shitholes like this every night. Anyway, she'd claim the cats were dependents and ream me."

I hesitated and Sparky's desperation went up a notch.

"I'll have the hotel comp your room and dinner," he threw in.

"That's awfully sweet of you, but I've got a bit of a backlog right now and it would take me a couple of weeks to get to it."

"Perfect. I'll be in Europe doing a bunch of dates next month. You could make it look like an accident so no one will suspect a hit."

Wilma gave me a *whatever* look.

What the hell. It would be a simple in-and-out-hair-dryer-in-the-bathtub kind of gig.

I nodded and Sparky's relief was palpable.

"I'll leave your down payment at the front desk in the morning." He stood up and offered his hand. "Any time after the fifth. I'll be in Belgium then. I'll leave our address in the envelope. And I'd appreciate it if you could take out a few of those cats as well."

"Sorry, Sparky, we don't do animals."

Sparky shrugged and headed backstage to get ready for his midnight show. I wondered how big the crowd would be for that one.

Finishing the wine, I left a hefty tip on the table.

We had a show of our own to get to.

HYPOTHERMIA

Tim Hortons is the perfect port in any storm.

This famous coffee and donut chain is an institution for our neighbors to the north. Recently Tim Hortons moved south to New York, Michigan, and Ohio. I like their coffee and I'm especially partial to their honey dipped donuts.

Imagine my delight when I spotted their familiar logo blazing through the raging storm just a short walk from our hotel.

~

We went out the side door of the casino a few minutes after 1:00 in the morning. It wasn't a surprise that nothing was moving on the streets, except for the occasional snowplow.

Huddling in the shadows at the edge of the parking lot, we watched a convention of snowplow operators drinking coffee and eating Timbits. They were having a great time picking up the latest gossip and earning double-overtime for sitting around on their donut-enhanced asses.

Most of them had left their plows idling in the parking lot while they went inside.

I mean, who would be stupid enough to steal a snowplow, right?

A large plow sat about fifty feet away, its motor still running. The driver finally returned, hunched against the wind as he protected his coffee and jelly-filled.

Wilma slipped from the shadows and gave him a jolt with her Taser. He did a little mambo and flopped to the ground. We hauled him into the plow's cab and stuffed him into the space behind the seats. I hopped behind the wheel and Wilma crouched on the floor of the passenger side.

With the driver's baseball cap pulled down to hide my face, I put the rig into gear and gave a jolly toot on the air horn as I drove off.

Driving a snowplow wasn't as tricky as I'd first thought. I'd once owned a Hummer H3 and the plow handled better than *it* ever did.

~

You'd think driving a snowplow along a slick road next to a high gorge in a raging blizzard might cause me anxiety but, *au contraire*, it was strangely exhilarating.

I was six years old again playing with my Tonka dump truck in the sandbox.

The big rig handled the icy roads really well. We made excellent time by using the angled blade to push the drifts out of our way.

Letting the GPS be our guide, we left the main road and went down a narrow lane.

We had toyed with the idea of ramming the main gate but decided a more subtle ploy was called for.

Our plan was to leave the plow nearby and approach on foot. Wilma would go to the far side of the compound and create a diversion. There was a perfect way in for me near the river where a large tree overhung the security fence. I'd climb up and wait for Wilma's signal. Then I'd drop to the ground inside the compound and head for the main house.

~

We left the warmth and safety of the truck and moved through the woods. Much to my dismay, my fashionable winter ensemble was entirely useless. The jacket did next to nothing to prevent the icy, damp wind from penetrating my bone marrow and my wet feet were quickly turning to frozen lead.

"Fuck, it's freezing!"

Snug and warm in her Michelin Man jacket, Wilma smiled smugly. She took immense joy in allowing me to uncoil lots of rope.

Well, it's too late now.

I hugged myself in an attempt to generate some warmth.

"Buzz me when you're ready," she said and jogged off.

I made my way through the woods until I came to a ten-foot high, thick steel mesh fence topped with razor wire. Signs with large angry red lightning bolts hung from the wire. Their message was very clear.

Visitors will be electrocuted.

But grabbing onto it had a certain appeal at this point. I would die warm.

Twenty feet away and just barely visible through the snow was an old maple. Although gnarled and broken, it had one redeeming feature — a long branch that overhung the fence. Crawling along it and dropping into the compound looked simple enough.

The reality was a different story. The limb was a lot thinner than I'd expected *and* it was fifteen feet off the ground.

Suddenly the thought of climbing up there seemed like the worst idea I've ever had. My balls, already flash-frozen by the storm, tingled unpleasantly and I held back nausea.

In that instant of terrifying clarity, I realized my mistake. Wilma should've been the one going up the tree while I caused a fuss to lure the guards away.

I had not thought this through. I could only imagine Wilma grinning to herself as she visualized my tortured climb.

Of course, she could have pointed all this out to me when we were still in the planning stage, but that would have spoiled her fun.

Resigned to my fate, I strapped on a pair of lineman's spikes and began to climb carefully. I tried to focus only on the branches above, but couldn't resist glancing down. My brain twirled like a badly maintained carnival ride and I wrapped my arms around the tree trunk and hugged it for dear life. I sucked in deep breaths of frigid air and chanted a new mantra.

Asshole, asshole, asshole, asshole ...

I started climbing once more, pulling myself up inch by inch until I reached the limb.

I looked down again.

Big mistake.

The ground shimmered like a mirage on a desert highway.

I almost let go.

Bile rose in my throat and I struggled not to throw up.

A flashback to the swinging cable car overwhelmed me. I could feel it swaying in sickening arcs back and forth. Darkness invited me to join it and I fought to stay conscious.

Asshole, asshole, asshole, asshole ...

I shut my eyes and forced myself to crawl along the branch. It groaned under my weight.

Had it gotten thinner, or had I gotten fatter?

I prayed that a strong gust of wind wouldn't knock me off.

When I finally opened my eyes again, to my horror I saw that I still had six feet to go.

That was another thing I hadn't thought through, hanging from the branch and dropping.

The moisture in my mouth evaporated and my heart tried to hammer its way out of my ribcage.

Asshole, asshole, asshole, asshole …

But I had no choice. I had to continue.

Little by little I slid my gloved hands along the branch and slowly dragged my body behind them. With every move I made, the branch creaked and groaned in protest under the added strain of my weight.

There's a spot in every Roadrunner cartoon when my hero Wile E. runs off the edge of a cliff, stands in mid-air, and has time to contemplate the inevitability of gravity.

But in real life that doesn't happen.

I just dropped like a stone against the background of a brilliant flash of sparks.

With the ugly sound of a firecracker exploding in a trashcan, the fence was crushed by the limb.

I lost my grip and flew through the air.

Fortunately, a thick layer of snow cushioned my fall. I was momentarily winded, but at least, I was inside the compound.

All hell broke loose!

Intense spotlights turned night into day and deafening sirens screamed my name.

Asshole, asshole, asshole, asshole …

So much for the subtle approach.

~

The frenzied barking of guard dogs got louder and louder.

Flashlight beams stabbed the darkness.

It was time to find somewhere to hide, and quickly.

I burrowed under an umbrella of evergreen branches. With luck, no one would spot me.

Three large Alsatians burst through the blowing curtain of snow, each tugging a guard behind it.

The guards stopped with their backs to me, assessing the damage.

"It's a fuckin' branch," the middle one said into his headset. "It took down a section of the fence."

Sparks continued to snap, crackle, and pop from the damaged fence.

"The fence is still charged. We can wait until morning."

I prayed he meant they would wait until morning to repair it and not that they were going to guard the breach all night.

Meanwhile, the Alsatians had picked up the delicious scent of yours truly. They strained at their leashes and tried to tug the guards in my direction. I shifted uncomfortably in my hidey hole, certain I was about to become a chew toy for a pack of raging beasts. The guards, however, were having none of it. They had their answer: a branch had broken the fence. Besides, it was freezing cold and the snow was blowing. They must have decided the dogs had caught the scent of a rabbit or something and dragged the frustrated animals away.

The guard took a final look at the fence and walked away in disgust. The other two followed him and they all disappeared back into the blizzard.

I breathed a sigh of relief.

My choppers were chattering like a joke shop novelty and I was glad they hadn't given me away.

If I didn't get moving soon, I was going to freeze to death.

Little Rip was giving me hell for not wearing long johns. To warm up, I thought about when I was kissing the inside of Mandy Shugar's incredibly silky thighs.

My body temperature rose a couple of degrees.

I visualized the two of us joined together at the hips, her erect nipples rubbing against my chest as she moaned in my ear. Her warmth enveloped me.

Suitably Mandyfied, my core temperature shot up another ten degrees.

I resolved right there in the icy grip of the storm, with my marrow frozen as hard as peach ice cream, that I would get out of this alive. Then I would jump on the first flight to South Carolina, book a suite in the finest hotel, and invite Mandy over for my personal Olympic challenge. We would have fifteen days of non-stop sex, interrupted only by naps and deliciously fattening foods.

Just the thought had Little Rip radiating more heat than a runaway reactor.

He'd saved me again.

I jumped up from my hiding place with renewed vigor and followed the guards. They would lead me to the main house. Their footprints were already beginning to disappear beneath the relentless blizzard so I picked up my pace to catch up with them. With luck, there would be at least one straggler.

There was.

One of the guards had stopped to have a cigarette. His dog was straining against its thick chain, desperate to get out of the cold.

Coming up behind them, I put the business end of my Taser against the back of the guard's neck and pulled the trigger. The charge knocked them both off their feet. The guard exhaled a long stream of smoke on his way down. It looked like his soul was leaving his body.

I stripped off his uniform, coat, gloves, and balaclava and put them on. He wouldn't last too long in his underpants.

I juiced him again with the Taser just for fun. His circular convulsions reminded me of the jerky style of dancing we did back in the 80s.

I had a brief flashback to a *Talking Heads* concert I'd gone to at the Masonic Temple.

Once in a lifetime ...

~

Promod answered on the first ring.

His hissing whisper told me he was in bed and not happy about being disturbed.

"Sorry to call so late. Did you have any luck finding the schematics?"

"Yes. The property's owned by the prison corporation, the International Correctional Management Group. They're a private company and don't have to file any kind of public financial statements, so I can't figure out who owns them."

"That's interesting, but right now I need you to shut down the alarm system."

"Right now?"

"Stop groaning and get out of bed, I'm fucking freezing out here and I need a way into the house."

~

The house was barely visible through the blowing snow. Waiting at the edge of the woods, I was worried that they would notice one of their guards was missing and come looking for him.

With this level of security, it was a sure bet the doors were monitored. If I suddenly showed up on their screens, it would cause bedlam.

More flashing lights and screaming sirens!

Promod needed to cut off the security system and open the way for me but he was taking his time. He was punishing me for disturbing him in the middle of the night.

Even wearing the guard's heavy winter garb, I was starting to feel the bite of the cold again.

~

Three frozen minutes later my phone vibrated.

"They have incredible security," Promod told me. "I can't get directly into their system. They would detect the intrusion. But I found a vulnerability. They have a backup generator that takes several seconds to kick in. During that time, they'll be wide open. I can kill the power to the house from here. As soon as the lights go out, go through the door. Make sure to close it immediately, before the lights come back on."

"Okay, but I need a minute to get there."

"Buzz me when you are at the door."

I stepped out of the woods and headed toward the back door. To anyone watching from the house, it would look perfectly normal, just another guard on his way in after taking a smoke break.

I reached the back door and hit speed dial on my phone.

~

A second later the entire complex went black. When I heard a loud click, I pushed the door open, stepped through, and shut it quickly behind me.

Promod strikes again!

The lights came back on and there was a dull thud as the electronic bolt slammed back into place.

I was safely inside.

Well, maybe not *safely*, but I was inside.

THE SHIBUYA DISTRICT

I was standing in a mudroom, melting snow dripping from my coat.

A row of coats hung on the wall above a wooden bench and heavy boots were on a metal grate running under it. A pair of cozy slippers called invitingly, but they wouldn't provide any protection in a fight. I decided to be a bad house guest and keep my wet boots on. Me tracking mud on the floors would be the least of their worries.

After waiting a few moments to see if my presence had been detected, I decided it was safe to go exploring. At this time of night, there should be minimal security. The fence incident was probably the most excitement they'd had all day, if not all year.

I moved along a hall and, to my surprise, heard the sound of at least two voices coming from what I guessed was the living room. While I couldn't make out what they were saying, the tone was relaxed and friendly.

The distinct pressure of a gun barrel against my spine disrupted my plan to disturb their pleasant evening.

"Well look who it is," said a familiar voice. "How about a taste of your own medicine?"

Something pricked the side of my neck and then everything faded out.

~

Nauseating waves of reality washed over me like a Pink Floyd song.

Where the fuck am I?

Blurred signs shifted into focus. From the park bench where I lay, a vast city spread out before me. The style of the buildings and the flashing neon characters on the signs told me I was in …

Tokyo? What the hell was I doing in Tokyo?

"How do you like it?"

The amplified voice sliced through the ether. I continued to marvel at the city spread out before me. Elevated high-speed trains raced among the skyscrapers and thick lines of traffic clogged the streets like donut fat in a cop's arteries.

How do I like it?

Something was off. I focused on the shimmering buildings that stretched to the horizon.

The horizon.

That was it!

The background was fake. The entire vista was a very elaborate model of a Japanese city.

"Two million dollars."

I turned my head painfully and saw Godzilla glaring down at me. "You were thinking about how much it cost."

I'd also been wondering who'd be crazy enough to build it.

Godzilla clomped up beside me. "It's an exact replica of the Shibuya district of Tokyo. It's one of my favorite stomping grounds."

The giant lizard chuckled.

A human laugh.

The Godzilla costume was almost nine feet tall and must have weighed a couple of hundred pounds. The creature moved toward me with a slow, shuffling gait.

"I had it built by the same special effects artists who stole the suit for me from Toho Studios in Japan. I'm a stickler for detail. Ever since I was a little kid, I've loved Godzilla movies. And now that I'm rich enough, I want my fantasies to be as real as possible."

He leaned over and the lizard's mouth flopped opened. A thin black fabric hid the face inside, but the eyes were clearly visible and gleaming with excitement.

"I love to see things destroyed. Things like planes crashing, race cars exploding, or buildings imploding. Spectacular. Makes me feel all warm and fuzzy inside."

Since I'd recently experienced a building implosion up close and personal, I knew what he meant, although *spectacular* is not exactly the word I would use to describe it.

"They modified the suit for me and put on a sound chip so I can roar."

The giant head reared back and a painfully loud roar shook the entire room.

"And they even rigged up a flame thrower so I can breathe fire. I'll show you that a little later. But first …"

He turned toward the city and I ducked as his tail swished over my head.

"Up and at em, pal!"

I was jerked to my feet and my arms were pinned to my sides. Twisting my head, I saw my old buddy Scuggins. I realized he'd been the one who'd drugged me.

Scuggins held up a syringe filled with clear fluid.

"No thanks, I've had my quota for the day."

"Love Potion Number Nyet, ordered on eBay," he said with a wicked grin.

A single, mesmerizing drop of the liquid glistened on the tip of the needle.

"I expect you want me to talk," I said.

"You already have."

Icy fingers ran up my spine like an Olympic sprinter.

Had I spilled all the details of our mission?

Did I give Wilma away?

Or worse, had I confessed my real name?

My head throbbed like I'd been kicked in the balls.

In the bed of my psyche, fear rolled over to make room for dread. A deep and profound fear, like the kind you experience just before watching the latest *Star Wars* sequel.

Struggling against Scuggins iron grip, I used the only weapon in my limited arsenal — useless bluster.

"What are you going to do about it?" I shouted to Godzilla.

"Well, right now I have a city to destroy. But when I'm finished, I have another new toy that you can help me out with."

He activated the sound chip and tore into Tokyo. His bellowing hurt my ears.

Before I could react, Scuggins stabbed the needle into my neck again.

The scene swirled like dirty water going down a drain. The last image I had was of Godzilla breathing flames onto an office building.

~

I was trapped inside a bag of gelatin.

Everything was wavy and curled up at the edges, with the surreal quality of a cosmic lap-dance.

Little pieces of time dropped away like chips of paint.

Was this death, or was it purgatory as dreamed up by Dante's giant lizard?

I was no longer the star of my own show. Instead, I was forced to watch it from a distant balcony in the back of a theater.

Large portions of reality were missing. There were only snatches — the vague sensation being dragged along hardwood floors, the hollow sound of a door opening, the clunk, clunk, clunk, clunk of the toes of my boots hitting stone step after stone step.

~

I was in a cable car, cowering in a corner as far away as I could get from the open door.

Godzilla stood next to the yawing egress. Snow swirled around him, and for a moment, I thought he looked really cool.

Why didn't they set a Godzilla film in wintertime?

Do they even have winter in Japan?

He looked over at me, eyes twinkling from inside his open mouth. "Look what I can do!" he roared just before jumping.

The bungee cord trailed behind him.

Well, that's that.

The car lurched as Godzilla's massive weight pulled it down.

Sliding toward the opening, I desperately grabbed for something to hang on to.

I reached the edge and looked down into the snow.

Munchkins danced around in my chest.

A muffled "Wheeeee …!" was followed by the iconic Godzilla roar.

The car lurched again and I tumbled out.

Falling backward, I watched the cable car above me get smaller and smaller until it was lost in the swirling snow.

As I passed him, Godzilla reached over and grabbed my shoulders.

The added weight snapped the bungee cord and we both tumbled ass over teakettle, the giant lizard squealing in delight like that annoying pig in the Geico commercials.

It was pissing me off and I hoped the fall would be over quickly to shut him up.

Glancing over my shoulder, I saw we were approaching the ground really, really fast.

We hit and the ground broke away beneath us.

Suddenly Godzilla was gone and I fell alone into a deep chasm.

The patch of sunlight at the top of the hole got tinier and tinier until it was just a pinprick.

I was deep inside the earth now and ...

~

My brain rejoined my body and I was having a difficult time adjusting. What part of the looking glass had I passed through this time?

I let my brain flop around for a bit like a beached whale. I trusted all would make sense again. When reality finally returned, things had taken a decidedly medieval turn.

The Japanese city was gone and I was in a much different place. It was dank and cold and the echoing of dripping water had a distinctly ominous feel.

I closed my eyes and tried to go back to sleep, but it was no use. I was too uncomfortable. Opening them again, I attempted to figure out what was going on.

I was at the bottom of a deep well-like room. Curved stone walls disappeared into the darkness high above.

Metal shackles bound my wrists and ankles. I lay spread-eagled on a table of narrow planks stretched across a deep pit.

The only light was from sputtering torches set in the walls. They illuminated stone stairs that spiraled upward. The steps reminded me of the grooves inside the barrel of my weapon. I wished I had my warm gun with me, but my pistol was long gone along with my clothes.

I was now dressed, if that's the right word, in a robe that smelled like dung. My garment was made all the more unpleasant by lice, which I'm sure had had been added for extra authenticity. I struggled to scratch myself but it was impossible because the shackles clamped me tightly.

All I could do was suffer the death of a thousand itches.

Luckily, I didn't have to wait long.

Squealing hinges at the top of the shaft announced the arrival of my host. He grabbed a torch and descended slowly.

I struggled to relieve the prickly sensation of tiny critters crawling all over me by frantically rubbing my back on the wooden boards. That didn't help and it was driving me crazy.

Another figure stepped through the door and started down the stairs. My anxiety level ratcheted up to eleven.

The first figure towered over me.

Scuggins.

He looked extremely uncomfortable in his woolen monk's robe. I wondered if his outfit had lice too.

Scuggins held his torch high and waited for the other person to join him.

This guy was dressed in a red silk monk's habit, his face hidden by the darkness within. The figure in red took the torch from Scuggins and stepped closer to me.

A chill ran up my spine like a mouse with its tail on fire.

What new kind of lunacy is this?

"I am a man of many obsessions," he said.

I recognized my tormentor's voice. He was the same person who had been wearing the Godzilla costume.

"For instance, I have an incredible collection of early American first editions," he continued as he stepped even closer. He was a little more subdued like stomping Toyko had worn him out.

"My most prized books are by Edgar Allen Poe. Perhaps you've heard of him."

"Sure. I read him in lit class when I was in school."

"Of course, you did. Everybody did. But did you really *appreciate* him?"

The pointed hood of his robe reminded me of the Ku Klux Klan. It made me uneasy.

We had once killed a Grand Dragon or was it an Imperial Wizard, or a Sith Lord. I can never tell them apart. All I remember was that he hadn't taken kindly to being lynched.

He handed the torch back to Scuggins and then stepped to the wall and pulled on a wooden lever. Lights flickered to life above me, illuminating the entire chamber.

In the weak light they cast, I saw a large mechanical apparatus with a long arm extending down into the shaft. On the end of the arm was a curved six feet blade.

I recognized it immediately; it was from *The Pit and the Pendulum*.

I'd seen the old movie numerous times and gleefully rooted for Vincent Price. But now it was hanging directly above me, and I didn't feel like cheering. Instead, I pulled against my restraints in desperation.

"No, use in struggling. Those are made from chrome steel."

His laugh reminded me of Vincent Price.

This guy was taking the whole supervillain thing *way* too seriously.

"I had those Japanese craftsmen put this together for me as well. They do excellent work. It's entirely authentic. Well, at least, I think it is. I haven't had a chance to give it a real test yet. And that's where you come in."

He pushed a larger wooden handle. With a creak, the gigantic mechanism groaned to life. The pendulum quivered and then began to move.

I watched it in sickening fascination.

The arm swung back and forth in ever-widening arcs until it almost brushed the chamber's walls.

With a loud *click*, the blade dropped and carved an arc through the air five inches closer to my chest. It swung once again and there was another *click*. The blade dropped another five inches.

My heart skipped a beat and the room began to spin around me.

Reality deteriorated into madness and I held my breath.

When I did, I involuntarily sucked in my belly but I knew that no amount of stomach holding was going to stop the inevitable agony of the blade carving me asunder.

THE PIT AND THE HUMDRUM

The man in red took out a small book and flipped it open.

> "Down — still unceasingly — still inevitably down! I gasped and struggled at each vibration. I shrunk convulsively at its every sweep. My eyes followed its outward or upward whirls with the eagerness of the most unmeaning despair; they closed themselves spasmodically at the descent, although death would have been a relief, oh! How unspeakable! Still I quivered in every nerve to think how slight a sinking of the machinery would precipitate that keen, glistening ax upon my bosom."

I wasn't particularly paying attention to what he was reading. All I could focus on was the blade relentlessly dropping closer and closer.

I felt like vomiting. But why bother? In less than a minute, the contents of my stomach would be all over the place anyway.

He shut the book and went up the steps. He paused and turned to look at me. "Sorry, I've got to leave you now. The messy stuff is dreadfully upsetting. I'll leave it to Mr. Scuggins to pick up the pieces."

The blade cut the air closer to my chest. I could feel the swish as it passed over me. A brief sparkle glinted off its finely-honed edge. I looked down at my plump belly, wishing I'd lost a lot more weight.

I would even give up second breakfasts.

"I just wanted to shoot you," Scuggins said in disgust, "but he loves his toys."

As the blade swung closer, I thought about reincarnation. It's one of the few beliefs that make sense to me. I'm hoping to come back as a mongoose.

I discussed this with Wilma one time. She said I'd probably come back as a tapeworm.

Tapeworm or mongoose, it didn't matter very much at this particular moment. The curved blade flashed by a few inches from my flesh. I figured there was one, maybe two, swings left before it cut me in half.

Scuggins leaned in close, his eyes shining with excitement. He obviously was not in the least bit squeamish and wanted to enjoy every gory moment of my demise.

I was pissed off and wished for the thousandth time my hands were free to wrap around his scrawny neck and ...

Scuggins' eyes almost popped from his head. He grabbed his stomach and doubled over in pain. A reddish glow coming from inside him reminded me of ET's heart light.

The blade swished past me again and nicked my belly.

He screamed and farted smoke and flames, just like a label on a bottle of hot sauce.

Wonder what he had for lunch.

Across the room, the blade reached the end of its arc with another loud *click.*

Death was just inches away.

Pounding footsteps distracted me from the inevitable. I looked up to see Wilma running full-tilt down the stairs.

Scuggins stumbled blindly into the path of the blade. It sliced through his chest and came neatly out his back, dragging him toward me.

I closed my eyes and braced for the agony of being cut in half.

A deafening screech echoed through the chamber.

Time stood still.

Then I looked up into Scuggins' bulging eyes. He was still impaled on the blade, which had stopped a few inches from my stomach. Blood leaked from the corners of his open mouth.

The tiny explosive charge inside the tracker we had fed him had done its job after Wilma sent the signal via her cell phone.

I bet he wasn't expecting that.

She fiddled with several switches on the wall until the blade started to clank its way upward, carrying the impaled Scuggins along for the ride.

A large drop of his blood smacked my forehead.

"Release me," I begged.

She hit a button on the side of the table. The metal shackles snapped open. I jumped up and began scratching myself like a maniac.

"What took you so long?"

"I needed to search the house. You were a good distraction."

I pulled the robe over my head and tossed it into the pit, oblivious to my nakedness.

"Did you get him?"

"Get *who*?"

"The guy dressed in red. He would've gone right past you."

"I didn't see anyone."

~

We found a secret door near the top of the stairs. It was practically invisible in the dim torch light. We couldn't find any way to open it and finally gave up. This had to be how my tormenter had gotten away without Wilma seeing him.

~

When we reached the main floor, I saw that he had indeed stomped Tokyo flat.

Whoever he was, he'd obviously escaped with his bodyguards.

I was furious. I kept flashing back to the pit and the pendulum and needed to kill someone to satisfy my insatiable lust for revenge. But all the hens had fled the henhouse.

Short of shitting on his furniture, there wasn't much I could do but find my clothes and get dressed. My unrequited bloodlust was literally making steam come from my ears.

"Here." Wilma passed me a thermite charge from her pack. "Why don't you do the honors."

I grabbed the charge and shoved it under the couch in the living room. For the next five minutes, I jammed multiple charges into every nook and cranny I could find.

I felt a little better when I had finished.

~

There had been no let up in the raging storm. The full brunt of it slammed into us when we left the house. The cold froze the tears in my eyes and after twenty minutes of struggling through the woods, I was convinced my face was frostbitten.

Luckily, the snowplow was where we had left it. Surprisingly, the driver was still out cold in the back and I wondered if Wilma had given him too big a dose. But then he groaned and I knew he was okay.

The big rig shimmied and shook when I started it, its frozen cylinders chugging to warm up. Once the engine was humming again, I put it into gear and we began to plow through the massive drifts that had built up in the hours we had been away.

Once we'd reached the Parkway, I stopped. Wilma passed me her cell phone. I pressed *Send* and sent a signal to the charges I had planted in the house.

A brilliant flash cut through the storm and lit up the night around us. Large pieces of the house and all its toys rained down into the woods around it. A second later we heard a dull crump and the heavy truck shook from the shockwave.

I breathed a sigh of *release*.

Hope *he*, whoever *he* was, got the message: *We are an unstoppable force and we're coming for you.*

~

I parked the plow where we found it with its engine running and left the driver slumped over the steering wheel. When he woke up, he'd have one hell of a headache and probably think he'd just fallen asleep.

~

A day and a half later we bid goodbye to western New York. The storm had finally worked out its anger issues and moved on but while the blizzard was still in full fury, it held us prisoner in the hotel. It was frustrating. I wanted to find the bastard who had held me prisoner and raped my mind with truth serum.

My experience in the torture chamber played over and over. The pendulum had been within a few inches of chopping me in half. When I found the guy in red, I'd show him a thing or two about Edgar Allen Poe.

Perhaps he'd enjoy being bricked up behind a wall.

Or maybe being buried alive.

Or having a raven peck out his eyes.

While I stewed in my thoughts of revenge, Wilma was struggling with cabin fever. She hated being cooped up and prowled around the suite constantly looking out the window to see if it had stopped snowing.

Too bad there wasn't a Costco around to help her relax.

Unfortunately, Niagara Falls was an economic disaster area. It should have been packed with visitors but wasn't. People avoided the American side of the Falls like an Ebola outbreak. The Canadians had the best views and had created a miniature Las Vegas. Casinos, wax museums, and arcades made Niagara Falls, Ontario, one of the top tourist destinations in the world.

By contrast, the New York side was down to a few dumpy hotels and restaurants. The only people who visited now were just passing through on their way to the outlet malls.

What a shame. It should have been a busy place.

I asked the room service waiter about it when he delivered our breakfast. He'd lived here all his life.

"It used to be a lively place with plenty of tourists. But the planners fucked it all up and the whole town turned into one big dump."

I asked how the planners had messed up.

"They built that highway next to the gorge. It cut off the view, plus the Canucks built all those casinos and shit."

"That's a shame."

"Damn right it is," he replied and walked off.

His depression was infectious, so I drank my way through the mini-bar. *What the hell, it's all on Sparky Fletcher's tab anyway.*

When we finally checked out, I figured Sparky would be doing gigs here for the next ten years to pay off our bill. I decided to cut him a break and used one of my phony American Express cards to cover the tab.

~

Wilma slumped in the passenger seat and brooded as we headed west toward home. We both felt uneasy. Things had not gone well. We were no closer to finding the person behind the Judge's murder.

I was sure that Godzilla-cum-Vincent Price was the man behind the Judge's killing.

But why?

I assumed the Judge's untimely demise had something to do with a pissed-off former felon. God knows there were enough of those around.

But what if it was something else?

He'd been a state senator when we killed him. Maybe it was something involving his legislative career. I decided to explore this possibility with his daughter.

Of course, that wasn't the *only* possibility I wanted to *explore*.

Wilma agreed when I explained what I wanted to do next.

I put on NPR, which had a calming effect on Wilma. They were interviewing a famous Canadian science fiction writer who was talking about his atheist views.

When the program finished, I asked Wilma if she believed in a higher power.

"Of course not," she replied. "Would a caring God have created us?"

She had a point.

MRS. POUNDCAKE

We kept ratcheting up the pressure on Promod to find out who owned the compound.

So far he'd had no luck.

"It's almost as if they don't exist," he told me. "They have a website, of course. But it really doesn't say anything about them."

In other words, a typical corporate website.

"And they have all the required social media outlets but, again, nothing. It's like they're going through the motions and putting up a good public front."

Promod's frustration disturbed me.

After all, Promod was a man who had hacked the Pentagon, CIA, and NSA just for fun. He could bankrupt a billionaire with a few keystrokes. He'd put the profile of a key conservative congressman on a gay dating site. He had even manipulated the trading software of a leading hedge fund. It started making wild random buys and sells that caused the fund's returns to spike up and down like a heart attack victim's ECG.

My personal favorite was when he hacked the World Wildlife Fund's website and offered African lion hunting safaris as an inducement for making a generous donation. The shit storm this caused was fun to watch. The outrage trended for weeks on Facebook and Twitter.

His talents knew no bounds, so I was surprised that he was stymied by this seemingly innocuous corporation.

"The problem is their website sits on a *backwater* server. It isn't connected to anything else. It begins and ends right there."

Each time he'd broken through the digital wall he found another black hole.

"But they're a large company. There has to be some sort of public record."

"That's what I'm working on," he replied, "but they're registered offshore and it requires a bit more finesse. Don't worry. I'll have something for you in a couple of days."

I was happy to see he was so enthusiastic. When we'd first asked him to find out about ICMG, he gave off his usual resentful vibe. Once he hit a digital roadblock, however, the beast inside was released, turning Promod into a raging maniac.

To add to our frustration, there was nothing on the news about the fire at the compound — no television coverage, not a word in print.

Nothing. Nada.

It was as if the conflagration had never happened. Maybe house fires weren't that big a deal in Western New York, but I doubted it.

Who could cause a complete media blackout?

I had a feeling the lack of coverage was due to the power of the International Corrections Management Group, and the man in the Godzilla costume.

~

Since we were at an impasse in locating the Judge's killer, we decided to turn ourselves to another piece of unfinished business, dealing with Sparky Fletcher's wife.

Wilma's research revealed Belle Fletcher had been one of Sparky's backup dancers. A picture from back then showed a gorgeous young woman. I could understand why Little Sparky took a liking to her. She had a dancer's body with legs that went all the way to her shoulders.

A more recent photo told a different tale. It was taken at a charity event she and Sparky had attended. The best way to describe the way she looked today would be *ample*. Her once lithe, sinewy body was buried in rolls of fat.

In short, she looked like a jelly-filled donut.

Wilma put the photos side-by-side on the screen to show me the before and after.

"Take a good look, Butterball. Here's where you're headed."

Two days trapped in the hotel suite stuffing myself with rich casino food, plus all the mini-bar liquor had done nothing to improve my waistline or my self-esteem.

"I got you this at Costco." Wilma handed me a small package. Inside was a pedometer, the kind that wirelessly downloads all the steps you take into an app on your phone.

She showed me how it worked. "It calculates the number of calories you should consume every day. Use this and you'll be slim again in no time."

Bouncing the pedometer in my palm, I considered throwing it out the window. Wilma made it extremely clear that tossing it would be a mistake.

"I suggest you use it, or the other alternative is that I carve six feet out of your lower intestine."

I pretended to be enthusiastic about my gift.

Wilma rarely gives presents to anyone, except for her brother. I believe she sends him something at Christmas and on his birthday. She never talks about him and all I know is that he lives somewhere on the west coast.

On the other hand, I have a sister in Flint, which is my hometown. She's married to a useless twit who is always between jobs. They have two children who love their dear old Uncle Rip though they know me by another name.

It's a shame dear old Uncle Rip doesn't love them back.

To compensate, however, I spoil them with lavish gifts. That makes my brother-in-law squirm.

I turned on the pedometer and clipped it to my belt. The little unit chirped and gave me a cheerful smile.

I hated it already.

"You either shape up, or I'll ship you out in a box."

I knew she meant it.

Wilma often made threats. Most of them were idle. Some were not. For example, she once threatened a UPS driver who stole the parking spot she'd been about to back into. He gave her an apologetic grin and hustled off with his package, ignoring her glare. He hasn't been seen since.

I'm not exactly afraid of Wilma. It's more that she disquiets me.

There's a clear understanding we each have a role to play in our partnership. Mine is the outside man, the public face of our enterprise. Wilma is the back office. I meet with clients, come up with a strategy, and she executes it while at the same time watching my back.

I could see where my weight gain might, in her mind, threaten to upset the balance, but this was the first time she'd actually intruded into my personal life. Well, that isn't totally accurate. She'd killed a couple of my lady friends in the past.

But that had been for business reasons.

I tapped the *after* photo of Mrs. Poundcake. "Thoughts?"

Wilma contemplated the picture. Her mouth curved into an evil smile.

FRANKENMUTH

What would you have if you carved a village out of Bavaria, filled the parking lots with oversized American cars, and plopped it down in the picturesque Michigan countryside?

You'd have Frankenmuth, a place where every day is a festival set to the soundtrack of a glockenspiel, complete with gaily painted storefronts beckoning gullible tourists to buy useless knick-knacks, polka bands playing in the square, and cavernous beer halls serving Bratwurst and fried chicken.

Needless to say, Frankenmuth attracts a lot of tourists. And this is what makes it a good out-of-the-way spot for a client meeting.

Laura Petrie stood next to the river waiting patiently while I got us soft pretzels. We strolled along the bank.

"I hate this place."

"Because of its forced jolliness?"

She shook her head. "Because all that's missing are swastikas and torchlight parades along the main street."

I bet the Frankenmuth Chamber of Commerce wouldn't see it that way.

"Have you tried the all-you-can-eat fried chicken at Zehnder's?"

Laura ignored my question. "Have you had any luck finding out who killed my father?"

"Well, we've made some progress."

I didn't elaborate on our "progress" which at last count included several victims, a stint in solitary confinement, a burned down house, a stolen snowplow, and the major prison riot which occurred after a white supremacist leader woke up in the arms of a molester.

Personally, I thought they made a perfect couple.

"How soon before you kill whoever was responsible?"

I had to admire her forthrightness. I was also admiring her breasts heaving against the tight sweater she wore. As if sensing my admiration, she pulled her coat tightly around herself.

I felt cheap and obvious.

I was beginning to suspect this attractive young lady and I were not going to ride off into the sunset after all.

Little Rip expressed his displeasure. I would have to find some way of mollifying him.

"It won't be long now. We're getting close to your father's killer."

I didn't add that she was, in fact, standing right next to one of them. That would only shake her confidence in me.

"It would help if you could remember anything your father might have been working on when he was in the Senate."

"Like what?"

"Oh, I don't know. Like any legislation he might have been sponsoring. That sort of thing."

She thought about it for a few minutes. I broke off pieces of my pretzel and tossed them to the ducks. I wondered what all the salt would do to their blood pressure.

"We didn't discuss his work."

I detected a note of sadness in her voice.

"In fact, we didn't talk about much of anything."

The relationship between Laura and her father became apparent to me.

It was that age-old story — the estranged daughter compensating for a lack of parental affection. I guessed that her father was a mean old prick who was absorbed in his career and ignored her when she needed him most. She was left feeling bitter with her daddy issues unresolved.

Now I was glad that I had killed him.

"I have a bunch of his papers and things at my place."

Little Rip stirred, the image of that tight sweater firmly in his mind.

"If you need them, I can get them for you."

"Yes. Yes. Yes," cried the happy little fellow.

"I would be pleased to drop by and pick them up," I said casually.

"That would be sweet of you."

She wrote down her address in Royal Oak.

"Tomorrow evening around 8:00?" My too casual tone sounded creepy to me, but Laura didn't seem to notice.

She just smiled. "Okay. I'll see you then."

I hesitated and did my best impression of sincerity. I took both her hands in mine and looked into her eyes.

"I'm going to find your father's killer, and I'm going to take care of him. Don't you worry."

~

I drove to the giant Christmas store on the edge of town where Wilma suggested we meet.

Her cart was half filled with Christmas ornaments and doo-dads.

"Look at this stuff." She held up an ornament in the shape of an assault rifle, her eyes full of shopping lust. "I've never seen these at Costco."

It isn't that Wilma loves Christmas; she doesn't. She just loves to shop.

"Let's go," I said impatiently.

"I need a while longer. They've got these full-sized plastic reindeer for the front lawn."

"You don't have a front lawn. You live in a condo."

She ignored me.

"Okay, but then we're stopping at Zehnder's," I said.

"Sure, and *you* can enjoy the all-you-can-eat salad bar."

I didn't say anything, but visions of fried chicken legs were dancing in my head.

While Wilma shopped, I wandered around.

Thousands of square feet of Christmas decorations were overwhelming. I had never seen so much holiday gaiety in one place. It reminded me of the time we had strangled the pedophile Santa with a string of lights.

Ho! Ho! Ho!

~

The meeting with Laura had left me feeling uneasy, but I couldn't put my finger on why. A faint red light began to flash in the back of my lizard brain.

It wasn't *what* she said. It might have been the *way* she said it.

Her tight sweater had distracted me. Lust almost always trumps caution, however, this time I overrode Little Rip and listened to the voice in my big head.

I was going to make certain I was well protected when I went to Laura's place.

~

Wilma didn't laugh when I told her about my uneasiness. In fact, she was downright alarmed that I wasn't following the dictates of my dick.

Her brain shifted into lethal efficiency and a cool look filled her eyes. I could almost hear her inner voice debating about which weapons to bring.

~

Wilma got a box of Zehnder's fried chicken to go and the car filled with its lovely aroma. She munched while I drove. I picked at my rubbery spinach salad and watched longingly as she stripped the meat from the chicken. Wilma licked her lips and purred in delight at every bite. I could feel the crunch of the crispy coating and taste the juicy flesh.

"Hey, save some for me."

She showed me the box. It was empty.

"Sorry. It was soooooo good."

~

We arrived in Royal Oak after midnight.

Laura lived just south of the Red Run Golf Club in a modest brick bungalow with a tiny front yard. A three-year-old Honda Civic was parked in the driveway.

This was the kind of neighborhood where people would *notice* if you were staking out a house, so we parked down the block.

Wilma got a GPS tracker from the trunk and disappeared to plant it under Laura's car. She returned a few minutes later rubbing grease off the palm of her hand.

She opened an app on her phone and checked to make sure the device was sending out a signal. It was. Now we could monitor Laura from a safe distance.

~

After Wilma had dropped me back home, I went to sleep.

My phone rang a little after 3:00 a.m.

"She's on the move. I'm outside your place."

Jesus, does that woman ever sleep!

LUGNUTS

Laura was heading downtown.

We moved to intercept her. She got off I-75 on East Grand, went up a side street, and stopped. I shut off my headlights and turned into the street. I could see her Honda a block away. We waited.

Wilma got out her trusty Nikon and fixed it with a night-vision lens. She focused in on Laura's car and watched. We didn't have to wait long before an edgy looking guy came down the street. He got into the Honda and they talked for a few minutes.

I wished I still had my micro drone so I could eavesdrop on them, but I'd already returned it to Steve.

When the guy got out of the car and leaned over to say some final words to Laura, Wilma snapped a series of pictures.

"Gotcha," she whispered.

Laura drove off and the guy watched her go.

To my dismay, he continued along the street heading right toward us. We were too obvious, parked here at this time of the morning.

Without saying a word, I pushed Wilma's head down. She slipped the camera under the seat.

As the guy walked past our car, I moaned softly and Wilma's head was bobbing up and down in my lap. We trusted his imagination to do the rest. He was most of the way down the block before I tapped Wilma's head to signal the coast was clear.

"But while you're down there …"

"You're pathetic." She reached under the seat and retrieved her camera. "Let's get a good look at this guy."

~

143

After Laura had headed back to her place in Royal Oak, we drove to the Walmart Supercenter in Southfield.

Wilma made prints at the photo kiosk in the electronics department. I flipped through them while we had coffee at the McDonalds at the front of the store.

"Any idea?" Wilma asked.

I shook my head.

Even though the picture was tinted green from the night-vision lens, his features were clear enough to make out the acne scars on his nose.

"He looks like a real thug."

"I can color correct it in Photoshop. Why don't you show it to Del. Maybe he can make the guy."

~

The next morning, I found a parking spot off Woodward and walked over to the Art Institute.

I believe in supporting culture in all its forms. That's why I have a membership at the gallery. I can spend an entire afternoon looking at a single painting, parsing it, trying to sense what the artist is attempting to tell me.

It's also a great spot for picking up women.

I asked Del to meet me there so I could show him the photograph. Wilma had color-corrected it and blown up the face of the man leaning against Laura's car.

Del joined me as I stood admiring *The Nightmare* by Henry Fuseli. "That thing always gives me the creeps."

"I think it's inspiring."

The painting actually lived up to its title. A little demonic creature was perched on the chest of a sleeping woman. It was one of the cornerstones of the Institute's collection.

"Inspiring?"

"Well, it's sexual don't you see. The demon is the woman's repressed desires manifesting themselves ..."

Del looked at me like I'd just grown a third eye in the middle of my forehead.

"Any idea who this gentleman is?" I slipped him the photo.

He glanced down and his eyes widened.

"Lugnuts Johnson." He handed the picture back like it was radioactive.

Boris 'Lugnuts' Johnson.

While I obviously didn't know him to see him, I knew *of* him. He was a competitor, a contract killer and an enforcer for a local loan shark. He lacked our finesse and style, but more than made up for it in pure terror.

If someone pointed Lugnuts at you, you were toast.

Why the hell would Laura be mixed up with a meat bag like Lugnuts?

"You didn't get on Lugnuts' bad side did you?"

"Isn't he *all* bad side?"

Del glanced around nervously and backed away a few inches. He looked as if he was ready to make a dash for it.

I smiled reassuringly to calm his fears.

"Nope, just professional curiosity."

From his expression, I knew he didn't believe me. But he let it go anyway.

Del waved his hand around the gallery. "I hear the bankruptcy court's going to make the city sell all this shit. Maybe you can pick up the crypt keeper there for your bathroom."

He walked off laughing to himself, but the joke was on him.

I had once done a little favor for an art forger and ... well, you can guess the rest.

Needless to say, *The Nightmare* will be staying in Detroit for years to come.

~

The Greektown restaurant was filled to capacity with noisy Finnish tourists. I had to strain to hear Wilma over the din.

"Lugnuts Johnson? What the hell is that bitch up to with a touchhole like him?"

Wilma was sawing at a piece of chicken souvlaki so dry it was practically petrified. She dipped the desiccated morsel in watery tzatziki and made a face while she chewed it.

"That's an excellent question, and it deserves an answer." I contemplated both while picking chunks of fat off my lamb.

I finally gave up on the lamb and picked at my salad instead.

A loud crash was followed by screaming. Several of the Finns had started a fight by the front door. Beer bottles began to fill the air. Wilma deftly caught one and threw it back. The bottle exploded on the back of the head of a blond ape.

The manager and a couple of the waiters pulled the fighting Finns apart before they could do significant damage to the Greekery.

We went back to our dinner conversation.

Why the hell was Laura talking to Lugnuts?

His face popped into my mind. It was the face of a prize fighter. Lugnuts had taken a lot of punches over the years. While he didn't have much in the way of brains, he made up for it by being a brute. He once ripped a guy's leg clean off and beat him to death with it.

Then I had a thought that made me sick.

What if Laura had found out who had actually killed her father?

Maybe she'd sicced Lugnuts on me.

We needed to know what the hell was really going on, and there was one person in Detroit who could tell us.

"Let's go see Lightbulb. He'll know if there's anything buzzing around town."

I laid fifty bucks on the table.

Since the Greeks and the Finns were still fighting on the sidewalk out front, we ducked low and ran out the back.

~

We drove around the east end for a bit and finally spotted Lightbulb Lugosi standing on the corner of Mount Elliott and Heidelberg. We joined him and strolled down the street together admiring the works of art.

The Heidelberg Project is one of the city's most visited tourist attractions, which is strange considering it's in a really rough neighborhood. Still, it's a refreshing oasis of color and whimsy in the midst of urban decay.

Lightbulb believes we're cops. We never correct him.

I handed him a couple of crisp hundred dollar bills fresh from an ATM.

"Anyone out soliciting for contract killers?"

He held the hundreds up to his nose and sniffed.

"This is Detroit, man, someone's always hiring here."

I had to agree with him about that.

"Lugnuts Johnson is flashing bills around."

Tell me something I don't already know.

"Maybe someone's trying to hire more than one."

He mulled this over and nodded thoughtfully.

"Neil Brunner and his brother are up to something right now."

Yikes!

The Brunners were real dangerous characters. They were extremely cruel and, unlike Lugnuts, pretty smart.

I wouldn't want to be at the top of their hit list, but I had the sinking feeling we already were.

Slipping Lightbulb another fifty, we parted.

~

This is worse than I thought.

Laura's obsession was getting way out of hand. At some point, one of these coffin fillers was going to connect us to the Judge's murder. If they served up our heads to Laura, it would be too bad. The real person behind her father's death would remain undetected. She would believe what she was supposed to believe, that her father was killed by a pair of contractors who were hired by a disgruntled ex-con.

If that happened, Laura would never learn the truth.

"We have to nip this in the bud," Wilma muttered.

I knew what she meant by "nipping it in the bud."

The situation involving Lugnuts Johnson, the Brunner brothers, and, of course, Laura, was rapidly escalating into a classic clusterfuck. At some point, we were bound to be fingered as the Judge's killers and then things would turn ugly.

And what a tragedy that would be because we'd miss out on our final payment from the lovely Laura.

It was also a matter of personal pride. Wilma and I hate to leave anything unfinished, especially if it would mean leaving the real person responsible still breathing.

In our business, it's not good to leave anyone alive.

Except ourselves.

Again I thought of the mystery man, first dressed in the Godzilla suit and then playing Edgar Allen Poe in his own pit and pendulum. I shuddered at the memory of how close that blade had come to giving me a permanent tummy tuck.

He obviously had tremendous resources behind him and I had the uncomfortable feeling he would bring all of them to bear on us. And that would not be good. In fact, it would be a disaster. Lugnuts and the Brunner Brothers were a mild annoyance compared to this guy. We needed to find out who he was, and we needed to find out in a hurry.

But first, we needed to take some of the pressure off.

"I've got an idea."

Wilma looked at me dubiously. In her mind, she was already feeding little pieces of Lugnuts, the Brunner brothers, and Laura to the fishes.

ARTS AND CRAFTS

I arrived in Royal Oak a little before 7:30.

Parking several blocks from Laura's house, I took a stroll through the neighborhood, looking for any sign of either Lugnuts or the Brunners. Satisfied that the immediate vicinity was contract killer free — well, except for yours truly — I rang the doorbell.

Laura was wearing another of what must have been a vast wardrobe of tight sweaters.

Little Rip perked up.

Then I thought about Lugnuts and the Brunner brothers.

Little Rip withered on the vine.

"Come in," she said and held the door wide open.

Although I was nervous, I resisted the urge to look over my shoulder.

I glanced down at the doormat and saw **ABANDON HOPE ALL YE WHO ENTER HERE.**

WELCOME was all it actually said.

~

"Any other hit men around I should know about?"

I'd injected Laura with the Russian truth serum as soon as she let me in.

She smiled lazily and giggled. "Nope. Just you. You're cute, you know. For a killer."

Laura leaned her head on my shoulder and I maneuvered her over to the couch.

Little Rip came to life and it took all my willpower to resist the temptation to lift up that sweater and feast upon the goodies beneath. But while my moral compass spins faster than a politician after a debate, I don't believe in taking advantage of a drugged woman. That would not be playing fair, and there's no satisfaction in it. If a woman wants to sleep with me, she has to give herself freely. I'm like Dracula in that respect. You have to invite me in.

"How about you and I have a little chat."

She bobbed her head drunkenly.

I looked around. Her living room was decorated in the Arts and Crafts style, with plenty of wood and built-in bookshelves. It reminded me of a cozy cottage on a rainy day. She even had a log blazing in the fireplace.

How romantic.

I regretted doping her up.

"How many other killers have you hired to look into your father's death?"

"A couple."

"Why?"

"I figured the more, the better. I have lots of money, and one of you was bound to get lucky."

It wasn't a bad strategy, but it upset me. Wilma and I were the best in the business.

At least the best in the Detroit metropolitan area.

Hiring those other goons meant we would be falling all over each other.

That would be awkward.

"Call them off. I've got it under control."

"I can't."

"You can't?"

"No, I won't. I have an obligation.

"An *obligation*? What obligation?"

She rolled her head and smiled.

"An obligation to my father's memory to use everything at my disposal to find his killer, and I'll keep hiring people until I do.

"Anyway, what do you care? You told me that you weren't a detective."

She had a point.

We were excellent killers but lousy investigators. It was ironic that we had spent all our time on this case trying to learn who the real killer was. We are much more efficient when you just point us at a target.

Laura began blinking. The serum was wearing off so I moved away from her and smiled.

"Yes, thanks, I will."

Laura shook her head. I could tell what she was thinking. *Did I just gap out?*

"Scotch, if you have it." I wanted her to believe she had just offered me a drink.

Laura gave her head another shake, got up, and went into the kitchen. I felt sorry for her. She had no idea that she'd been under the influence of a potent truth serum.

She returned a few minutes later carrying a small silver tray with two tumblers of whiskey.

~

"Someone powerful is definitely behind your father's murder. I'm hoping something in his papers will point me in the right direction."

Her father's files were in a banker's box on the floor next to me.

Laura took my hand and rubbed it gently.

"Please find whoever did it." Her eyes were moist. I reached over and wiped away a tear.

I was rewarded with the flicker of a smile and resisted the urge to pull her into my arms and kiss her. Having to earn it first would make it more exciting.

~

We decided our safe house, Fort Knox Secure Storage, would be a good place to examine the Judge's paperwork.

Wilma set to work immediately and loaded all the papers into the hopper of our high-speed OCR scanner. Digitizing everything would make our search a whole lot easier. It took most of the day but when finished, we had an entirely searchable database on our server.

Next to eviscerating someone with a potato peeler, this was the kind of work Wilma loved most. She was a natural researcher and would happily go looking for the tiniest connection in mountains of data.

While she was busy doing that, I had my own mission.

It was time to take the other hounds off the scent.

CHUBBY HUBBY

As a strict vegetarian, hot dogs were like kryptonite to Detective Sergeant Delbert Newell.

I, however, love them and took every opportunity to pig out on tube steak. If you live in Detroit and love weenies, you are either a fan of American Coney Island or Lafayette Coney Island. Of course, if you're a vegetarian like Del you won't have an opinion on the matter.

When I insisted on hot dogs for lunch, he groaned as always and said he'd meet me at Detroit One on Woodward because he wanted to go to Whole Foods up the street.

I suspected Del, like Promod, was starting to resent our relationship. But he was pragmatic and knew that I had the goods on him. In his case, it was where he'd buried an honest cop after he'd murdered him. I'd tucked away incriminating pictures of Del doing the deed so I had leverage with him. This advantage also allowed me to delight in pissing him off at every opportunity.

Everyone needs a hobby, right?

"What now?" Del was sullen and didn't even bother to look at the menu.

"Actually, this time I have something for *you*."

If he was interested, he didn't show it. He stabbed a straw into his diet soda.

"Oh yeah?"

"Yes, and if you play your cards right, it might even mean a promotion."

"And *why* are you so generous?"

I smiled. "Because a happy Del is an accommodating Del."

After a few minutes of munching my Coney Island, I explained what I had in mind. When I finished, Del was smiling. Before we parted, he even shook my hand. He had never done that before.

~

Wilma wasn't moved when I told her about Del's reaction to my plan.

Her frustration after spending three hours trying to parse something from the database was palpable.

"Anything?" I asked.

She frowned. "A couple of things … The Judge was pretty passionate about preserving the great outdoors, especially in the Upper Peninsula, and that really pissed off a lumber baron named Earl Krynkle."

Earl Krynkle?

Everyone in Michigan had heard of 'Chainsaw' Earl Krynkle. He was a throwback to Michigan's past when timber barons ruled the state. He'd acquired a vast portion of the UP which he was ruthlessly turning into pulp and paper. His mills were also poisoning the air and water up there.

To put it not-so-subtly, Chainsaw Earl Krynkle was a one-man environmental disaster.

If anyone had a motive for wanting the Judge dead, it was Chainsaw Earl. The Judge had been a real thorn in his side for years after thwarting Chainsaw's plan to clear-cut several million acres of old growth pine adjacent to the Ottawa National Forest. There had been a court challenge by the environmentalists to stop him and the Judge had ruled in their favor.

Later, when he became a Senator, the Judge had sponsored a bill that would have permanently protected those lands.

I suggested we focus on Krynkle as the most likely suspect in the Judge's murder.

When I Googled his name, I got over 100,000 hits and discovered Krynkle was not well liked by the tree-hugging crowd. Descriptions of him included "earth-raper", "an enemy of the forest", and "a pine weasel".

The more I read about the man and his brutal ways, the more I came to admire him. Quite honestly, I didn't care if he mowed down entire forests. That would just mean fewer trees for our enemies to hide behind.

Wilma, on the other hand, took a more holistic view. She gave a lot of money to protect wood ducks and turtles and believed firmly that if we cut down trees, we'd destroy the future of our planet. It was a matter of self-preservation.

I began to wonder what this monster looked like. I expected he'd be one of those burly Hemingway-types, and I wasn't disappointed. In fact, he looked like he'd stepped out of an Ayn Rand novel, with his gap-toothed grin shining out of a bushy, jet-black beard. He dressed the part of a lumberjack in red plaid shirts, jeans, and tan Timberland boots. Apart from a belly that overhung his belt, he looked like he was in excellent physical shape and would probably put up quite a fight.

I dug a little deeper and discovered more useful information in a secret eco-terrorist chat room. Apparently they'd been planning an attack on him and had valuable intelligence on his compound. It was a vast estate on the northwest shore of Lake Michigan, located on a small bay just outside Manistique. He was right next door to the Hiawatha National Forest, which many environmentalists suspected he planned to grind into toilet paper.

I called up a Google map of the area and didn't like what I saw — a single road in and out of that entire area. The eco-terrorists' intelligence indicated the local sheriff's department was an extension of Krynkle's own security. They had decided to mothball their attack because it would be impossible to escape.

I zoomed out a bit and saw the estate was almost directly across the lake from Badger Island. This gave me an idea, and the timing was perfect because bad weather was on its way.

For the past few days, the forecasters had been warning that Michigan was going to be hit by a late fall snowstorm coming in from the west. Of course, in their normal restrained way, they made it sound like the apocalypse was coming.

I, however, saw a window of opportunity.

The impending storm would give us the perfect cover. If we could get to Badger Island, we might be able to find someone to take us across to Krynkle's place.

I showed Wilma where Krynkle lived. She traced a line from the island to his house and frowned.

"Maybe you can swim it. You've got the blubber for it." Her reply reflected her nasty mood.

Wilma's comment didn't bother me, but I resented her sarcasm. Since she'd been preparing dinner and was holding an eight-inch chef's knife, I resisted the temptation to respond in kind.

She tapped the map with the tip of the blade. "What about ice?"

"It's too early for that. Anyway, the lake rarely freezes over."

I had given a lot of thought to my plan. I'd even calculated the distance — fifty miles.

"With a fast enough boat it would take about three hours, maybe a little more. And Krynkle wouldn't be expecting anyone coming in from the water at this time of year. There'll probably be next to no security."

Wilma wrinkled her brow. "Do you know how to drive a boat?"

"Just one of those jet-ski things, but how hard could it be?"

Wilma gave a sarcasm-laced chuckle. "You have to know about navigation and how to tie secret sailor's knots. It's like being a Mason."

I rolled my eyes.

"So we hire someone to take us across."

"And how the hell do we find someone — *craigslist?*"

"I bet there are lots of smugglers on the island who would like to pick up some easy cash. Let's have Promod check the DEA intelligence files to see if they're watching anyone there."

~

And that's how we found Lumpy Carmichael.

He ran summer fishing charters out of the north harbor of Badger Island. In the off-season, the DEA suspected he ran something else. Being on the Coast Guard watch-list of drug smugglers made him the perfect person to help us make our little jaunt across the water.

I showed Wilma the DEA stuff while we were eating our steaks.

She was skeptical. "So five minutes after we leave the harbor, the Coast Guard and the DEA will be shoving AR-15s up our asses?"

"Not if we give them something else to do," I said.

I explained what I had in mind and she agreed that it made some kind of sense.

"What do we do about this Lumpy person when we finish?" She licked a drop of blood from her steak knife.

I smiled. "I don't think that will be a problem."

In fact, the only problem I could see was my steak. The piece of meat was roughly the circumference of a golf ball. This was Wilma's idea of portion control, which I guess was preferable to having her carve off part of my lower intestines to help me lose weight.

I began to plot ways to get into the freezer after she'd gone to bed. A carton of *Ben and Jerry's Chubby Hubby* was calling my name seductively.

GLECKEN SPA

Badger Island sits in perfect isolation forty miles off Michigan's Sunset Coast.

Fifteen miles long and ten at its widest point, most of the island is a state park. There are, however, two tiny villages, one at the south end and another half-way up the west side. Both villages have small harbors. The best way to reach Badger Island is on the small car ferry that sails once a day from Sunset.

Wilma and I know the area well. We have a safe house there.

Our next door neighbor is a cop by the name of Molly Parsons. She knows us as Fred and Bernice, a lovely couple who own an antique business in Detroit. I wonder what she'd think if she ever discovered that her neighbors were actually a pair of contract killers.

Hopefully for her sake, she never will.

~

We arrived in Sunset just after 1:00, which gave us plenty of time to have lunch before the ferry sailed at 3:00.

Sunset is quiet in the off-season, but there are still some restaurants open. In fact, we knew the perfect spot to eat — the Villager.

The owner, a big guy named Hank Summerville, greeted us warmly and led us to a table.

"Haven't seen you folks for a while, you up here for a stay?" He handed us each a menu.

"A romantic getaway at the Glecken Spa," I replied.

Hank gave me a knowing wink.

"Too bad you weren't a few minutes earlier. You just missed Molly."

Yeah, that is too bad.

"She's got her work cut out for her," he said.

"Yeah, we read about it. It was in all the newspapers."

"It makes you sick to think about it, doesn't it?"

It would, of course, if you had a conscience and cared about such things.

I nodded again and considered the menu options.

The food here was always good, especially the pizza. I was ready to order a large one smothered in pepperoni and sausage when I remembered the five pounds I had managed to lose over the past week. I looked for a low-carb alternative.

There wasn't much. The people of Sunset were mostly hard working stiffs who needed a shit load of calories to give them the energy to make it through the day. I finally decided on the *Dieter's Special*, a small piece of meatloaf with a side salad.

~

That afternoon the lake was choppy and the tiny ferry rolled with the waves.

The town of Sunset was far behind us and I stood at the bow rail feeling the icy spray on my face. In my mind, I was one of those intrepid explorers seized with demon wanderlust. As the boat rose and fell, I scanned the horizon for any sign of the island. The fresh air was invigorating. Just breathing it was burning up the minuscule amount of calories I'd consumed for lunch.

Wilma was also getting rid of calories by depositing her pulled pork sandwich over the rail. Her chili fries followed as she held on for dear life, moaning in agony. Watching her obvious distress warmed my heart.

"I thought you enjoyed cruises."

She shook her head and then treated the fishes to the pecan pie she'd had for dessert.

I hoped her reaction to rough sailing wasn't going to be a problem. Because as rough as it was now, this was nothing compared to what it was going to be like once that monster storm out west hit. It was currently dumping massive amounts of snow all over the Great Plains and was fast heading our way. We would have to time our visit to Chainsaw Earl's estate with precision to avoid being caught on the water.

Our plan was to capture Krynkle and dose him up with truth serum. Once we were satisfied that he was indeed responsible for the Judge's demise, we would dispose of him in a suitable manner.

I was leaning toward squashing him with a stack of logs. Wilma was holding out for something involving an ax.

Either way, it was going to be a messy demise for Chainsaw Earl.

I had packed my most robust set of disposable coveralls for the trip.

~

The ferry reached its berth in the south harbor of Badger Island just before dark. When we entered the shelter of the harbor the waves calmed down and Wilma's face seemed a little less green.

After I had checked us into our luxury suite at the spa, I went to get Gravol for Wilma from the gift shop. Back in the room, I made her swallow a dozen or so to knock her out. I left her sleeping and eagerly headed down to the dining room for dinner.

With Wilma safely snoring away, I would celebrate dietary liberation and order a double portion of everything deep fried.

~

What the fuck is this?

I re-read the menu. It was entirely meatless. In fact, everything seemed to feature something called quinoa as the main ingredient.

I waved to the waiter.

"Can you get me a steak about two inches thick and smother it with mushrooms and fried onions."

My server, dressed in tight black jeans and a matching tee shirt, reacted to my request as if I had just cut off his grandmother's hands while she was holding out a fresh-baked apple pie.

"I'm terribly sorry, sir, but we *only* have the items on the menu."

And then it dawned on me.

Wilma booked this place.

The luxurious rooms, king-sized beds, and two-person tubs made it sound fantastic. But that was all dressing to disguise this resort's evil purpose. It was a health spa! And now I was its unhappy prisoner.

Damn that woman! She can be so cruel and unfeeling.

I could hear her diabolical laughter reverberating in my head.

"Is there another restaurant ... a McDonalds or something like that nearby?"

He looked at me in shock. "Oh no, sir, all the other restaurants are closed for the season."

Shit!

I desperately looked for a way out of this hell. Unfortunately, the ferry had already sailed back to the mainland. I briefly considered chartering a plane, but finally surrendered to the inevitable and ordered dinner.

The chili tasted like beet-flavored oatmeal. The bread they served was so thick it hurt my teeth.

According to the menu, my entire meal totaled three hundred and fifty calories and was low in carbohydrates, sugar, and sodium. They forgot to mention it was low in flavor as well.

I washed the sludge down with a tea that was made from milkweed. The only positive thing I could say about it was that it was wet and hot.

~

Wilma was still sawing logs when I got back to the room and I thought about smothering her with a pillow. But I figured she'd suffered enough on the trip over, until I thought back to my dinner.

I then realized *my* suffering was just about to begin.

My stomach kept me up half the night begging for more food. When I did sleep, I was tortured by visions of juicy, thick hamburgers dancing merrily through my dreams.

LUMPY CARMICHAEL

After a breakfast of a pair of poached quail eggs swimming on the surface of a bowl of gray gruel, I was ready to face the day.

I marveled at the abilities of a chef who was able to produce all those tasteless entrees with surprising skill. After I asked for a large cup of coffee, our noir-clad waiter haughtily told me that "coffee was poison" and offered me a cup of dandelion tea instead.

Needless to say, all this made me very grumpy.

Wilma suggested we go for a walk.

~

Three miles later, we reached the village of West Harbor, a cluster of wooden buildings clinging to the water's edge. This place looked like something out of a *Popeye* cartoon. The village hadn't seen a straight angle since the 1930s when most of the houses had been built.

We read the names off mailboxes until we found **Carmichael**.

When we knocked, the door rattled loosely in its frame.

~

I imagined Lumpy Carmichael would be a grizzled old salt with one eye pinched closed and a corncob pipe clenched in his teeth. He would use liberal doses of *arrrrrs* to liven up the conversation.

A very attractive woman opened the door and looked at us quizzically. "Yes?"

I caught the most heavenly scent of fried eggs and freshly brewed coffee.

"We're looking for Lumpy Carmichael," I said.

"Yes?"

"Is he in?"

"I'm Carmichael. What the hell do you want?"

She was on the verge of slamming the door in our faces.

There was nothing the least bit Lumpy about Carmichael. She was, in fact, quite beautiful, with just the right amount of ass and breast to make Little Rip rise from the icy prison of my Calvin Klein's.

"You have a boat for charter?" Wilma flashed a smile.

Lumpy shook her head and started to shut the door. I rammed my foot in the gap to stop her. She looked at me like I was a cat turd.

"Look, I'm eating my breakfast. What do you want?"

"And it smells delicious," I replied putting a lot of not-too-subtle emphasis on the word *delicious*.

"We want to book a cruise," Wilma told her.

"Season's over," Lumpy shoved hard against the door, mashing my foot.

I yelled in pain and then fanned a wad of $100 bills. "How about reopening it for us?"

She looked greedily at the money and motioned us in.

~

I would have offered Lumpy a thousand dollars for her bacon and eggs if Wilma hadn't been there. Lumpy did pour me a cup of coffee, however, and I fell in love. Little Rip was wide awake after his dandelion-induced coma and he entertained me with nautical fantasies of Captain Lumpy and myself on the good ship Lust-e-Pop.

While we enjoyed our coffee, I put ten big ones on the table in front of her. She eyed them suspiciously.

"What kind of cargo are we talking about?"

"No cargo, just two passengers on a nocturnal cruise to the northwest shore of the lake near the Wisconsin border."

"The northwest shore? Why the hell do you want to go up there?"

"That's our business."

Wilma laid another bill on the pile in front of Lumpy. "And no questions asked."

"We've got a big storm heading our way." Lumpy nodded to the marine radio on the counter.

It periodically buzzed to life with end-of-the-world type warnings from the Coast Guard about the approaching storm.

"We've got maybe a day and a half at best before that blizzard reaches us. I plan to be sitting right here in my cozy little shack when it does."

"And you will be, but you'll have lots of money to keep you warm."

I pushed a Michigan roadmap toward her. It had our destination circled in yellow highlighter. She looked at it and then got out a navigation chart. She spread it out on the counter and traced a path.

"That's fifty-seven miles. It'll take three hours over and three hours back, and that's if the lake is calm. Plus it'll be damn cold and my heater is mostly fucked. So dress warmly."

"Could we go over tonight, after dark?"

"Yeah, I guess. Be here at 7:00. I have to warn you, though, there's a good chance the Coast Guard will board us either on the way out or on the way back. So make sure you're not carrying anything that would get us into trouble."

Wilma and I smiled reassuringly.

"Oh, I don't think that will be much of a problem," I told her.

"Yeah, I hope not. It's my boat."

THE CROSSING

We drove back that evening and parked in Lumpy Carmichael's driveway. It was well back from the road so no one could see us.

As a precaution, however, we wore our LED necklaces to make our heads glow in case there were any surveillance cameras around.

I hauled a couple of heavy duffel bags down to the boathouse where Lumpy had her thirty-five-foot trawler idling in its slip. The motor wheezed ominously every few seconds. I set the bags down carefully in the wheelhouse.

Lumpy had been right, it was damn cold. Luckily I had discovered the island's general store that afternoon and picked up a heavy snowmobile suit and boots.

She looked at me and smiled. "If you go overboard, you'll sink like a stone."

"It's better than freezing to death."

"Maybe," she said. "Just be careful, that's all. The deck gets icy from the spray."

Wilma had prepared herself with a Gravol suppository and conked out immediately in the forward cabin. I would have Captain Lumpy all to myself for the duration of the crossing.

Does this boat have autopilot?

"What's in those bags?" Lumpy asked.

"Just our golf clubs. We never leave home without them. You want to play a round?" I wiggled my eyebrows suggestively and then caught myself.

By the look of disgust on Lumpy's face, I knew it was a juvenile thing to say

"I'm the captain of this vessel and I have to know what I am carrying. The Coast Guard is out there and they might also want to know."

"Don't worry about them," I said. "Let's get going."

She shook her head.

I was beginning to admire her tenacity.

"Why would the Coast Guard stop you?" I demanded.

Lumpy averted her eyes.

"Could it be because they think you're smuggling drugs?"

She stood stock still.

"Look, don't worry about the damn Coast Guard, I'm taking care of them."

"Taking care of them, how?" She looked at me dubiously.

A clatter from behind startled us. Pistol in hand, Wilma had emerged from the cabin. She swayed in groggy confusion.

"Are we there yet?"

"We haven't even left the dock. Go back to sleep," I told her.

Wilma nodded, yawned loudly, and scratched her nose with the barrel of the pistol.

Lumpy's eyes were wide in fear. "I'm in over my head, aren't I?"

"No, not really." I shrugged. "Let's get moving."

The ship-to-shore radio burst to life. The operator started giving more urgent warnings for all shipping to take shelter and then stopped mid-sentence.

"All stations, all stations," he resumed, "Report of a vessel in distress … " The operator gave the coordinates.

I looked at Lumpy and smiled. "There, I told you it was taken care of. This should clear the way. Let's go."

~

The lake was fairly calm with only a six-inch swell and we were making great time. Lumpy hadn't said a word since we left the harbor. She stared grimly ahead, knowing she was taking a one-way voyage.

We had planned to feed Lumpy to the pickerel. However, that was before I'd met her when I still believed she was a grizzled old pirate. Now, I wasn't sure what to do with her.

Lumpy looked stricken. I decided a distraction was in order.

"So what do you usually carry?"

"Summer tourists, fishing charters, that sort of thing."

I gave her a skeptical look. "I mean, what do you *actually* carry?"

She sighed. "Drugs mostly. From Canada."

"What? Like weed?"

She shook her head. "Blood pressure meds, prescription stuff for Parkinson's. There's a pharmacist up there who supplies them under the counter."

"Drugstore drugs? What's the point of that?"

"Have you priced out a prescription for cholesterol medication recently? It's a third of the cost in Canada."

"But those are substandard drugs aren't they?"

At least, that's what I'd heard on FOX News.

"It's exactly the same damn stuff we get in the drugstores down here, just a whole lot cheaper. The Canadians force their drug companies to sell at a more reasonable price."

"So what you're saying is that the pharmaceutical industry here is gouging us."

"More like holding us for ransom. They know that health plans pay for most prescriptions but, if you don't have insurance, you're screwed. It's either pay for your life-saving medication or starve."

I was starting to see the drug industry in an entirely new light. Up to now, my opinion was informed by those heart-warming commercials that ran on the nightly news. And the pharmaceutical industry had been responsible for Viagra, that miracle of modern medicine. But they were actually ruthless bastards, and that made them my kind of people.

Those guys were right up there on my most-admired list along with Republican congressmen, the folks who write cell-phone contracts, and most Hollywood agents.

I could see from the look on her face that Lumpy's smuggling activities were less about making a buck and more about doing something good for her fellow man. If I had a conscience, I might have even admired her.

"Look, I know you're planning to kill me, so why don't you tell me why we're going over there?" Lumpy kept her eyes on the lake ahead.

"I understand the scenery is breathtaking."

"Don't be glib. As far as I know, there isn't anything along the coast."

Her eyes flicked to the map again.

"We're going to drop in on a friend of ours."

"Your friend have a name?"

Once she had come to terms with the inevitable, Lumpy seemed to have vanquished her fear. She was becoming downright defiant, and I have to admit it was making Little Rip very excited.

I like a woman with spunk.

"His pals call him Chainsaw."

"You're not talking about Earl Krynkle are you?"

I smiled. "The very same."

Lumpy was smart and I could see her putting it together. She looked at me with something close to admiration.

"You know he's surrounded by an army of lumberjacks, don't you?"

I had uncovered this fact from the eco-terrorist chat room. His private security detail was entirely made up of former woodsmen. They even carried broad axes as weapons, which gave those of us who labor with guns a distinct advantage.

"He's completely paranoid about being attacked. I'm pretty sure he has radar."

I pointed at the rubber dinghy lashed to the bow deck.

"It can only scan a few thousand feet. You can drop the dinghy in the water and we'll row into shore. Its profile on the water is so low the radar won't detect it."

A ghost of a smile crossed her face. Even though she tried to disguise it, I saw faint hope in her eyes and knew what she was thinking.

I'd better cure her of that little delusion.

"Look, I don't expect you to believe me, but if we pull this off, we won't kill you."

I tapped her forehead. "I know right now you're considering making a run for it after you drop us off in the dinghy. That's why my partner has planted a nasty device down below. If you're not exactly where you should be when we get back, she'll press a button and down will come Lumpy, cradle and all."

Lumpy turned a whiter shade of pale.

"Oh, and if you find our little package and try to mess with it — BOOOOOOM!"

WINKIES

An hour later, Lumpy slowed the trawler and cut the engine.

While she dropped the sea anchor, I knocked on the cabin door to wake Wilma.

"We're here, darling. Bring the luggage."

A minute later, a disheveled Wilma poked her head out. I handed her the thermos of coffee Lumpy had thoughtfully packed. Wilma looked at the thermos, trying to figure out what it was. Finally, she opened it and drank down all the coffee.

The scalding liquid put the fire back into her eyes.

~

My partner in crime jumped onto the back deck and sucked in some fresh air. Steam poured from her mouth.

I checked my watch. It was after midnight, the witching hour, the perfect time to pay a visit to Earl Krynkle.

Lumpy sniffed the air as if she could smell the storm coming. The boat bucked up and down in the rising wind. She joined Wilma on the back deck and hauled out the dinghy. After it had been inflated, she pushed it over the side. The raft was a lot smaller than I'd imagined.

Lumpy pointed at my snowmobile garb. "That suit's too bulky for the raft. You need something lighter."

"But I'll freeze."

"I've got something for you."

She opened a locker in the fore cabin and pulled out a black rubber suit.

"This should fit. It's a diver's dry suit. It'll keep you warm and, if you happen to go into the drink, it'll help you stay alive."

Lumpy dragged out a second suit and reluctantly offered it to Wilma.

We changed quickly into our new togs. The suits were toasty warm, and a flat black which made us practically invisible in the dark.

~

"How do you feel?" I asked Wilma.

She gulped in a draft of cold night air. She had spent more time leaning over the side than paddling the raft.

Luckily, I was able to pilot the spunky little craft on my own. We were close to shore now and I guided the dinghy carefully between large sheets of ice.

I checked the GPS.

"I sure as hell hope Promod got the coordinates right," Wilma muttered.

If he hadn't, her tone made it clear that she would fillet him.

The wind smelled like Pine-Sol.

Wilma took another lungful and frowned. "I can't believe that bastard wants to chop down all these trees."

I smiled. "Why don't you discuss it with him when you see him."

With a cinematic segue worthy of Stephen Spielberg, we rounded a small point of land and there was Krynkle's estate sprawling along the shoreline.

Powerful sodium lights lit up the small bay in front of his property. Less intense lighting illuminated the grounds around the house, a French-style chateau that looked like it would survive anything Lake Michigan could throw at it.

Over a hundred feet long and three stories high, it was constructed from heavy gray stone. Facing the lake along the back of the house was a full-length deck. A pair of cigarette boats hung in slings. A large Zodiac bobbed against the dock.

~

We back-paddled around the point and beached the raft. I looked at our small rubber dinghy and thought about the two speedboats. If anything went wrong, there was no chance we could outrun them.

But hey, what could possibly go wrong?

Wilma unzipped one of the waterproof duffle bags and took out a high-powered rifle. Then she handed me a pair of Glocks in a double shoulder rig with a dozen spare clips. Finally, I had hooked a Taser to my belt.

I was ready to do battle.

The woods were thick and reached almost to the beach. They would provide excellent cover.

Wilma fixed a large suppressor to the end of her rifle and took a position behind one of the pines. With the night vision scope, she would be able to cover the side of the house.

Steve had been experimenting with new silencer technology. It used a combination of carbon baffles and a suppressor which would cancel out the sonic boom of the bullet.

Wilma sighted on Krynkle's Zodiac, aiming at the outboard motor on the stern. When she pulled the trigger, we heard a faint plunk and the engine vibrated briefly. I checked the damage with my night vision scope and saw dark liquid running from a hole just above the *Mercury* label on the side. We waited to see if this had attracted any attention. All remained quiet.

A few seconds later, a pair of axe-carrying guards dressed in bright plaid jackets, jeans, and heavy boots walked down to the edge of the lake. Their nonchalance told me security was pretty lax. These guys weren't expecting anything to happen, especially on a shitty night like this one.

The guards split up and one walked down the beach. He unzipped and began to piss in the water. Through the night scope, I could see steam rising.

Wilma let the other one get to the edge of the woods before bringing him down. His head jerked to one side and he crumpled to the ground. She shifted position and waited until the pissing man finished. As he turned in our direction, she put a neat cluster of bullets in the center of his chest. He staggered forward, dropped to his knees, and then fell face first into the water with a faint splash.

Crouching down, I ran to the body and dragged it into the woods. I carefully stripped off his jacket and boots. His coat was tattered from the cluster of bullet holes but, hopefully, no one would notice until it was too late.

I walked casually onto the lawn and then up to the house.

~

A massive guy was standing guard outside the front door. I kept my head down and hoped he wouldn't make me.

I had a strategic advantage; he had an ax and I had a pistol. While an ax might look intimidating, it makes a lousy weapon. It's no match for a bullet between the eyes.

I caught his ax before it hit the porch and alerted the guards within the house. I hefted it and felt its power course through me. It might be fun to try it, but only in the right situation.

The ax did an excellent job when I snuck up on a guard and split his head open.

I liked the ax and slung it over my shoulder feeling like one of the Wicked Witch's Winkie guards in the *Wizard of Oz*.

It was better than being a flying monkey.

Oh he-ho, yo-ho.

MR. KRYNKLE

Chainsaw Earl was full of surprises.

The biggest was finding him asleep in a massive log bed dressed in a fur-trimmed nightie and curled up in the arms of the burliest bear of a man I've ever seen.

I put the blade of the ax across Krynkle's throat and pressed it slightly to wake him up. His eyes popped open in surprise. I let the pressure of the blade do the talking. I lifted it from his throat and Krynkle sat up.

His grizzly lover woke up with a snort. He looked up at me in alarm and reached for an ancient Colt .45 on the nightstand.

"What the fu…" I cut off his question — and his head — with a mighty swing of the ax.

I was starting to really like this weapon. It made me feel positively medieval.

Krynkle looked over at his bed partner in shock. The guy's head rolled off the pillow and thumped against Krynkle's thigh.

"Get up," I ordered with deadly intent. "You've had enough head for one night."

He started to scream and I Tasered him.

~

We bundled Earl Krynkle into the rubber raft and set off among the pack ice at the edge of the lake. He was shivering uncontrollably, which was understandable since I'd removed his nightie and used it to gag him.

Wilma leaned over and administered a dose of the truth serum.

"So, Earl, we need to know a few things," I said slowly.

"Yessss," he slurred.

"I need to ask you about the late Senator Walter Armstrong."

"That asshole? He took my campaign contributions and still wouldn't support my forest project."

"So you took care of him?"

"Yes. Well, I was going to but then he died and the problem went away."

He slipped into a dream fugue. I prodded him with the ax, which I'd insisted on bringing along.

"You mean you had him killed, right?"

He blinked several times and shook his head slowly.

"Nooooo ... I don' ... I didn't."

"But you know who did."

He continued to shake his head.

"Why would I do that? I was going to fund his opponent in the next election and defeat him."

"But you were pissed off at him because he wouldn't let you cut down that forest."

"Sure, but revenge isn't good for business."

He had a point.

The adrenaline began to flow and a headache set up camp behind my eyes.

Wilma looked at him and then at me. She pointed at Earl. He had started to hum the theme from *Winnie the Pooh*.

"What now?"

I looked at the naked man shivering in the bottom of the boat and shook my head.

Earl Krynkle was another dead end.

Were we ever going to get to the bottom of this?

~

Our final view of Earl Krynkle was of him sitting cross-legged on a floating piece of sheet ice. He waved goodbye to us wearing the stupid grin of pure enlightenment.

I wondered if he'd feel the same way when the dope wore off.

~

We used the motor to make a fast return to Lumpy's trawler, which was exactly where we'd left it.

"What did you tell her?" Wilma was looking green around the gills again.

"That you'd planted a remote device in the cabin."

"Nice …" She leaned over the side and threw up.

I maneuvered the dinghy beside Lumpy's boat and she tossed me a rope.

Lumpy looked drawn, resigned to the inevitable fact that she was going to die before this night was over.

~

I made a good case with Wilma for leaving Lumpy alive.

After all, she was wrapped up in the illegal pharmaceutical trade and we had paid her $6,000 for our little cruise. Plus she could be tied to the disappearance of old Chainsaw and the messy attack on his home. I was confident she would keep her mouth shut.

Who knows, we might even need her again in the future.

~

On the way back, the mood was lighter. Lumpy accepted my promise that we weren't going to kill her. To pass the time, she even showed me how to drive a boat and, after a few minutes, I found myself really enjoying it. By the time we reached her dock, I was entertaining ideas about picking up a little cabin cruiser of my own.

Maybe I'd keep it on the island so Lumpy and I could go out for the occasional *pleasure* cruise.

THE NO-CARB HILTON

The blizzard hit just after dawn.

Badger Island is the most exposed piece of dirt in Lake Michigan, with wind driving the snow into high drifts that make roads impassable. Of course, the ferry wasn't sailing because of the rough weather so we were trapped at the No-Carb Hilton, which was good because it was bitterly cold outside.

The dining room, however, was warm and cozy when I came in for breakfast. The waiter had stoked a large fire in the fireplace and Wilma had taken the table next to it. I joined her and my heart leaped for joy when I saw she was devouring a huge breakfast of bacon and eggs.

They served real food here after all!

After our night's undertaking, I was starving and my stomach was grumbling loudly.

"Morning," she said and dipped a piece of toast into a perfectly cooked egg yolk.

I reached for a piece of bacon on her plate.

Wilma's arm shot out and the tines of her fork quivered an eighth of an inch from the back of my hand. She has excellent control of sharp implements.

I released the bacon.

She nodded to the waiter and he slithered over to the table with a steaming bowl.

"Your quinoa porridge, sir," he announced. His voice had just the right degree of condensation.

Here's your feed, piggy.

He was as thin and pale as a vampire. I was tempted to use my butter knife to slash his throat to see if his blood was green.

I dug into my breakfast. Wilma was really enjoying my discomfort so I decided to ignore her and eat my slop.

"Hey, this is exquisite." I licked my spoon clean.

Her lip curled cynically.

But I wasn't joking. It really *did* taste good.

Was I starving to the point where anything would taste good?

Wilma smiled. "I booked us into the spa this morning."

The spa?

Visions of lying in a sauna with the temperature set to broil and then jumping naked into a snowbank filled my head. That would be followed by an invigorating full-body massage from a beautiful Chinese girl who would walk up and down my spine and curl her toes around my balls. Finally, there would be a warm mud bath lasting until my afternoon nap.

It will be glorious.

I finished my breakfast with renewed enthusiasm and washed it down with a steaming mug of carrot tea. I was ready to face the day.

~

And what an unpleasant day it was. For this was the day I discovered *where* the Fourth Reich was born.

I came to this conclusion while I was physically restrained by a couple of black-clad attendants during my colonic irrigation treatment. Any doubts were erased when the torture continued during my body shaping massage with a huge woman who bent my limbs at mathematically impossible angles. Next I was off to the pressure cooker to rid my body of unwanted toxins. Then my wrists and ankles were firmly strapped to a traction table and I was pulled until my joints popped. When I was a foot taller, I was taken to a treatment room where a gorgeous Asian woman waited.

After all the torture was this my happy ending?

She smiled demurely and took the sterile shroud off a tray of very long needles.

"Now please hold still," she told me as she slid one into the skin next to my eye. She twirled it delicately between her fingers.

Five minutes later, I looked like Pinhead from *Hellraiser*. But, to my surprise, the aches and pains disappeared with each new needle. I began to feel warm and drowsy.

She consulted my chart. "I see that you suffer from a deficiency of Qi. This is not good. It affects your energy, you see."

I didn't see but I was feeling so good I just went along for the ride.

She inserted a series of needles into my back.

Little Rip sprang to attention. I tried to hide my embarrassing erection.

She smiled and felt under my towel. "Yes, I can feel that your Qi is restored."

"I'm not sure, maybe we should test it."

She giggled and shook her head.

"Sorry, but it is not that kind of treatment. However, I think your wife will be very pleased tonight."

~

We all laugh at drug ads that warn you to seek medical attention if you have an erection lasting more than four hours. I didn't think that was funny anymore.

My Qi was raging and Wilma was delighted to play the tease. When I staggered back to the room after my treatments, she was reclining on the bed in her skimpiest bikini bottom. She'd spent the afternoon baking under sunlamps and had the kind of healthy glow that usually led to skin cancer.

She looked up and pursed her lips, blowing me a kiss. I tore off my robe and practically leaped onto the bed beside her. But she rolled off with a little laugh and locked herself in the bathroom. No amount of door pounding or pleading could get her to come out.

She just stayed in there and laughed and laughed while my Qi continued to rage.

Did I mention that Wilma is a really cruel woman?

Later that night, however, she did come to appreciate my combination of cleansing and Qi in a session I could only describe as the *Marathon des Sables* of sex.

~

By the time the storm had passed and the ferry was running again, I felt like a new man. The toxic effects of my liquor and hamburger diet had been reversed and my mind was sharp and clear. It needed to be. We still had no clue *who* was behind the Judge's murder.

The news that morning was filled with stories about the attack on Earl Krynkle's home and his abduction. Much to our relief, the FBI had been called in to take over the case.

They would completely fuck up any investigation.

The local sheriff's department was incompetent, ironically thanks to Krynkle's sponsorship. They were giving out regular press briefings to the effect that they were looking at some an eco-terrorist group as the possible suspect. They were also optimistic that old Chainsaw Earl was still alive and had been taken into the woods.

Will our Earlsickle be discovered?

If he weren't, then we could add his name to the long list of famous people we had made disappear permanently.

~

The final piece of business we had on the island was Lumpy Carmichael.

I had promised our faithful captain we would leave her alive, but now Wilma was having second thoughts.

"We need to kill her."

"That would raise unnecessary suspicion. One of those FBI morons might actually put the two and two together and guess what happened. Anyway, I don't think Lumpy is the talking kind."

Wilma still wasn't convinced. The FBI was offering a huge reward and it might lead Lumpy into temptation. To placate Wilma, I agreed to drop by Lumpy's place to remind her that her continuing silence was paramount.

~

"You've come to kill me, haven't you?"

Lumpy held the door open for me. Her expression said she was already resigned to her fate.

On the large screen TV in her living room, CNN was speculating that Earl Krynkle had been kidnapped by "terrorists."

As I shook the snow off my jacket and took it off, Lumpy backed away in fear.

"Have you got anything to eat?" I tried to keep the pleading tone out of my voice.

"What? You want me to cook something for you before you kill me?"

I shook my head. "I'm not going to kill you."

"You might not want to, but I bet your partner does."

I had to hand it to Lumpy, she was very perceptive.

"I can keep Wilma under control. I told her you might come in handy in the future."

I wasn't sure Lumpy bought it, but for once I was telling the truth.

"I have some pork chops in the freezer."

An electric charge shot down my spine and I smelled ozone.

Lumpy's eyes dropped and then widened in shock. She was looking at my crotch where my Qi was in its full glory.

I smiled. "It's from a treatment I got at the spa."

"I see they renewed your Qi," she said. "I have a shortage of Qi myself." Lumpy took my hand. "Let's see if you can spare some of yours."

All thoughts of pork chops were chased from my head as she led me to her bedroom.

~

There were no preliminaries with Lumpy. She obviously had a lot of desire bottled up. When my Qi was exhausted, we lay back and listened to the wind shrieking as it tore the shingles off the roof.

Lumpy caressed the small of my back and licked my ear. "That was wonderful."

I closed my eyes and focused on her hand making small circles on my left buttock. Little Rip was beginning to twitch again. Her fingers slid between my legs and started to encourage the little fella to come out and play.

My Qi answered the call.

~

I looked up from kissing her belly and asked the question that had been nagging at me since we first met. "How did you get your nickname?"

"It's not my nickname, it's my given name. My father thought I looked all lumpy when I was born so he convinced my mother to let him name me that. He was always doing goofy shit."

When she said the last part, I detected sadness.

"How long has he been gone?"

She grimaced. "Five years. He sailed out one a beautiful spring day and never came back."

"That's an awful way to go," I said, implementing what I hoped was a reasonable facsimile of sympathy.

"I ended up with this place and an insurance settlement that paid for the boat and that's about all."

She looked deeply into my eyes, trying to find the truth within.

Good luck with that.

"So you're not going to kill me?"

I shook my head.

"What happens if anyone comes around asking questions?"

"No one will."

She nodded. "But the DEA is already watching me."

"Then you need to keep a low profile, no more drug runs for a while."

She frowned.

I resumed kissing her belly.

"Anyway, who knows, we might need your services again."

This seemed to satisfy her and her taut stomach muscles relaxed under my tongue.

"Why not, I can always use the cash," she groaned.

She pulled me into a close embrace and I tapped into my endless supply of Qi.

THE TEMPLE OF DOOM

I left Lumpy's place a little after 4:00 to catch a 5:00 ferry.

Even though the storm had passed, the lake was still rough. Leaving Wilma in a Gravol-induced coma in the front seat of the car, I walked to the bow rail to feel the icy splash on my face once again. The stars had come out and it was a beautiful night.

I thought about what we should tell Laura. Maybe she'd be satisfied if we blamed Earl Krynkle for arranging her father's death. While that might satisfy her, I still had a personal score to settle with the man in the Godzilla costume.

In my mind, I was still shackled to the table as the pendulum swished overhead with its razor-sharp blade brushing across my belly. I felt like screaming.

I vowed I would find that bastard and show him what real fear was like.

~

I called Promod from the ferry.

"Any luck?"

The long pause on the other end told me what I needed to know.

"It's a bitch. Once you get past their public site, you fall into some sort of rabbit hole. It's full of hacker snares and boomerangs."

I knew *boomerangs* were little traps that could lead back to an attacking hacker. Ukrainian and Asian gangs used them to dissuade intruders. I'd even heard rumors they'd killed a couple of teens in Holland to make their point after an Indonesian gambling site was hacked. These guys were smart and brutal.

Boomerangs were also a challenge for Promod. And he loved a challenge.

"I've been digging around the edges and staying away from their traps. I did manage to learn a little about that house of horrors you visited. For instance, the title deed is registered in Niagara County and the owner is listed as the International Corrections Management Group. It's designated as a training facility for their personnel.

"That's the standard bullshit that companies use to write off these executive retreats for tax purposes. Just try to do that for your cabin on the lake. The IRS will mail your ass to prison."

"Spare me the anti-corporate rant will you."

Promod went silent.

I didn't give a shit whether or not I hurt his feelings. Promod drove a Bentley, lived in an upper-class neighborhood, and took his wife and daughter on luxury vacations. And I figured he was a dues-paying supporter of the GOP.

He was hardly the proletariat type.

"I'm at a standstill here," I told him. "I need to know everything about ICMG and who's pulling their strings."

"Well, I have to be really careful. Like I said, I'm tiptoeing around the edges right now. Give me a little more time to see what I can find."

"Alright ..."

I hoped the annoyance in my voice would send the right message.

~

I let Wilma sleep all the way back to Detroit. It gave me time to think. Since Promod was having no luck out there in the digital forest, I decided to call Del and see if he might be able to shake a few trees for me. I figured he was bound to have contacts with other police forces, and hoped he might know someone in the Buffalo PD as crooked as he was.

~

As always, we met for lunch.

This time, I surprised him by suggesting a small café near the Wayne State campus just off the Ford Freeway.

Del was impressed when I ordered a quinoa salad and tuna wrap. When the food came, he doused his veggie wrap in hot sauce and slurped it down.

"What's the matter, you burn a hole in your guts eating all that nitrate-laced shit?"

"Del, you of all people should understand the concept of the body as a temple."

"Yeah, sure. The Temple of Doom." He snorted at his feeble attempt at humor.

Del's enormous girth made him more like Vatican City than a temple.

I unscrewed the top of a bottle of wheatgrass juice and poured some.

"What do you want this time?"

"I need the name of one of your band of brothers in the Buffalo area."

He looked at me suspiciously.

"I need you to introduce me to a cop who is just as dishonest as you are."

Del looked down at his empty plate and traced a finger through a puddle of hot sauce.

"Sure, there's this guy I know in the Genesee County Sheriff's Department. Paul Reese. Everyone calls him Pee Wee. We shook down a Toronto drug gang together, helped them make sure their product moved unimpeded into Michigan and New York. We split it fifty-fifty."

Del licked the hot sauce off his finger.

"And I can trust him?"

"Almost as much as me."

"Which is to say not at all."

He frowned. "Well, he likes money and once he's paid he stays bought."

Del looked around for our waitress.

"You want dessert? They make really great pastries here."

"No, I want you to give him a call and arrange a meeting ."

"I'll see what I can do," he shrugged.

He waved over the waitress and ordered a plate of sugar cookies.

I got up from the table to spare myself the disgusting sight of Del shoveling down the sweets.

"I expect to hear from you within the next three hours." I let the implication hang in the air between us.

The cookies arrived and Del's eyes went wide with delight.

"I'll call him when I get back to the office. What do you want me to tell him?"

"That I'm an old army buddy who needs some intel."

Del popped a cookie in his mouth and chewed. "Okay, I'll let you know."

Bits of sugar cookie flew in all directions. He picked up another one and jammed it into his already cookie-filled maw.

If the Keebler elves were around, Del would probably eat them too. I put a twenty on the table and left.

WE ARE SIAMESE IF YOU DON'T PLEASE

"Why don't we take care of Sparky Fletcher's feline problem?"

I was still waiting to hear back from Del and, frankly, I was bored. We'd had no luck so far resolving who was really behind the Judge's murder. The issue with Sparky Fletcher's wife would be a good distraction.

~

I'd checked Sparky's website. It was pathetic like a kid had put it together in the 1990s, with spinning globes, counters, and flashing marquees.

I clicked on the spinning globe that served as his *Performing Live* link to check the venue and show schedule. He was playing Antwerp, an excellent alibi for when we stopped by to visit his wife that night.

~

Sparky Fletcher's home was in a beautiful neighborhood in Farmington Hills.

We had driven past the house earlier in the day just to get a sense of the place. It was the perfect location for our kind of business. Lots of bushes came right up to the house and the nearest neighbor was almost a hundred feet away.

Sparky told me one of the cats had chewed through the wires of their alarm system and he hadn't bothered to replace it.

The alarm system or the cat? I guess we'll find out.

He also mentioned his wife popped Ambien every night to help her sleep over the din of the cats.

No alarm system and a comatose victim. Could we ask for anything more?

I hate to use the expression *Piece of Cake*, but this one practically screamed Double Dutch Chocolate.

~

Wilma remembered there was a Costco nearby in Novi where we could kill some time.

She said she needed some toilet paper. Just one of those monoliths of toilet paper rolls they sell would keep her in bathroom tissue for at least twenty years.

But we needed to wait until Sparky's spouse had gone to bed and what better place to do it than in the *Dawn of the Dead* splendor of a giant warehouse store.

Wilma stocked up on toilet paper, along with several dozen other essentials. After she had finished, we killed a couple more hours at the movies watching a John Travolta film that was so bad it made Adam Sandler look like *Shakespeare in the Park*.

~

It was after midnight when we finally arrived at Sparky Fletcher's house.

I picked the lock on the back door and pushed it open gently. Sparky had made good on his promise to oil the hinges before leaving for Europe.

A nauseating bouquet of soiled cat litter and sour milk hit us as soon as we entered the house. Wilma gagged and grabbed the doorframe for support. I covered my nose and reluctantly shut the door behind us.

"I'm gonna burn my clothes when we're through," Wilma hissed.

I knew what she meant. I was going to take a two-day shower to get rid of the feline stink.

The kitchen smelled worse than a tiger's cage at the zoo.

Wilma put her foot in one of the large food bowls.

"I hate cats," she muttered scrapping a goopy mass of *Salmon & Whitefish Supreme* from her sneaker on the side of the bowl.

Belle Fletcher was covered in a blanket of kitties on the living room couch where she'd passed out from the Ambien.

We'd agreed to stage her transition from this world to the next as an accident. I'd run the usual scenarios such as the radio in the bathtub or the scarf caught in the garburator and finally decided in her semi-conscious state that a neck-snapping tumble down the stairs was in order.

I could just see the investigating officer's report: *Subject woke up, became disoriented, and tripped on the top step.*

Thumpa, thumpa, thumpa.

The only complication was the fact that old Belle weighed about three-fifty naked and was dead weight when we tried to drag her to the top of the basement stairs.

"I think we need a forklift."

Wilma strained to get Belle standing upright. "Put your back into it!"

The Ambien was doing its job and Belle was completely out of it.

Belle patted the top of Wilma's head.

"Nice kitty," she slurred.

I had to stop Wilma from biting off Belle's nose.

With some cajoling and no small amount of effort, we finally managed to get Belle to the top of the stairs where, ironically, we didn't need to give her a push after all.

Belle tripped over a sleek Siamese and tumbled forward head-over-tail into the basement.

Thumpa, thumpa, thumpa.

When she hit bottom, her head was completely twisted around facing back toward us. It gave me the creeps.

I checked her pulse and sure enough, she had gone off to join the *dance company invisible*.

The cats surrounded her and began to mew expectantly, wanting her to get up and feed them.

"Sorry, fellas. It's going to be a while before meantime."

Some of the bolder cats were rubbing against her.

"Think we should feed them before we go?"

Wilma sniffed. "They'd better start looking out for themselves."

I leaned down and petted a pretty little calico. It mewled and arched its back against my hand.

"Sorry, honey, your sugar mama's gone."

~

"Ever think about getting a pet?"

We were in the car heading back downtown.

Wilma smiled. "I already have one."

"Amusing. But you must have had a dog or a cat or something when you were a kid."

She shook her head. "Nope, but my parents were rats."

I thought of the dog I'd had when I was little. His name was Dodger and he'd had the cutest way of cowering in the corner and growling at me.

"I don't understand the whole pet thing," Wilma said. "Why would anyone want to bring a wild animal into their home? What purpose does it serve?"

"In the old days, they used them for protection and hunting."

"But she had about a hundred cats in there and they didn't protect her. Anyway, it's not healthy. You can get worms and shit from them."

"I wonder how long it will take before they find the body."

~

As it turned out, it was almost a month before a nosy neighbor peeked in the front window and saw a cat trotting by with a human finger in its mouth. We didn't have to be concerned about the cats' welfare after all. They'd made out just fine with over three hundred pounds of meat to keep them satisfied.

You think that someone would have noticed the noise of the cats and the smell of rotting Belle before a month had passed.

But, after all, it was Detroit.

~

There's nothing like a personal tragedy to work wonders for a faded celebrity's flagging career. Sparky was in Barcelona doing a two-night gig when they contacted him about his wife's "terrible accident".

He rushed back home, stopping briefly to pick up his press agent on the way.

It didn't hurt that his wife's death had a lurid touch. In fact, the details set off quite a debate around the country. It's not every day that a minor celebrity's wife is consumed by her cats. I wondered if a lot of people were now nervously eyeing their own pets after reading about Belle.

Of course, by the time the story broke, Wilma and I were consumed by troubles of our own.

NOT MY CIRCUS, NOT MY MONKEY

With Sparky's wife out of the way, I thought it might be a good idea to pay another visit to Laura and give her a *progress* report.

Or, in our case, a *lack of progress* report. I decided not to tell her about Chainsaw Earl, our latest dead end. Instead, I did the next best thing and made shit up.

We sat side-by-side on her couch.

"I am very excited about a new possibility."

"So you don't know anything new."

Her lack of enthusiasm told me she was getting the same stories from her other two contract killers.

I wasn't afraid of those killers. Wilma and I had dismissed our rivals as common thugs and had deluded ourselves into thinking we were just *that* much cleverer. The chance they would learn about us was just as remote as us finding out about them. That's the problem with having a monster fucking ego. It can get in your way and cloud good sense.

Our rivals were probably doing what Wilma and I had done, keeping Laura under observation.

The thought that we had popped up on two very dangerous radar screens made the hairs on the back of my neck stand up.

Do those guys feel the same as we do about having competition?

Feeling I was in a set of crosshairs motivated me to gather Laura in my arms and kiss her. If someone were aiming at me, they hopefully wouldn't risk killing their client.

I expected Laura to pull away or to slap me, but instead she hugged me tight.

Interesting indeed. I was about ten years older and wondered if she had any unresolved daddy issues.

But my doubts were forgotten when she tore off my clothes like a horny teenager.

~

Laura screwed like a panther, tearing at me and growling her desires. She knew exactly what she needed and how to get me to give it to her. It was like a whirlwind tour of Laura Land. I only had impressions of what we were doing before her back arched and she howled in pleasure.

Five wordless minutes later she was back in her tight sweater, and I was going out the front door wondering what the hell had just happened.

~

The next morning, Wilma and I met for coffee at our favorite diner on Michigan Avenue in Dearborn.

I dragged myself to the booth and flopped down.

"You look exhausted."

"Client relations."

Her eyebrows lifted slightly and then narrowed.

"Did it ever occur to you that our competition might be following us?"

Wilma stared at her coffee thoughtfully. "Of course," she replied. "But I've been following them while they followed each other and you. It's like a big daisy chain."

"So what do you think we should do about it?"

"I think you should call Del. He hasn't gotten back to you yet about his contact in Buffalo. And while you've got him on the line, here's what you should tell him."

She spent the next few minutes detailing her scheme. It was brilliant. I was reminded yet again why I have the best partner a fellow could hope for in this line of business.

~

"I talked to Pee Wee and he's expecting your call."

Del was tense.

"Something I should know, Del?"

Loooooooooong silence.

"Yeah, I'm not sure you should trust him. We go back, but not that far. I got the feeling that someone's pulling his strings."

"What makes you say that?"

"He sounded like he was *expecting* my call. Asked a shitload of questions about you. It didn't feel right to me."

I took him seriously. Was I walking into a trap if I went back to Buffalo? *Probably.*

But we needed some intel and it had to be local. Anyway, I always hedged my bets, and I was not walking in there alone.

"Thanks for the insight, Del," I said. "I've got something for you. Play it right and you might get another gold star on your chart."

I told him what we were going to arrange. He laughed unpleasantly.

~

"Are you serious?"

It was a rhetorical question.

Of course, I was serious.

"Ummm … my little worm on a hook." Wilma poked me playfully in the belly.

"Yes, well worms do draw out the big fish."

"I thought we had Promod for that."

She was right, but Promod kept putting us off. I was starting to get the distinct impression that we were not his first priority.

What was he up to, fiddling around with the North Korean economy?

"It might help if I dropped by and gave him a little additional motivation," Wilma said.

The image of Wilma sticking a gun in his ear popped into my mind.

"I'm not sure that's the kind of inspiration he needs. I wonder if he feels like we're taking advantage of him?"

Another rhetorical question.

My phone rang. It was a moment of synchronicity. Promod had finally learned something of value to us.

~

"I'm a genius. Say it."

I ignored him and waited.

"What?" I finally asked to make him happy.

"I found something good."

"Okay, spill it."

"There was nothing filed with the SEC because International Corrections Management Group is a privately-held company. I tried the IRS database and voila, I hit the jackpot. There's a whole treasure trove of stuff there, including an investigation."

"For what?"

"They set up dummy headquarters in Holland to avoid paying taxes at the U.S. corporate rate."

"So?"

"Nothing. Lots of companies do it. The investigation was terminated in 2012. However, the file contains all kinds of goodies about them, including the identity of their real owners, the Franklin-Stroud Group of Companies."

He paused for dramatic effect.

"Never heard of them."

"It's an international consortium of companies. Besides ICMG, they own a diverse collection of businesses."

"Like what?"

"Well, a couple of arms companies, a software group, an agri-business, and ZOTZ, the energy drink maker."

I was familiar with the latter. I'd tried ZOT when it first came out. It was a delicious combination of grapefruit juice, sweet tea, and a massive dose of caffeine. I couldn't sleep for three days.

"So what do we know about the Frankenstein Group?"

"Franklin-Stroud," he corrected me. "They're huge. And very protective, the kind of people who start wars to goose their quarterly returns."

"Do we know who's in charge?"

He laughed. "Funny you should ask. The public face of Franklin-Stroud is their CEO, Tesla D'Urberville."

Tesla D'Urberville!

"He's a clown," I said.

Tesla D'Urberville had created and hosted the very popular reality show *You're Fired!* He was also a right-wing nut who had been teasing that he would run for president. He pledged to manage America like a business. No one actually took him seriously, but he thrived on the publicity.

"So why would he be interested in killing a state senator?"

"Because *this* senator was sponsoring a bill to stop the privatization of Michigan's prisons. It would have cost them almost a billion dollars in lost revenue."

And we only took fifty thousand to do the job.

"I'm still not convinced. Guys like D'Urberville spend a billion on lunch. Why would he risk everything?"

Promod didn't respond. He'd apparently been thinking the same thing. It didn't make any sense. D'Urberville was a celebrity. And he had more money than God. What could he possibly get from killing the Judge?

I decided we still needed to take a closer look at Tesla D'Urberville as a possible suspect.

"Keep digging," I told him.

"I will." Promod sounded unhappy, like a child whose father ignores the A+ he got on his spelling exam.

I decided he needed a little pat. "Thanks, Promod. Good work. We appreciate it."

I'd read in one of the endless streams of management books Wilma was always foisting on me that singling out an employee for a job well done goes a lot farther that a monetary reward.

"Yeah, well I'd appreciate a little cash now and then."

This management technique was lost on Promod.

I moved on to my second favorite management motivation skill, *the empty promise.*

"Sure. We're picking out a beautiful gift basket from Hickory Farms for you."

I hung up.

Wilma's reaction was the same as mine. Tesla D'Urberville would fit right in with Ringling Bros. and Barnum & Bailey.

He brought to mind an old Polish proverb, *nie mój cyrk, nie moje małpy,* which meant *not my circus, not my monkey.*

BEEF ON WRECK

So we shuffled off back to Buffalo.

On my way to lunch with Sheriff's Detective Pee Wee Reese, I dropped Wilma at a large mall. She needed to pick up another car so she could discretely follow me and, for some reason, mall parking lots are usually full of them.

Of course, it started to snow again. Local forecasters were masturbating over 'another fall blizzard' on the way. I was beginning to think this town only had two seasons — raging snowstorms or bad snowmobiling weather.

Wilma picked out a rusted Toyota Corolla parked on the far edge of the lot where store employees were *encouraged* to leave their cars. It wouldn't be missed for hours.

If it were my car, I wouldn't miss it at all.

~

Reese had suggested we meet at the Sawyer Creek Hotel in North Tonawanda.

I got there first and sat at a table in the dining room. I ordered a Coors Light and settled back to wait.

According to a framed newspaper article on the wall, this was a favorite stopping off place for the stagecoaches running between Buffalo and Niagara Falls. The dining room looked like Aunt Bitty's parlor with garish red paisley wallpaper and a worn oxblood carpet.

Wilma sat at the bar and watched the table through an open door connecting the two rooms.

Reese was twenty minutes late.

He brushed snow off his cashmere overcoat and hung it carefully to dry on a coat rack.

Reese was the polar opposite of Del, tall and slim with a bald head buffed to a shine. I discovered he was also vain when I shook his hand. It was as soft as calfskin and professionally manicured. With such a sophisticated look, I was puzzled that he would pick a shop-worn location like this to have lunch.

"Everyone eats here," he said as if anticipating my question. "The food is excellent. You should try their Beef on Weck sandwich."

Beef on Wreck?

My knowledge of Buffalo cuisine was limited to stuffed peppers and chicken wings.

"Sure. Sounds good."

He ordered a sandwich for each of us and I had to admit he was right. It was *great.*

Weck, I learned, was a German roll topped with caraway seeds and large grains of salt. It was filled with shaved roast beef and you slathered on fresh horseradish and dipped the whole thing in au jus.

After we'd finished our lunch, he got down to business.

"Del tells me you need some information."

"An expensive house burned down a couple of weeks ago."

"This is Buffalo. Houses burn down here every day. We're famous for our fires. Can you give me specifics?"

"This one was north of Niagara Falls, on the river."

"I don't recall hearing anything about it."

"There was nothing in the papers or on the news. But it was the kind of place that *should* have been noticed."

"I can look into it for you."

His intense, unwavering eyes and casual manner made me nervous.

"You planning to be around here for a while?"

"At least for the next couple of days."

"Got a number I can reach you at?"

He took out a cop's notebook.

I gave him the number of the burner phone I was carrying.

"I'll get back to you."

Without any preamble, he stood up and got his overcoat. He didn't offer to pay for lunch and left the dining room without saying another word.

I waited a few minutes, finished my beer, and paid the check.

~

The snow was getting serious.

What had been a light dusting when I went into the restaurant had become a fierce blast of winter. Blowing snow made it difficult to see more than a hundred feet.

Luckily, I was able to find the Hampton Inn we had booked. After shadowing me to the restaurant, Wilma returned her stolen car to the mall and took a cab to the hotel. She registered separately and got a room on a different floor from mine.

~

Wilma knocked softly on my door a few minutes later.

"He had a partner, the porky little guy who was sitting next to me at the bar. He went out while you were having lunch with Reese and put something under your car."

A GPS tracker.

"Was Mr. Reese as smooth as he looked?"

I nodded. "Yup. He's a slick one."

"He's definitely bent. He drives a big BMW so he's not trying to hide it."

A Beemer and a $1,000 topcoat.

This guy was an operator.

"I don't trust him."

No surprise there. Wilma doesn't trust anyone.

~

All I could do for now was wait for Reese to call.

It was a good time to catch up on some sleep. I drifted off and dreamed of climbing a mountain made from Beef on Weck.

The phone woke me up late in the afternoon.

"I found out some interesting stuff for you," Reese said.

"Oh yeah," I yawned. "What's that?"

"Not on the phone. Meet me tonight around 11:00 at Three Sisters Islands."

"Where's Three Sisters Islands?"

"You've got a tourist guide," he said and hung up.

THE THREE SISTERS

Wilma looked up Three Sisters Islands online and showed me the location on a Google map.

My stomach lurched when I saw the Islands were a couple of hundred feet from the brink of the Falls.

"What a delightful spot for an ambush," Wilma said.

"It certainly is isolated."

She laughed. "I think you're going for a swim tonight."

Of course, I was. Reese wouldn't have picked this spot otherwise. But it was also encouraging. If he was planning to kill me, that meant he was taking orders from someone.

And I was going to find out who that someone was.

~

It was early evening before the snow let up.

The ever efficient snowplows had the road in front of the hotel cleared by 10:00. Since they'd already put a tracking device on my car, I didn't think they would be camping on me.

Wilma opened the trunk and took out a duffle bag. She walked down the row of parked cars and selected a late model Ford Focus. It took her six seconds to open the door, disable the alarm system, and turn on the ignition. I was impressed. Even for Wilma, this was a new record. My confidence was boosted.

She's sharp tonight.

I certainly hoped so because if she weren't, I was going over the Falls without a barrel.

~

The visitor parking lot on Goat Island was empty.

I sat in my car patiently. I was sure that Reese wouldn't keep me waiting like he had at lunch. He'd want to kill me quickly so he could get home to his nice warm bed.

It wasn't long before his BMW pulled into the lot. I got out of my car and waved. He nodded and headed toward me.

"Let's go." He pointed to a small foot bridge leading to the Islands. "We can talk out there."

Playing stupid, I followed him.

A **DANGER DO NOT ENTER** sign hung from a chain across the entrance:

Reese unhooked the chain.

"Isn't that against the law?"

He ignored me and led the way onto the Island.

I was glad I'd abandoned my stylish coat for something warmer. My new Gore-Tex jacket did an excellent job of preventing the frigid wind from turning me into a Dilly Bar.

The roar was unbelievably loud. I watched huge chunks of ice race past and then disappear over the lip of the Falls.

"I don't see why we couldn't talk back there in the parking lot."

Reese's answer was to point a massive pistol at me.

"It's easy to see why Detroit is going down the shitter if it's full of dumbasses like you," he smirked.

I stuck out my chin. "No one gets to talk about my hometown like that. I have civic pride."

His gun didn't waver. He cocked the hammer, confident that he had the upper hand.

And that was just the way I wanted him.

When my fake look of desperation made him laugh, I stepped forward and twisted the gun from his hand in a smooth, well-practiced move. I turned it on him.

Reese smiled smugly, totally unfazed by this turn of events.

So I decided to *faze* him and shot him in the knee. Reese collapsed on the ground. Although writhing in agony, he remained defiant.

Then a loud bang came from the parking lot.

"It sounds like your backup just met my backup," I said as I dragged him to the edge of the water.

Fear filled Reese's eyes as he came to the dark realization he'd overplayed his hand.

"So who planned this little excursion?"

I pulled him to his feet and he balanced precariously on his uninjured leg.

"Juke," he gasped.

"Juke? Like in *joint*, or *box*?"

"Juke Warfrin. Look no hard feelings. Remember, I'm a friend of Del's."

"That's interesting because Del told me not to trust you. What kind of friend is that?"

"I'll tell you all about Warfrin." He looked around desperately for a way out. "He's the leader of a bike gang, the Demon Stompers, up in Empire."

"Where the hell is that?

"Near Lockport." Reese bounced around on his uninjured leg trying to keep his balance. "Please ... don't ...," he begged as I edged him closer to the river.

"Anyone else I should know about?"

"No one else," he gasped.

As frustrating as it was, I believed him. Reese was probably just a hired gun and not privy to the bigger picture.

"Too bad then."

"Please!" he screamed as I kicked his good leg out from under him. With wind-milling arms, he fell backward into the raging Niagara River. A second later his head bobbed up a few feet away and he dog paddled frantically against the current as it propelled him toward the brink of the Horseshoe Falls.

"Enjoy the view," I shouted to him. "I hear it's spectacular."

Reese's screams ended a few seconds later.

~

Back in the parking lot, Wilma was bending over a goon lying face down in the snow. The air steamed out of a massive exit wound in the back of his head. Holding her high-powered rifle under her arm, she flipped through his wallet. I caught the glint of a badge.

"Amateurs," she sniffed.

"Well, at least I found out something." And I told her about Warfrin and his bike gang.

"Why would bikers want to kill the Judge?"

"I'm not sure."

It didn't make sense to me. Bikers were technically our competition. Some of them were hitmen, but they lacked a sense of style. They tended to use way too much brutality, and their personal hygiene left something to be desired.

"Who the hell are the Demon Stompers anyway?"

I shook my head. "Never heard of them. They must be local."

Wilma walked over to Reese's BMW.

I followed and watched her jack open the trunk and root around inside. She pointed at two neatly-wrapped bricks Reese had hidden under his spare tire.

I made a small slit in one of the packages. I lifted out a tiny amount of white powder with my knife and rubbed it on my lip. It went numb instantly.

Cocaine.

"He must have liberated these from the evidence locker." I bounced the package in my hand.

Wilma took it from me and tossed it back in the trunk.

"Let's make it look like a falling out over drugs," she said pointing at the dead man on the ground.

I picked up the brick again and slipped it into my pocket.

"Leave it," she said sternly.

"It might come in handy."

I could see she was unhappy and I understood why. Drugs, unlike contract killing, have a bad reputation. They give off the same creepy vibe as watching *The Bachelor.*

To my knowledge, no one had ever declared war on contract killing, or arson, or even shoplifting for that matter. But drugs, well, that was an entirely different story. They attracted unwanted attention from law enforcement.

But a pound of coke might come in handy as a great door-opener for the criminal element. I was thinking specifically about the Demon Stompers Bike Club.

Wilma tossed Reese's pistol next to his dead partner and I took the rifle back to Three Sisters Islands to drop it near where Reese had gone into the river. To the cops, it would look like a shootout. When the remaining cocaine in Reese's trunk was discovered, they would assume it was a falling out between partners in crime.

~

After leaving the Falls, we went back to the Hampton Inn. I took the GPS tracker from under my car and stomped on it. I tossed the remains into the creek that ran behind the hotel.

Then we got a good night's sleep.

~

The next morning we Googled Empire, New York, and discovered it was only a few miles from Lockport, which in turn was only a few miles from where we were.

Wilma picked up a car at the Niagara Falls airport and followed me.

It was a lovely day in Western New York for a change, postcard pretty with the sun sparkling on the freshly fallen snow.

A perfect day to go calling on the Demon Stompers.

THE DEMON STOMPERS

Lockport, New York, is a charming little town at the ass-end of the Erie Canal.

The name comes from two massive lift locks located just off the main street. We could see them from our table in the back of the diner where we went for breakfast. I was shocked to learn they didn't serve quinoa and instead I had to settle for bacon and eggs and a half pound of hash browns.

Wilma was searching for references to the gang on her phone. "They have a website."

Their logo was a cartoon that resembled *Hot Stuff*, a favorite comic book of mine from childhood. But I didn't remember the lovable little devil in it giving the finger to the world.

Under their Wikipedia entry was loads of useful information, including the fact they ran the village of Empire and had several legitimate fronts. The main one was the local sawmill which served as their headquarters.

"They must think they're the *Sons of Anarchy*."

"More like the Sons of Absurdity," Wilma chuckled.

"It's a smart move having an entire town under their control. Strangers will be noticed."

Wilma called up a satellite view of the area and zoomed in on the sawmill located on the south side of town. "Motion sensors and CCTV for sure."

"Bikers like Nazi shit so they'll probably have Alsatians too."

Alarms and TV we could easily deal with. Dogs were another matter. They are unpredictable and yappy. I thought back to the German Shepherds tugging on their leashes the night we invaded the compound by the gorge.

After Niagara Falls, I discussed the dog problem with Steve Carlson. He smiled and went into his shop. A few minutes later he came back and set a portable Bluetooth speaker and USB drive on the bench.

"Plant the speaker within a hundred feet and link it to your MP3 player. Play the file marked *Fido* on this drive. It sends out a frequency that only canines can detect. It'll make them want to chew off their own ears."

"That sounds like fun."

Steve looked at me askew.

"The pain only immobilizes them. It doesn't do any permanent damage. When you turn the signal off, they're back to normal in a couple of minutes."

I paid him an outrageous amount of money and added it to an arsenal of useful items we might never need.

Now I was finally going to get some return on my investment.

I looked at the satellite image of the sawmill.

"So I go in the front and you go in the back."

"I'm not sure what that'll accomplish. They'll probably stomp your ass as soon as you show up at the gate."

"I'm hoping to win their respect," I said. "Plus I'm bringing along a little house warming gift."

I held up the brick of cocaine.

~

The biker guarding the gate at the lumber mill made no attempt to hide the AR-15 he cradled like a lethal baby. He yawned loudly when I approached. The dark circles under his bloodshot eyes told me he'd been partying all night.

I calculated how long it would take to get the gun away from him.

A millisecond, maybe two if I permanently cripple him.

Instead, I showed him an official-looking ID. He read it slowly, mouthing the words.

"New York State Department of Forestry? Never fucking heard of it."

"It doesn't matter," I said. "We've heard of you and your mill and this is a snap inspection."

He pointed the rifle in my direction.

I pretended to be intimidated but, like any good bureaucrat, I annoyingly stood my ground. He finally lowered the gun and spoke softly into his headset. Then he opened the gate and waved me in with a smile that revealed stained and crooked teeth.

"Be my guest."

~

I parked my car next to the trailer which served as the gang's clubhouse. A row of Harleys sat under the roof of a nearby shed. A couple of troglodytes wearing Demon Stompers colors stepped out of the trailer and watched me warily as I went around and opened the trunk. I reached in and their hands instinctively slid to their waistbands. They relaxed when they saw me lift out a briefcase.

"I need to speak to the manager," I demanded.

They looked at each other in amusement.

"Inside," one grunted.

~

The trailer smelled like well-aged beer, cigarette smoke, and the kind of perfume you get at Walmart. A man sat behind a desk with his feet up and regarded me through hooded eyes. From the back came the unmistakable sound of frenzied humping and a woman was moaning loudly. A couple of biker thugs were leaning against the door listening to the action inside.

"We're doing orientation on our new secretary this morning." The man behind the desk smirked. "What the fuck do you want?"

I started to tell him but he held up a hand.

"And no bullshit about the New York State Department of Forestry. There's no such thing."

I hesitated.

"Do I have the privilege of addressing Mr. Warfrin?"

He touched the patch on his cut-off jacket. **PRESIDENT.**

I nodded and opened my case. I put the brick of coke on the desk.

He looked at it casually. "So?"

"It's 80% pure and I have access to nearly a ton more."

"Not interested."

I picked up the coke and put it back in my briefcase.

"Okay. I'll go talk to the Banditos then. I'm sure they can use the money."

His eyes narrowed and he slowly got to his feet. He came around to my side of the desk and looked at me intently.

"You know, I can't figure how an asshole like you could ever get the drop on Reese, so I guess I'll have to finish the job myself."

He pulled out a pistol and pointed it at my nose. From where I was standing, the barrel was as deep and dark as Wilma's soul.

"Let's go." He poked my nose with the hand cannon.

Behind us in the back office, the woman was crying out with unbridled passion.

Warfrin looked at the two bikers who were patiently waiting their turn.

"Let's show him around."

Casting regretful looks toward the closed door they took my arms, lifted me off my feet, and propelled me out of the trailer.

Everyone froze.

All the guards were on the ground with large bullet holes neatly drilled through them.

Bikers' chests on either side of me exploded a heartbeat later and tattoos rained down all over the place.

A screaming naked woman covered in blood and brain matter burst from the trailer and ran across the yard. She continued running down the street.

"That'll give the locals something to gossip about for months," I said as I deftly wrenched the large pistol from Warfrin's hand.

The camo-colored Desert Eagle had given this asshole a false sense of security.

Too bad for him he'd left the safety on. I flipped it off and held the gun against his forehead.

"Now that we won't be disturbed, let's have a little talk."

~

The scope of the sawmill surprised me. I expected it to be a half-assed operation, but it was a state-of-the-art affair. The main attraction was a computer-controlled ten-foot saw blade. This monster was designed to cut thick tree trunks into thin planks in seconds. The saw could be operated by a single person using touchscreen controls. At the push of a button, a large hopper fed the logs onto a cart which pushed them through the saw blade.

Wilma held her rifle on Warfrin while I tied him face-down onto a log. He lifted his head and looked at the edge of the blade spinning six feet away from his nose.

His cool completely evaporated.

I walked to the controls and started the cart inching forward toward the saw.

"Hands and feet inside the car at all times, ladies and gentlemen," I shouted over the whine.

Realizing he had a very short amount of time before his beak was split, Warfrin peed his pants.

I walked beside him. "I have a couple of questions for you but, obviously, I'll have to make them quick ones."

He twisted to face me.

"Who ordered you to kill me?" I asked.

Warfrin looked frantically back to the blade.

"My brothers down in Charleston."

"Why do they want me dead?"

"I don't know. They just sent word they wanted it done. I told Reese to take care of it."

"I need names!"

"Pawnee and Loco," he screamed.

"Thanks so much," I said politely and walked away.

Warfrin stared at the controls willing them to shut down. Unfortunately, that kind of stuff only happens in movies and cheap fiction.

Wilma and I strolled from the mill. A blood-curdling scream followed us out. The pitch of the saw blade momentarily changed as it bit into something softer than pine.

I took a quick look back.

"There goes the *brains* of the operation."

Wilma shook her head.

"Stop pretending you're James Bond."

STARS AND BARS

We spent a leisurely half hour going through the office.

The place may have smelled like a public toilet, but the Demon Stompers turned out to be very meticulous bookkeepers. We quickly located their charter and discovered they were an affiliate of the Stars and Bars MC, a much larger club based in Rosewater, South Carolina. I looked up the town on my phone. It was on the Old Savannah Highway south of Charleston.

The current weather in Charleston was sunny and in the low 80s, a real contrast to the bitter cold here in Western New York.

"I think a trip to balmier climes is in order."

Wilma agreed.

"But first we have unfinished business back home," I said regretfully.

I needed to have another talk with Detective Sergeant Delbert Newell. I was curious to see if he was the duplicitous bastard who had set me up. For his sake, I hoped not.

Years before, when we first started doing business with Del, Wilma had carved his name into a Dum-Dum shell and put it away just in case it came in handy. At the time, I put it down to Wilma's state of constant paranoia. Now I wasn't so sure.

Reese had been a bad recommendation on Del's part. In his defense, though, he had warned me not to trust the guy. But that might have just been a diversion in case things went wrong in Buffalo.

And they had, especially for old Reese.

While I'm not always the most perceptive person on the block, I do have a knack for determining if people are lying. Forget strapping a person into a polygraph. Just ask a question and look into their eyes. Watch for a

206

twitch or a sudden slight dilation. That will show you whether or not they're telling the truth.

And if that failed, just shoot 'em up with good old fashioned Russian truth serum.

~

Del was the Detroit media celebrity de jour.

The night before, he'd brought down three of city's most notorious hired killers in a violent shootout. The *Free Press* hailed him as a hero. His smiling fat face was plastered under the headline.

Of course, we engineered the entire thing.

Using Lightbulb's street contacts, we'd gotten word to each of Laura's hired guns that the other was the target they were looking for. They stalked each other while Wilma and I went happily about our business.

They'd finally received separate tips that the other would be in a certain place at a certain time. I was disappointed we weren't there for all the fun as Lugnuts came out of a liquor store on Mack just in time to see the Brunner brothers get out of their car across the street. Lugnuts thought it was an ambush and pulled out his gun. So did the Brunners and, lo and behold, bullets started to fly.

Del interrupted their playtime with a couple of well-aimed slugs from his hiding place in the alley next to the store.

In less than ten seconds, three of Detroit's most notorious killers lay dead in the street. Del modestly claimed he was in the right place at the right time and did what any self-respecting police officer would do.

He didn't add that he'd gotten a tip from me. That would have been difficult for him to explain.

It didn't take long for the media to deify Del.

He was a hero in a city that doesn't have a lot of heroes.

The following morning, the Mayor gave him a special commendation and the chief of police promoted him to Detective Lieutenant.

~

Del worked out of Central Division, an ugly cement building on Woodward.

I lurked nearby and waited for the newly minted hero to leave for lunch. He waddled out the front door just after noon and headed down the street to a little hole in the wall restaurant next to a tire store on East Grand. I browsed the Goodyears in the window and waited. A couple of minutes later, he came out carrying a paper bag.

I stepped into his path.

"Hi there, hero."

He didn't blink. "How'd it go in Buffalo?"

"You were right about Pee Wee."

"Oh yeah?" he said with mild interest.

His eyes were unwavering. I was reasonably sure he was telling the truth.

"You're going to have to find a new associate in Western New York."

"Out of the loop is he?"

"Yes, I'm afraid he went for a short swim in the Niagara River."

Del chuckled as he visualized Reese going over the Falls.

"I warned you not to trust that prick."

I nodded and relaxed my grip on the pistol in my jacket pocket.

Del flicked his eyes to my pocket and knew he'd just passed my lie detector test.

"Thanks for the tip by the way. They're moving me up a couple of pay grades and giving me a medal."

"I'm surprised they didn't name a school after you."

Del frowned at my sarcasm.

"Oh well, there is a plus side to everything. I bet detective lieutenants have better intelligence sources."

"Yeah, I never thought of that."

Access to more valuable information had likely been the first thing on Del's weasel-like mind the moment he heard about the promotion. He'd probably already put together a new rate card in his head.

"We okay?" he asked glancing at my pocket again.

"Yes. I think we are."

THE ORGAN GRINDER'S MONKEY

Wilma has a long list of people she wants to kill.

Some of the names on her list include all FOX News and MSNBC pundits, the guys who produce *South Park*, customer service reps, people who text during movies, and Facebook friends.

Her list seemed to get longer every day.

We'd be in the car listening to the radio and someone would rage about some new social atrocity. I would look over and could see her adding the name to the list in her head.

And then she would smile.

It reminded me of Tommy Souer and how he went off the farm. I realized there was a razor-thin line between killing for money and killing for pleasure.

On this cheerful note, we set off for the sunny south.

~

According to the GPS, we were thirteen hours from Charleston.

It was the day after Halloween and Wilma sat beside me munching her way through a bag of miniature Milky Ways. She didn't offer me even one and the tantalizing perfume of chocolate was slowly torturing me.

We keep a cache of supplies in an out-of-the-way storage facility on the north side of Columbus, Ohio. The unit we rent is packed to the rafters with false IDs, fake license plates and credit cards, exotic weapons, and various surveillance devices. We have several similar depots in different parts of the country. You never know when you might need to make a run for it.

We decided to go there and pick up some things for our trip to the Old South. Before we did, however, we stopped at a nearby outlet mall and Wilma stole a late-model Toyota minivan.

When we got to the storage facility, I swapped out the van's Ohio plates for Virginia ones. Then we dropped my car off in the long-term parking lot at the airport and were on our way.

I love minivans. They're the perfect vehicle for not being noticed. Thousands of them clog the interstates like gas-powered cholesterol and no one gives them a second look, which is handy if you're trying to blend in. And, as an added bonus, they have plenty of room for carrying bodies, or heavy equipment.

I could never understand why spies in the movies always drive luxury sports cars that scream out for attention. If James Bond were a real person, he'd probably drive a Dodge Caravan.

~

As we headed south, I tuned in the weather station on the Toyota's satellite radio. Behind us, the Midwest was getting clobbered yet again with another blizzard and Detroit was already buried in six feet of snow. I was very pleased to hear the meteorological conditions for the next few days were warm and dry in the Carolinas. Walking on the sunny side of the street would be nice for a change.

I turned to the 80s channel and the miles floated past on the sweet chords of Flock of Seagulls, The Jam, Talking Heads, and The Clash.

A phone call from Promod interrupted *Red Sky at Night*, one of my favorite new wave classics.

He was as excited as a prom queen with her panties off.

"I got in! It was tougher than hacking the NSA, but I did it."

"That's wonderful. Your mom and I are so proud of you."

Promod ignored my sarcasm and plowed ahead. "They have holding companies inside holding companies on six different continents.

Were there six continents?

I did a quick count in my head.

"Nothing in Antarctica then?"

"They tried to put a development company there, but the U.N. charter forbade it."

"So where are they actually headquartered?"

"The financials say Belgium but when I got into their secure server, I discovered their real headquarters is in the U.S.A."

"New York?"

I figured that an egomaniac like D'Urberville would probably own the biggest skyscraper in the city.

To placate his penile inadequacy no doubt.

"Nope. The entire company is run from a gated compound on Sullivan's Island."

"Never heard of it."

"It's across the river from Charleston, South Carolina."

Wilma sat up, dumping candy bar wrappers on the floor.

"It's D'Urberville's principal residence and he spends most of his time there. It's pretty impressive. He even has a zoo."

"I don't care about that. What else did you discover about D'Urberville?"

"He takes pride in being a major league asshole. He loves publicity, absolutely thrives on it.

"His mother was a Serbian countess who came to America during the Cold War and his father was from an ancient Southern family. They trace their roots all the way back to before the Revolutionary War.

"He inherited some serious old money but really amped up the family fortune by playing the real estate market. He made some acquisitions and has gone bankrupt more times than General Motors. But he always bounces back. The man has incredible luck."

So why would a publicity whore like Tesla D'Urberville be mixed up in something like this?

"I don't think he's the real power," Promod said. "I get the feeling he's an organ grinder's monkey."

It made sense. If you wanted to keep watchers distracted, make an egomaniacal clown your public face.

One of those giant blow up things with flailing arms that car dealers put out front to attract customers popped into my mind. It was supposed to make car buying seem like fun and distract you from the real evil lurking on the sales floor.

I wondered if Wilma had car dealers on her list.

I sincerely hope so.

"Any idea who's behind the curtain?" I asked.

"There are a couple of possibilities, but I need to do some more checking."

"All right, but we need to know what we're walking into here, so make it quick."

I disconnected and looked at Wilma. She was deep in thought.

Possibilities were tumbling through my head as well. None of them seemed good.

Whatever this was about, we appeared to be caught in a weird vortex that was pulling us straight into the heart of Charleston.

~

It was late in the day when we finally arrived in Folly Beach just a few minutes south of Charleston. Wilma had found an excellent off-season rate on a luxury condo there. The town reminded me of a miniature version of Key West, with dive bars, funky restaurants and tacky souvenir shops lining its main street. It had an outlaw vibe that I liked.

Our condo was six blocks from the beach in a gated complex. It was at the end of a cul-de-sac that backed onto the Inter-Coastal Waterway. The three-story condo was designed to withstand bad storms and was raised up to keep it dry during hurricane season. A garage ran the full length of the ground floor. The rental agents had thoughtfully provided an automatic door opener so we could come and go in privacy.

After we'd hauled all our stuff upstairs, I opened the door to the back deck. The warm air felt good after the bitter weeks we had just experienced back home. We sat on comfortable deck chairs and looked out at the channel that ran behind the condo.

"We should buy a place like this." I sipped from a bottle of ultra-light beer.

"And what would we do?"

"We could relax and decompress from all our stress and worry."

It would be nice to stop and smell the roses, and dream up imaginative ways to dispatch our targets.

"It would be like a retreat or something," I continued. "Business executives do it all the time."

"It sounds terrible," Wilma snorted. "Why would anyone want to relax?"

So they don't grab an assault rifle and start randomly picking off everyone in sight.

I kept that thought to myself and watched dolphins frolic in the water.

"We know anyone in Charleston?" Wilma asked.

I knew we did, but she wasn't going to like it.

Wilma grimaced when I told her who it was.

"See, I told you it was a good idea to not kill him," I said.

Wilma clinked her glass against my bottle. "Now we have another chance."

THAT GREAT PHILOSOPHER
VITO CORLEONE

According to the great philosopher Vito Corleone, *keep your friends close but your enemies closer.*

The same rule applies even if you don't have any friends.

Donald Douche had been an associate of ours for years, and one of our earliest clients. With his eidetic memory, Donald was a human version of Wikipedia, only more accurate.

Unfortunately, he had a couple of weaknesses. The first was his passion for rare first edition books, an obsession that had caused him to make some bad decisions. His second weakness was that he was a treasonous son of a bitch who had betrayed us and then set us up to be killed.

Needless to say, we found this very upsetting.

Wilma was so pissed with Donald that she'd wanted to give him a tonsillectomy with her immersion blender. He'd only narrowly escaped her wrath because we had to make a deal with him. Donald had something that was worth millions and he'd agreed to split it with us if we left him alive.

We did, with the provision that he had to vanish from our lives forever, and if he crossed our path again, we'd kill him.

So Donald Duchée had disappeared from Detroit.

I figured he would lose himself among the illuminated manuscripts of Europe. Instead, he'd settled in Charleston like a blue bottle fly on a fresh turd.

And just how did I know this you might ask?

I made it a point to keep tabs on him. It was laughingly easy.

In fact, I will offer some advice to anyone who may be thinking of disappearing: make sure you leave every aspect of your old life behind, especially your passions. If you love baseball, abandon it. Develop a love of opera instead. You can change your appearance and your location, but it's your passions that will give you away every time.

Donald's weakness was books and I knew this would lead me to him. I just monitored the members' roster of the Antiquarian Booksellers Association of America. Eight months after our unfortunate falling out, a new member appeared on their list — Francis Elliott Toucann.

A quick check showed Toucann didn't have a past. He was a complete cipher but had a very impressive collection of classic American literature, including a rare first printing of *Moby Dick*. Bells went off in my head. I was sure Toucann was actually our old associate Donald Duchée. According to the ABA website, he had a shop on Meeting Street in downtown Charleston.

Wilma interrupted my chain of thought. "How do you want to handle this?"

"Let's do a little sight-seeing in the morning."

~

Wilma and I haven't spent much time in the South. We avoid it as much as possible because of its draconian capital punishment provisions. Those who live below the Mason-Dixon Line seem to enjoy executing prisoners almost as much as they enjoy fried chicken and mint juleps.

I suspect it comes from a very long and proud tradition of midnight rides and lynchings. Now I don't want to give the impression that I believe all Southerners are overweight, cousin-marrying, God-fearing, tobacco spitting primates.

Reality television does a superb job of that already.

Charleston is not hillbilly country. It is sophisticated and well-mannered, with an undercurrent of decadent rot. There is plenty of old money here and if you trace it back far enough, you will find that much of it came from the slave trade.

Today, the gentrified citizens of Charleston have both rejected and embraced their long history of race relations. Monuments and plaques around town celebrate milestones in the civil rights movement. The former slave market is now a tourist attraction and there is an enormous business in plantation tours.

Taking one of those tours can be like a Disney version of *Twelve Years a Slave*.

~

It had rained before dawn, but by noon the sun had been out for several hours and the air was soupy with humidity.

We parked the van in the center of town so we could explore a bit of the city. We absorbed three hundred years of history during our short walk. Most of it was concerned with pestilence, disease, earthquakes, killer storms, war, and death.

It was our kind of town.

~

Poogan's Porch has the best biscuits and honey butter I have ever tasted. Wilma had a fried chicken salad while I tried the shrimp and grits. It was the kind of place where ladies still dressed for lunch and the men wore suits. I felt out of place in my khaki pants and polo shirt. Still, by the time we had finished our peach cobbler and sweet iced tea, I was beginning to feel like a Southern gentleman. I imagined myself all elegant in a wrinkled seersucker suit, strolling through the old town with a tittering southern belle on my arm.

Little Rip reminded me Mandy Shurgar was not too far away and I started plotting a way to distract Wilma so we could have a little tryst. But sadly any Mandying would have to wait. We had business to take care of here first.

After lunch, we walked down Meeting Street toward the water.

Donald's bookshop was located in the front of a grand old house. A small brass plaque read **TOUCANN FINE EDITIONS**. There was a buzzer directly below the plate and a CCTV camera above. It was obvious that Donald was prepared for unwanted guests. We'd have to figure out a way to drop in on Donald unannounced.

Won't he be surprised to see us!

I was tempted to make a full-frontal assault on Donald. We could just kick in the front door and wave our guns around. Somehow, that didn't fit in with the decorum of the neighborhood. Our reunion with Donald would have to take a more subtle form.

Anyway, it was all for naught. A neatly hand-lettered sign informed us the shop was closed. We were going to have to wait until tomorrow to reacquaint ourselves with Donald.

Since we had plenty of time to kill, it was an excellent opportunity for us to scope out D'Urberville's digs on Sullivan's Island.

TESLA D'URBERVILLE

Later that afternoon we drove over the Cooper River Bridge onto Sullivan's Island.

Sounds *so* easy, doesn't it?

I should mention the bridge was really high.

Wilma was behind the wheel while I covered my eyes in terror until she assured me we were on level ground once again.

She looked at me in disgust. "You're such a weenie. After all the money you wasted on your Swiss Miss and her magical treatment, at least you should have been cured."

"Yeah, well I had a setback."

That was putting it mildly of course. After the late Dr. Vessier's swan dive into the parking lot, my vertigo was stronger than ever. Luckily, Wilma was as fearless as Spiderman when it came to heights.

~

"Look at these places," Wilma said in awe as we passed one elegant mansion after another.

D'Urberville's compound was at the end of the island. A high stone wall surrounded the entire complex and prevented us from getting a good look.

Like any tourists, we slowed to a crawl to ogle the big houses. Each gate had a large, unfriendly sign warning against trespassing or loitering. We had no doubt those threats would be backed up by more than just some bored, overweight security guard.

~

We found a good spot for dinner next to the river and sat out on the deck watching the boats go by. The restaurant was island casual, with large ceiling fans spinning languidly. The waitresses moved quickly and

218

efficiently. I approved of their tight shorts and even tighter T-shirts emblazoned with **Got Crabs**.

It was nice of the restaurant to warn their patrons the wait staff had a sexually transmitted disease.

When I brought this to Wilma's attention, she just scowled. Wilma has no sense of humor, I guess.

The *Crabby Bucket* sounded delicious, but I finally settled on a seafood salad. If I kept on dieting like this, I'd soon be skinny enough to slip under Laura's tight sweater without her noticing.

After we'd finished dinner, Wilma showed me D'Urberville's place using the Google app on her phone. His home stood on a spit of land facing the Atlantic, defiantly screaming *don't fuck with me*. It looked like your typical villain's compound — a huge stone pile with broad lawns. A Jet Ranger helicopter sat ready on a pad jutting out into the water and a hundred foot yacht was anchored in a canal next to the house.

"The fence goes right down to the ocean." Wilma pointed it out on the screen.

"Electrified, no doubt."

Wilma nodded.

"See these enclosures? He's got his own zoo."

Lions and tigers and yachts, oh my.

D'Urberville certainly likes his toys.

~

"When you look up *self-centered* in the dictionary, there's a picture of D'Urberville to illustrate the word," Promod said.

I'd called Promod after we got back to the condo. We needed as much reliable information on D'Urberville as he could dig up.

Promod laughed when I mentioned seeing D'Uberville's private zoo.

"It's a tax dodge. They claim it's a research facility for breeding endangered species in captivity."

"Impressive," I said.

"Oh, there's a lot more. He has an entire fleet of aircraft, including the only remaining Concorde still flying. He also has the biggest yacht in the world. And get this, he has the only luxury submarine ever built. With D'Urberville, it has to be bigger and faster than anyone else's or it's not good enough."

"Wow."

Promod continued, "According to Forbes, he pays over a billion dollars a year in alimony to his eight ex-wives. His corporation owns significant chunks of real estate in Manhattan, central London, Moscow, Tokyo, and Singapore. They're currently negotiating to buy Barcelona."

"Which part?"

"The entire city. The Spanish government seems to be willing to sell."

"What about his compound?"

"Couldn't find out much. There was a reference to it in an article in Fortune a couple of years ago. D'Urberville bragged that it was built to withstand a force ten hurricane."

"Anything of a *personal* nature we might use?"

Promod consulted his notes.

"Sexual, you mean? From all accounts, he's straight. But he appears to have some obsessions according to the divorce filings. He loves fantasy and horror films, especially Godzilla movies."

Bingo!

I flashed back to the miniature Tokyo.

"Anything about Edgar Allen Poe?"

"Nope, though one of his divorce settlements lists a collection of priceless first edition books among his assets."

Wilma and I looked at each other and smiled.

Books!

We knew a seller of rare editions — our old friend Donald Duchée, and conveniently he was already in Charleston.

But before we could pay him a visit, we needed to fry some bikers first.

I wanted to find out who in the Stars and Bars MC gave the orders for Reese and the Demon Stompers to kill me.

I take that kind of thing personally. And I needed to know what they knew.

~

As it turned out, they knew nothing.

The headquarters of the Stars and Bars MC was located in an old general store at the north end of a dirt water town off the Savannah Highway south of Charleston. A motley collection of fat-ass thugs wearing cut-off jean jackets with the Confederate battle flag on the back sat on the front porch watching the traffic go by.

They should have been wearing those **Got Crabs** T-shirts.

Wilma and I were watching them through high-powered binoculars from the woods across the road.

"These guys look about as tough as the local Rotary Club," I whispered after observing them for a few minutes.

"Let's take one of them and see what we can shake out of him."

We still had plenty of the Russian truth serum left. I wondered if any of them would even lift a finger to stop us if we tried.

Not fucking likely from the look of these hounds.

"They must have had Quaalude Puffs for breakfast."

Wilma smiled and kept her eye fixed on the scope of her rifle. I stifled a laugh.

This is going to be way too easy.

The front door opened. What a shock. Bob Neill, my favorite Arian thug from prison, strolled out with his arm draped over the shoulder my former cell mate Marty Borman.

"Hey, isn't that ...?"

"Yes indeed," I replied.

Neill squeezed Borman's ass.

"Cell block romances are kind of touching don't you think?"

Wilma snorted, "Yeah, they make the perfect couple."

"And to think *we* played a pivotal role in sparking their relationship."

None of the other bikers seemed to care that they had their hands all over each other.

Must be the languid southern heat.

When Borman began polishing Neill's front hub, I turned away.

~

A black Escalade pulled up and Neill waited. A man got out and walked over to him. This mysterious visitor looked like one of those nerds who work at H&R Block in the mall. He wasn't the Escalade type, but from the way Neill responded to him he definitely had authority.

"Isn't that Drew Carey?" Wilma was watching him intently through her rifle scope.

I focused my binoculars on him. She was dead-on. This guy even had the same flattop buzz-cut as the comedian, but he was a lot thinner. Tiny scars crisscrossing his cheeks reminded me of what Yamahaha had said.

"He looked like he'd been necking with barbed wire."

Grabbing Wilma's Nikon, I snapped his picture.

Drew Carey looked pissed and got right in Neill's face. Too bad we were too far away to hear what he was screaming. After a few minutes, he got back in his SUV and drove off. Neill looked like he'd been slugged. He stormed over to his gang and started kicking ass. The bikers jumped on their Harleys and roared off in different directions.

"Now what do you suppose they are up to?"

Wilma shook her head. "I think they might be looking for us. I bet he's got them covering all the major roads."

Neill stood in the dust watching the last of his boys ride off. He rubbed sweat from his face and twisted the cap off a beer, which he downed in one gulp. Borman handed him another one and Neill chugged it as well.

Things did not look good in Neillsville and I wanted to find out why.

~

A few minutes later, I slammed on the minivan's brakes in front of the MC's headquarters and hopped out.

Neill and Borman were sitting on a porch swing holding hands and comforting each other.

"Hi there," I said with a friendly wave. "Do you know the way to San Jose?"

Neill spat beer foam across the parking lot as he recognized me.

I smiled and did a double-take. "Hey, guys, fancy meeting you here."

Borman leaped up, tugging a pistol from his belt. I let him get his gun out before I shot him between the eyes.

Neill let out an anguished cry and went for his gun. I fired a bullet into the dirt at his feet.

He froze.

I nodded at his pistol and he dropped it.

Then I waved him toward the back door of the van.

He looked over to where Borman laid face down in the gravel, his brains leaking all over the parking lot.

"Sorry about the mess," I said.

I grabbed Neill and slapped a pair of handcuffs on him.

"Let's go for a little ride. I'd like to see some of the Low Country."

BARREL OF FUN

Bob Neill looked suitably terrified.

We parked the van on top of a hill overlooking a drainage pond in the remote country just over the Georgia state line.

"Have a beer, Bob."

I handed him a longneck Bud. Neill took it gratefully, twisted off the cap, and drank it down. The alcohol gave him false courage.

He looked at Wilma and leered. "I remember you from Sawmill Grove, sugar tits."

I expected Wilma to tear him a new one. Instead, she just smiled sweetly.

"Would you like another beer?"

He held out his empty bottle.

Wilma nodded at a large metal oil drum. "In there."

Neill smirked and tossed his bottle into the drum so hard it shattered.

"Now, Bob, we just have a few questions and then we can all be on our way," I said handing him another beer to keep the wheels lubricated.

Neill took off the bottle cap and started to throw it on the ground. Then he had a second thought and tossed it into the drum. It clicked against the shattered glass.

He burped and swallowed the contents of the bottle.

And another.

And another.

And another.

Lucky, he wasn't driving.

The more he drank, the sloppier he became. His words became slurred and his aim got bad. Wilma picked up several of the bottles that missed the bin. She tossed them inside and the smashing glass made Neill's smile even wider.

He leaned his head back and let the sun warm his face. "It's nice up here." His words ran together.

"Bob, when did you get out?"

Neill looked over at me and grinned. "I was never really in prison. They just put me there to watch for whoever showed up to see Randy Yamahaha."

He held his hand out for another Bud. I passed him one and he drank it greedily.

"Then what?"

"I was supposed to tell Scuggins."

"Did you tell him about me?"

"Of course."

He put an arm around my shoulder like we were best buddies.

"He didn't like you at all."

I smiled at the memory of the surprised look on Scuggins's face when Wilma exploded the micro-charge inside him.

"What else can you tell me?"

Neill summoned up his alcohol-enhanced defiance. "I'm no rat."

I ignored him and continued pushing. "Who was the man in the Escalade?"

Wilma slid up to him and pressed her hip gently against his, rubbing it in a teasing way.

"Come on, Bobby, you can tell us."

She held out another bottle and took the empty from his hand. Wilma casually tossed it over her shoulder and it smashed inside the barrel.

Neill was impressed. He drank the beer and threw the bottle up in the air. It came down with a loud crash inside the barrel.

Wilma caressed his thigh.

Neill was sweating and his face had turned a lovely shade of beet.

"Stench," he gasped. "His name is Marvin Stench. He's a real asshole."

"And what else can you tell us about him?"

"I don't know much." Neill drew in a breath as Wilma swept her palm lightly over his crotch. "He uses us for protection sometimes, and to keep an eye on things."

"But you don't know who he is?" Wilma whispered seductively.

Neill shook his head. "Nope, just that he pays well."

"Oh, that's a shame."

Neill looked at her in drunken wonder. "A shame?"

Wilma pinched a muscle next to his bulging neck, a trick the late Leonard Nimoy had taught her. Neill went limp and sagged into her arms.

Wilma dragged him to the drum and I helped her dump him in. Then she picked up a large metal lid and hammered it into place, sealing Neill inside. He pounded frantically on the lid.

I tipped the barrel over and a muffled shriek filtered through the sealed container. "Don't worry Bobby, you'll have a barrel of fun."

Wilma gave it a kick and the barrel began to roll down the hill.

Neill's screams intensified as the broken beer bottles turned him into steak tartare.

~

"Marvin Stench. That's a lovely name."

We were sitting on the front deck of Taco Boys on the main street in Folly Beach. Colored pennants lining the deck snapped in the light breeze blowing in off the ocean.

I was hungry but knew better than to have one of those football-sized burritos everyone else was enjoying. Instead, I ordered a couple of grilled fish tacos and a light beer.

Dinner arrived and I watched resentfully as Wilma wolfed down her Carne Asada Plato.

"I think this Marvin Stench is a good candidate for the Judge's murder."

Promod was busy searching online for Mr. Stench. With any luck, we'd have some information before we finished our meal.

It should have been pretty quiet at this time of year, but the traffic heading toward Charleston was bumper-to-bumper. I looked at the line of cars and asked the waiter about it when he came to remove our plates.

"They're the early birds," he said without giving them a glance. "A tropical low is forming off Puerto Rico and the National Hurricane Center thinks it might hit us in a couple of days. This happens once or twice each season. The storm usually stays out to sea, but the early birds don't want to take any chances so they head inland and wait for the all-clear."

"You don't seem to be too alarmed about it."

He shrugged. "If it comes, it comes. I'll deal with it then."

Now I had a clear understanding of why people die in tropical storms.

"Think we should take off?" I asked Wilma, although I already knew the answer.

She was firmly in the waiter's camp when it came to responding to the threat of a hurricane.

"We've got work to do."

~

I tuned the car radio to the local NPR station. They were already dispensing information about evacuation routes and what supplies to stockpile.

"Let's swing by Costco and get some essentials," Wilma suggested.

The parking lot was jammed so Wilma hopped out and went into the store.

During the twenty minutes it took me to find a spot to park, I thought logically about what we would need if we were going to be trapped in the teeth of a storm.

The condo was probably safe. It was high enough to avoid a tidal surge, but the power might go off for a few days. So we would need flashlights, batteries, non-perishable food, a good supply of candles, and a stack of books to keep us occupied.

You know, practical stuff.

~

By *essentials,* I assumed Wilma had meant bottled water, condoms, and red wine but she was on an entirely different wavelength when it came to riding out a storm.

When I finally found her, she was standing in front of a display trying to decide on a 50 inch or 56-inch flat screen. I looked at her cart jammed with a six year supply of freezer bags, two gigantic beef tenderloins, and an exercise machine.

It was useless to argue with Wilma when she was in the grip of Costco fever.

I just added a couple of cases of bottled water, two giant containers of mixed nuts, some loaves of bread, six flashlights, a flat of spare batteries, a gross of candles, and James Patterson's twelve latest bestsellers.

That should see us through any storm.

~

We could hardly move in the living room once we had stacked up our $6,500 Costco purchases.

Looking at the pile of merchandise, I seriously began to question Wilma's sanity.

"This is fucking ridiculous."

She looked up from cleaning the Bolo Mauser pistol that had belonged to her father. The ancient weapon reminded me of Han Solo's blaster in Star Wars. Although almost a hundred years old, it was strangely modern.

The Bolo was a touchstone for Wilma, her good luck piece if you will. Generally, she kept it safely locked away, so I was surprised she'd brought it along. Although using it on her mother and father was not a bad way to work out parental issues, seeing the Bolo always made me nervous.

I knew the day Wilma used her father's gun would not be a good one for me.

~

The breeze had picked up during the evening and I could feel the familiar squeezing in my temples that told me the air pressure was dropping. I took this as a bad omen. Time was running out. I was sure of it.

Razor sharp clock hands were reaching out for us.

DOOMED IF YOU DO,
DOOMED IF YOU DON'T

A monster hurricane was bearing down on the Carolinas.

Mortimer, as it was named by the National Hurricane Center, was ripping up islands in the Caribbean and was predicted to make landfall within the next three days.

The normally goofy weatherman on the *Today Show* was now as solemn as a funeral director. Footage on the screen behind him showed large beachside homes being washed away by a tidal surge.

The weather map showed it was heading straight toward us.

I walked onto the balcony of the condo. The sun was sparkling on the surface of the water and a cabin cruiser was chugging along the channel. It was difficult to believe something so monstrous was heading our way.

Wilma put down the short history of Folly Beach she'd been reading.

"Did you know that Gershwin composed *Porgy and Bess* here?"

I shook my head. "We've got a huge storm heading our way."

Wilma looked across the calm water and began to whistle *Summertime*.

Come hell or high water, nothing fazed that woman.

The condo shook as a C-17 Air Force cargo plane heading inland flew low overhead.

"The Air Force must be moving their planes out of harm's way. We should think about doing the same thing."

Wilma was sipping her second cup of coffee. "We don't leave things half-done," she reminded me. "Anyway, I thought you wanted to impress Miss Tight Sweater."

My mind filled with images of naked heaving flesh, silky smooth skin, and Laura's liquid eyes open wide with pleasure.

"You will find my father's killer, won't you?"

Wilma yawned. "It takes more than a tropical low to make me run."

"I'm not suggesting we run, just retreat inland and let the storm pass."

She nailed me with her gunmetal eyes. "We're going to visit Donald tonight and see if he's had any dealings with D'Urberville. Then we're going to figure out a way to get into that compound and stop that asshole's clock and *you* have a personal score to settle. Remember his little medieval play toy?"

The very mention of it put me right back under the pendulum's blade, unable to move. Goosebumps covered my skin. I could still feel the brush of air as it swung back and forth in a deadly arc.

A flood of anger chased away any apprehension I had about the storm, plus I was insulted that he hadn't even bothered to stay around to see what his device would do to me.

And Wilma was right; we don't leave things half-done.

I thought about how I'd get my revenge. Maybe I'd bury D'Urberville up to his neck in the sand so he could face the approaching storm.

That would certainly tide him over.

~

Charleston was surreally quiet as the storm approached.

It was after midnight and Wilma and I sat in the van watching Donald's front door. He and his Meeting Street neighbors were snug in their homes.

I wondered if they would be making a run for it.

This area of Charleston was old money. The people who lived here were used to hurricanes and, even though Meeting Street was only a few blocks from the harbor, these folks would not leave until they were absolutely sure the storm was going to strike. Their houses were filled with valuable antiques and they would be reluctant to leave them unguarded.

Or it could be something more intrinsic.

Charleston had seen its fair share of hurricanes, fires, and war. An earthquake had even devastated the city in 1886. Maybe all these disasters had caused a sense of malaise in the population, leaving them with a philosophical attitude.

Doomed if you do, doomed if you don't.

~

229

Our jet-black Zentai outfits made us invisible in the shadows.

We worked our way down a narrow alley behind the houses on Meeting Street until we reached the fence behind Donald's home.

I figured Donald lived above the shop; he'd have to be near his babies.

Through gaps in the wall, we could see his carefully manicured backyard. A huge magnolia tree filled the space and a small fountain burbled in the sultry night air.

A massive iron gate was set in the cement wall and Wilma went to work on it. It weighed a ton and sagged on rusted hinges. Wilma quickly located and neutralized the alarm. Then she oiled the hinges and picked the lock. The gate swung open without a squeak and we slipped into the backyard.

"He's got motion sensors," I whispered to Wilma, pointing at a control box high up on the back wall.

Wilma aimed a small gadget that looked like a TV remote at the box. It sent a series of IR commands to shut down the motion sensors. However, we had no way of telling if her gadget actually worked until we moved into their range. If it hadn't disabled the system, we'd sure as hell find out real fast.

"You go first," I whispered to Wilma.

"You pussy."

Wilma slipped stealthily from one shadow to the next, moving closer to the house. She reached the porch and impatiently motioned for me to follow. She picked the lock and we slipped inside.

The faint aroma of coffee and freshly baked rolls lingered in the small kitchen. All was silent except for the tick-tick-tick of a clock in another room. Every floorboard creaked as we crept along the hall.

I paused to listen. The house remained silent except for the relentless ticking of the clock.

Donald's place gave me the creeps.

"Think it's haunted?" I whispered to Wilma.

I don't really believe in ghosts or any of that paranormal bullshit, but I do love those ghost story programs on the Discovery Channel. Not the shows where a group of morons traipses around wearing night-vision goggles and freaking out over camera flares. I like the ones that recreate hauntings with diaphanous ghosts terrorizing the living. They remind me of our work.

We sometimes have to wake up mortals in the middle of the night too.

Of course, their terror is very real, although sadly brief.

~

Wilma slid under the covers next to Donald, who was snoring loudly.

No wonder he didn't hear the creaking floorboards.

She gave him a sharp poke in the ribs.

I turned on the bedside light.

Donald woke up with a start and found the barrel of my pistol pressed against the tip of his nose.

"Oh Jesus," he moaned.

I took off my hood and smiled at him.

The color drained out of his face. "I thought we had an agreement," he squealed.

"We do. This is a friendly visit." I smiled reassuringly and put my gun away.

Wilma reached under his pillow and pulled out an ancient Colt revolver. She examined it with amusement. Finally, she broke it open and spilled the cartridges onto the floor.

I sat down in a chair next to his bed. "We keep our promises," I told him. "And we promised we'd kill you if we ever saw you again. But since we initiated this meeting, we're going to give you a pass."

"A get-out-of-hell-free card," Wilma added as she sat up and pointed her gun at him.

"In return, we expect a little favor from you."

Donald's eyes grew wary.

"Tesla D'Urberville."

"He's a good customer," he sighed. "I sold him a complete set of Lovecraft first editions last month."

"Have you been to his place on Sullivan's Island?"

"A few times," he nodded. "Why?"

"We want to have a private chat with him," Wilma said.

"Why don't you make an appointment?"

"We'd prefer to keep our meeting discreet."

"His security is state-of-the-art. You won't be able to get in."

Wilma tapped her pistol against the side of his head. "Then you get him to come here instead."

Donald shook his head. "Never. Tesla D'Urberville does not come to you. *You* go to him."

"Then we'll need to give him a splendid reason."

Donald thought about this for a minute and then smiled.

Something about his smile disturbed me.

"*The Black Tulip* …"

"What's that, a gardening book?" I asked.

"Edgar Allen Poe's first book, *Tamerlane and Other Poems*," he replied. "It's very rare. So rare, in fact, collectors refer to it as *The Black Tulip*. Poe supposedly wrote it when he was stationed on Sullivan's Island while serving in the army."

"And you have a copy?"

He shook his head sadly. "There is maybe a dozen still in existence. D'Urberville's been after one for years. The last copy sold for almost a million dollars at auction."

"So my chances of finding one on Amazon are pretty slim then."

Donald ignored me.

"But I do know where there *is* a copy," he said. "Give me a few minutes to get dressed."

~

Wilma and I sat in the kitchen with Donald. The coffee was excellent coffee and his sweet rolls divine.

"So, where is this copy then?"

Donald paced nervously. "It's in the library of Eugene Verlaine. He has an excellent collection of rare volumes. In fact, he has a rare tome that another customer of mine is lusting after."

"Why don't you make Verlaine an offer for both?"

"I already have. He's the scion of an old family and has more money than he'll ever need so he's not interested in selling. Plus he's crazy."

"Define *crazy*."

"He lives down the coast outside Beaufort on the family plantation. They made all their money in the slave trade and somehow managed to hang onto it after the Civil War. Eugene hasn't been seen publicly for years. He spends all his time in his decaying mansion."

"Dictating his memoirs to Tennessee Williams?"

"No, he leads some kind of cult."

"Everyone has to have some sort of hobby."

"They worship the devil."

A devil worshiping cult? Aren't there any normal *rich people in the world?*

"The grounds of the plantation are completely overgrown and no one goes near it because there are alligators and venomous snakes all over the place."

"If we got this Poe book would you be able to get into D'Urberville's compound?"

"Yes, and I'd split the money from the sale of the books with you as well."

"So what's this other book you want?"

"The *Arbatel de magia veterum.*"

The air went out of the room and the clock on the mantle stopped ticking.

"His copy is original, inscribed in Latin. It's reputed to be written with the blood of slaughtered infants and bound in tanned human flesh."

"With a cover blurb by Stephen King no doubt."

Donald ignored me again. He was genuinely frightened.

"Other than the man-eating alligators and poisonous reptiles, how's his security system?" Wilma asked.

"I don't know. I've never been out there. But I heard that a local book scout tried to get in there a few years ago and was never heard from again."

We jumped when the clock resumed ticking.

"Okay, we'll get the books but you need to set up a meeting with D'Urberville as soon as possible, Donald. We need to get this wrapped up quickly and get to high ground before the storm hits."

Donald nodded. "I'll call him first thing in the morning. The possibility of getting his hands on the Poe should keep him around."

"We're also interested in another guy who we think hangs out with D'Urberville."

"Who's that?"

"Marvin Stench. He looks like an actuary."

Donald shook his head. "He's one of D'Urberville's butt kissers. Vice President of Fun and Parties, or something like that."

I added Marvin in my Painful Death file.

"When are you planning to get the books?"

I looked at my watch. It was nearly 1:00 a.m. "No time like the present."

Wilma shot me a reproachful glare.

"Why not? We brought all our tools."

She dragged me out of Donald's earshot and nodded toward him. "Because I don't trust him."

"I don't trust him either, but if he's right about the book, it's the best bait we've got to snare D'Uberville."

She tapped her fingers nervously against her thighs. Finally, Wilma shook her head. "Okay," she said reluctantly.

I went to tell Donald the good news.

THE HIRED HELP

"Do I need to remind you what happened to us the last time we went after a rare book?" Wilma asked.

Our recent experience with an old book had gotten us into real trouble. We'd nearly been killed a few months ago when we went after an exceptionally rare copy of *Moby Dick*. The white whale led us on a wild clusterfuck of an adventure. We'd made a vow after that debacle to stay away from classic American literature.

And now we're at it again. We break more vows than Tiger Woods.

I swatted at a cloud of bugs as we paddled the canoe into a tidal estuary next to the Verlaine family plantation. Ironically, it was known as *Elysium*.

The stagnant water smelled like elephant diarrhea and the mud along the bank was even worse.

Wilma reached out to steady the canoe and whipped her hand back when something nearby hissed and slithered away. I steadied the boat and climbed up onto the muck.

Our black Zentai suits were certainly were going to need a good dry cleaning after this little excursion.

Whatever had slithered away from Wilma was still close by. Donald *had* warned us about the snakes and alligators out here. The riverbank was probably crawling with water moccasins. I'd already seen them in the water when we'd paddled up the estuary.

It wasn't the thought of venomous snakes sinking their fangs into our ankles that pissed off Wilma, it was my fool-hearty lack of planning and preparation.

I decided to toss her a bone. "I'll let you kill Eugene Verlaine if you like."

That, however, did not placate her. "This is just so incredibly out of my comfort zone, I can't fucking believe it."

Could it be any worse?

As if to answer, a swarm of mosquitoes decided we were going to be dinner.

~

We only had a vague idea where we were going.

Hidden under a thick canopy of trees, Elysium Plantation couldn't be seen on Google Earth. Only the outline of the mansion's roof was visible. But here on the ground, it was easy to spot.

The light of flickering torches guided us toward the house. As we carefully approached, the distinctive sound of chanting floated our way.

Torchlight illuminated a circle of hooded figures surrounding an altar on the front lawn where a little lamb was tied down bleating pathetically.

"Maybe it's a drumming circle."

That possibility was shattered when we saw a large curved blade raised high in the air by a figure in a crimson hooded robe. This had to be Verlaine. His followers were dressed in white, each with an embroidered pentagram on the front.

"No fucking way," Wilma hissed and brought up her sniper rifle.

Their rhythmic chanting grew louder. Then suddenly it stopped as a series of soft plunks downed them one by one.

Verlaine was left standing alone surrounded by bodies.

"Drop the knife, Verlaine."

He looked at me in stunned disbelief. His little ritual had apparently not gone as planned.

Verlaine set the knife down on the altar next to the lamb and pulled off his hood to reveal a thin, pinched face and comedic bulging eyes. He was the very definition of ugly — big ears, widely spaced teeth, and no chin.

"Who are you?" he gasped.

"We're the ASPCA SWAT team. Now hold still and keep your hands where we can see them."

I patted him down while Wilma released the grateful little lamb and it bounded away into the darkness. Seconds later there was a high-pitched *baaa ahhhh* and a sickening wet crunch.

We'd forgotten about the alligators, but they hadn't forgotten about us. Attracted by the smell of blood from Verlaine's fallen comrades, they arrived en masse for a midnight snack.

I suggested we move our conversation into the house. There was no argument from our host. He ran as fast as his red robe would allow.

~

I tied Verlaine to a chair in the sitting room. Wilma poked the side of his head with the barrel of her rifle.

"Gene ... Do you mind if I call you that?" I asked rhetorically. "Sorry to break up your little ceremony but we have a bit of a time constraint, so we aren't able to use our usual finesse."

Staring straight ahead, Verlaine said nothing. His body language told me he was royally pissed off.

I tried to cheer him up. "I'm sure your friends are sitting around with Satan right now drinking cosmopolitans and having a laugh over the absurdity of existence. We'll try not to hold you up so you can join them as soon as possible. But first we need to get hold of some of your reading material."

"My copy of *Tamerlane*," he said bitterly.

"Yes, for starters."

"I suppose D'Urberville sent you."

I shook my head. "We haven't had the pleasure of meeting Mr. D'Urberville, yet."

"What else?"

Verlaine struggled against his bonds.

"We're also interested in getting our hands on a delightful-sounding book entitled the *Arbatel de magia veterum*."

"Fuck you. They're both locked up where you can't get them."

"Then I'm afraid I'm going to have to ask my associate here to use her magical powers of persuasion on you."

Wilma shot off his left ear and Verlaine's scream reverberated through the decaying mansion.

I looked at the stump of his wounded ear and frowned. "Can you still hear me?"

He was shaking his head back and forth frantically. Blood flew from the ragged wound.

I leaned in close to his good ear. "Where are the books? Or would you like my partner to shoot something else off?"

He was tougher than I thought. It took two thumbs and four toes before he finally gasped out the location of the safe and the combination.

I went off to get the books, leaving Wilma to keep him company.

~

I had the safe open and was searching for the books.

"Hello," a familiar voice whispered in my ear.

An electric chill shot down my spine as cold metal brushed against the nape of my neck. I ignored the discomfort and found the two books I was searching for.

"Mandy Shugar. What a pleasant surprise to see you."

I took the books from the safe and turned to face my adversary.

Mandy stood there with an old-fashioned Derringer aimed right at my broken heart.

Why does every woman in my life end up betraying me?

"I thought you were going to give me a call when you got to town," she said.

"Well I intended to, but I got busy."

"So I see. Is your partner out there going to kill my brother?"

"Yes," I replied, nervously eyeing the derringer.

She smiled. "Good. How much do I owe you then?"

"Owe me?"

"For doing the job?"

"The job? What job?"

"The one I was going to discuss with you when I was in Detroit. I just never got around to it. You must have read my mind."

I didn't even bother asking who had referred her to us. I already knew. *Donald.*

"I guess you're splitting the profit from the books with him."

She nodded and lowered her gun.

"You know he's also splitting it with us?"

"As long as he pays you out of his share."

A loud bang from the sitting room interrupted our conversation. We turned in the direction the shot had come from.

"Or we just take it all," Wilma said from the doorway with her rifle leveled at Mandy.

Mandy scowled defiantly.

I held up my hands in exasperation.

"Ladies … Ladies … Please… Let's all take a deep breath here. I'm confident we can work it out so everybody gets what they want and we all walk away intact."

I stepped between Wilma and Mandy.

"Let's all be friends."

To my relief, Wilma and Mandy lowered their guns.

I helped Mandy drag her brother's corpse out the front door and down the stairs. We left him at the alligators' picnic.

Wilma tipped a burning candle from its holder onto a couch in the sitting room. The two-hundred-year-old upholstery burst into flames. We waited until the fire had a good foothold and then made a mad dash to Mandy's car.

~

"I thought we might go out for dinner some evening," I said after Mandy dropped us by the estuary.

"Sorry, Rip. Don't take it personally, but I make it a point not to get involved with the hired help." She drove off without another word leaving me gobsmacked.

Wilma started laughing.

A WHIFF OF BRIMSTONE

Hired help!

I obsessed on Mandy's pronouncement as we paddled the canoe back to where we'd left the car. Clutching the books tightly in my hands, I steamed. Wilma drove us back to Charleston while I glared out the window at the darkness.

"The *hired help* ..."

Wilma laughed again. She took great delight in watching me squirm.

"You have an uncanny ability to attract duplicitous women don't you?"

She was right. My luck in that department was pathetic. I chose to ignore her and looked at the books.

The Poe was protected by an elegant red leather slipcase. The book itself was quite plain. In fact, it looked like a cheap magazine printed on tan paper. The back cover even featured an ad for the printer. Poe's name was nowhere to be found. Instead, its authorship was attributed to *A Bostonian*. I had a hard time believing this piece of junk could be worth almost a million dollars.

The other volume was a different story.

Just handling its desiccated binding gave me the heebie-jeebies. It felt strangely alive and I swore it moved in my hands. That freaked me out. I was almost afraid to open it in case something otherworldly crawled into my lap.

Finally overcoming my fear, I looked inside.

The book was horrifying yet beautiful. The illustrations and text were hand-drawn. In places, the crimson lettering had faded to a light brown.

I closed the book and slid it out of sight under my seat.

~

Color tinged the clouds by the time we got back to the shop on Meeting Street.

"How did ... What ..."

Wilma pushed Donald aside and stomped into the foyer. The windows rattled when I slammed the door behind me.

"You double-crossing whore!" In one smooth move, Wilma twirled around and shoved her gun in Donald's face.

"Oh. Yes. Mandy."

Against instinct, I stayed Wilma's hand. "You could have told us about her."

"I didn't know she'd be there."

"And what the fuck difference does that make?" Wilma snapped. "Why didn't you just have *her* steal the books?"

"Well ... because ... in case you hadn't noticed, Verlaine is crazy."

"*Was* crazy," Wilma corrected.

Donald processed this news.

"Good," he smiled in relief. "Anyway, she was terrified that if she touched his books, his coven would come after her. They're quite dedicated to their beliefs."

"*Were* dedicated."

"Did you get all of them?"

"I don't know, ten or eleven I guess. How many were there?"

Donald counted on his fingers. "That sounds about right. I think you got them all. We don't need anyone showing up to spoil things for us."

"Did you call D'Urberville?"

"Yes, and he agreed to see me tonight."

"Here?"

Donald shook his head. "He refused. I have to bring the book to him."

"What time?"

"11:00. He wants to be gone before the hurricane gets here. He's sending a car for me at 10:30."

Donald took the books from me and put them on the desk. He pulled on a pair of white cotton gloves and slid the Poe from its case. His gaze was rapturous as he gently flipped through the pages.

"Magnificent," he sighed.

He treated the *Arbatel de magia veterum* like it was a diseased pancreas, holding it at arm's length while unwrapping its black silk covering.

"That thing gives me the creeps," I said.

He nodded and folded the cloth back over it.

"Don't you want to authenticate it?" Wilma asked.

"It's the real thing." Donald stared at the book. "Can't you feel it?"

I could. The temperature had dropped at least 10 degrees and the sound of a child's terrified screams filled my head.

Donald pushed it across the desk.

"It's one of a kind. The incantations it contains were only spoken up to the 15th century. The story goes that the monks of Lindholme Abbey in the Bavarian Alps sheltered a mysterious visitor who dictated the book to them. They became corrupted and perverse during this time and even had their novices steal children from nearby villages so they would have innocent blood to inscribe it."

"That must have upset their neighbors," Wilma said.

"The villagers stormed the abbey and burned it down, killing all the monks. The *Arbatel de magia veterum* was believed to have been destroyed in the fire. When they searched the ruins, there was no trace of the stranger.

"The book was discovered again in the 1930s and fell into the hands of the Nazis. Rumor has it Hitler kept it on his nightstand."

"So how did Verlaine end up with it?" Wilma asked.

"His uncle was in the OSS and found it on one of Hitler's bodyguards. The man was trying to escape after Adolf killed himself."

"So he brought his demon nephew a little souvenir."

Donald began to shake and I was afraid he was coming apart at the seams. Normally, he was as rational a human being as I've ever known, but this book was having a profound effect on him.

"How soon can we get rid of this thing?"

Donald rubbed sweat from his lips with the back of his hand and frowned. "My buyer is already on the way here from Europe. His private jet is scheduled to land in a couple of hours."

"How much are we talking about?"

"Five million in flawless black diamonds." He paused and then stammered, "Paid on delivery."

"And you don't trust the buyer."

He nodded.

"Then we'd better go along with you to protect our investment."

BLACK DIAMONDS

Thick, cloying air signaled the storm was definitely on its way.

A flat gray 747 with no markings flew out of an ominous dark purple sky. The massive jet rolled to a stop next to a hangar. We watched a couple of workers move a tall ramp to the front door then hurry away. The engines were left running.

I stood next to Donald on the tarmac holding an M-32 grenade launcher which I kept aimed at the jet's outboard port engine. Wilma was in position on the roof of the terminal with her sniper rifle trained on the stairway.

Donald approached the plane and stopped at the bottom of the stairs.

The front door opened and a bodyguard cradling an assault rifle stepped onto the ramp. He shielded his eyes from the sun and took in the scene. Then his gaze fixed on me.

A cold chill did a hundred yard dash up my spine and the faint buzz of insects filled my head.

Satisfied that everything was okay, the guard leaned into the interior of the jet. A moment later, a tall, thin figure emerged from the plane. At the top of the ramp, he paused and sniffed the air.

The buzzing in my head swelled and my temples began to throb. The figure shimmered as I tried to focus on his features. I shook my head to clear my funhouse mirror vision.

Pale sunlight glinted off a small metal case he held in his right hand as he glided down the stairs.

I resisted an overpowering urge to run away.

At the bottom of the ramp, he and Donald faced each other. Neither of them moved.

There must be trust issues between them.

Finally, the thin man handed Donald the metal case and Donald gave him the book.

The man turned and looked directly at me. At that moment, the sun came out from behind a cloud and I was momentarily blinded. I stepped back, feeling a numbing cold flow through me. I began to shake uncontrollably and clutched the launcher tighter. The insects in my head reached a painful crescendo and I looked away. When I looked back, Donald had the case open and a jeweler's loupe fixed in his right eye.

Although Donald is not a jeweler, I had no doubt he could tell a real black diamond from a fake. He pulled a stone from the bottom of the case and looked at it carefully as well. Satisfied, he shut the case and stepped back, signaling the transaction was finished.

The sun flared again and I lost track of the man for a few seconds. Raising the rocket launcher to my shoulder, I put my finger on the trigger. A cloud obscured the sun again as I glimpsed the man duck into the cabin of the 747.

The painful din of the insects faded and I became aware of my damp armpits as the humid air flooded in around us.

The jet's engines throttled up and I was relieved it was going back to whatever hellhole it had come from. The massive aircraft rolled onto the taxiway. The rumble of the engines changed to a harsh roar as the jet thundered down the runway and lifted into the sky. I was tempted to pull the trigger on the M-32 and send both the mystery man and his new purchase back to hell. But instead, I lowered the grenade launcher and watched as the jet disappeared entirely into the clouds marking the leading edge of the storm.

Wilma, holding a fiberglass gun case, joined us a few minutes later.

"That went well," I said trying to add a light tone to my voice.

Donald ignored me and continued to stare grimly at the jet's dissipating contrails. I wondered if he regretted selling the book. Somehow, I didn't think so.

I shivered again as I thought of the mystery man and his evil purchase. *Good riddance.*

~

We agreed to take a million out of Donald's share of the diamonds, which he'd divided into three neat piles on his leather desktop.

Donald pointed to the smallest pile. "That should be a million, give or take."

Wilma picked up the diamonds and weighed them in the palm of her hand. "It'd better be *give* and *not* take."

She held one up to the lamp. The stone absorbed all the light. Wilma rotated the diamond around, her eyes glistening as she examined every facet of the rock. Finally, she put it, along with the rest of our share, into a small black velvet pouch and dropped it into her bag.

"Do you want me to take them to market for you?" Donald asked.

"No," Wilma murmured, "we'll take care of it ourselves."

"See you at 10:00," I added.

~

On our way back to the condo, Wilma looked at the diamonds again.

They mesmerized her in a way that reminded me of Gollum from *Lord of the Rings*.

My precious ...

"You okay?"

She gazed out the window trying to view the clouds through the facets of a stone.

"You know it's a trap, right?"

I shrugged. "Sure, but let's play it through."

"Why?"

"Because I'm curious."

"They'll be expecting us to know it's a trap."

"I'm counting on it. And we can use that to our advantage."

"What do you think we should do?" She was still captivated by the stone.

"What we always do."

"They'll be expecting that as well."

"Then we'll improvise."

The odds against us were piling up like obscene profits at Goldman Sachs.

Wilma continued staring at the diamond.

I knew Wilma had been weighing the probability of dying and I could see that she'd already calculated the worst possible outcome. She smiled blissfully. Being hopelessly outnumbered inspired her.

There was no fucking way these guys were going to win.

Wilma slipped the diamond into her bra where it nestled between her breasts, close to her heart.

I wondered which one was harder, the diamond or her heart.

WE'RE FUCKED!

I should have rested after being up all night, but I was too keyed up and watching TV made matters even worse.

The storm had intensified into a Category 4 overnight and shrill warnings about the approaching hurricane filled the airwaves. According to the National Hurricane Center, Charleston was in the monster's direct path and it was due to make landfall in twenty-four hours.

Intermittent wind gusts rattled the condo's eaves. I wasn't concerned about the tidal surge — we were up high enough — but the wind might be a different story. The condo had been cheaply built and I was worried that it would give us about as much protection as a pup tent. But, if everything went according to plan, we would be on the highway home by the time the hurricane paid a visit.

Local television stations were having a contest to see who could be the shrillest. Channel 7 was the hands-down winner. Chip, their meteorologist, looked like he hadn't slept for a couple of days. I suspected that his producers weren't letting him wear makeup so he would appear particularly unkempt. In the gravest of tones, he pleaded with viewers to run away and seek higher ground. Under the grim façade, however, he was secretly having a ball. Being in the middle of a major hurricane was every weatherman's wettest dream.

Normally a weather forecaster is the idiot cousin of a news team, a meat puppet who provides a pleasant distraction from the reality of murder, mayhem, and economic disaster. He smiles and jokes about the sunshine or insincerely apologizes for rain. But when a hurricane is approaching, the good old weatherman goes front and center as the other anchors turn into screaming monkeys.

Like a general leading his troops, the noble meteorologist stands before his maps and lectures on hurricane dynamics. The closer the storm gets to landfall, the more he cranks it up. By the time it gets there, his map is continually flashing **WE'RE FUCKED!**

And when the situation becomes dire, he leads the entire team in the *Lord's Prayer.*

"We need to get out of here now." I looked at the pile of Costco debris filling the living room. "Is there enough room in the van for all this shit?"

"Sure. The seats fold down."

"But if we get stopped they might think we're looters."

Wilma looked at me. "Then we'd better not be stopped."

It would be ironic if, after all we'd gone through, we perished in a shootout with the South Carolina National Guard over fifty rolls of Kirkland toilet paper.

~

By 7:00 that evening Folly Beach was quiet. Most of the residents had already crossed the causeway to get out of harm's way. We sat on the balcony and watched the stragglers leave the island. It was now time for us to go to work.

Earlier I had called 911 and reported a heart attack at a unit three streets over.

When the paramedics finally arrived, I pretended to be a frantic relative and directed them around back. Then Wilma and I jumped them, stole their uniforms and their ambulance. Once we'd knocked them out, we tied them to stretchers so they would look like patients. I turned on the emergency flashers and we headed to Charleston.

The ambulance was our ticket through the roadblocks surrounding the city. At one point, the police generously provided an escort for us.

Once we'd reached downtown, we left the ambulance on a side street but kept the uniforms on. If anyone stopped us, we would have a good reason for being out on the streets during an emergency.

We headed for Donald's place.

~

"Nasty night." Donald closed the door against the rising wind and rain after he let us in.

"You planning to ride it out?"

"Sure, why not. This home has survived two hundred years of the worst mother nature and man has thrown at it," Donald smiled. "I've already moved the bulk of my collection to high ground. I have an electrical generator with a five-day supply of gas, an excellent cognac, and an ice chest full of *foie gras* to tide me over. I think I can weather this storm."

~

Donald put the Poe volume inside a waterproof case.

While we waited for the car to show up, he poured us each a brandy and we toasted to a successful night.

"Are you going to kill D'Urberville?" he asked me.

"With as much pleasure as possible."

"Good. I shudder at the thought of that Neanderthal putting his greasy fingers on *Tamerlane*. He has no real appreciation of its actual value. To him, it would just be another expensive possession, like his jet and his yacht, or those animals he keeps caged up."

It was nearly 10:30 so we finished up our drinks.

There was the beep of a horn and Donald glanced out the window. "The car's here."

He turned off the living room lights, picked up the case, and walked to the front door.

A minute later there was a sharp knock and Donald opened the door a crack. The driver stood under an umbrella. The rain was really hammering down and the wind blew some drops into Donald's foyer.

"Come in," Donald told the driver.

Before the poor man could respond, Wilma stepped out and punched him in the throat. He crumpled to the floor. She stripped off his raincoat and cap and held them out to me.

Donald looked at the blood leaking from the corner of the driver's mouth in alarm.

"What are you going to do with him?"

Wilma picked up the guy and dragged his body along the hall toward the kitchen.

"Have you got a blender?"

Donald blanched.

FAUX NEWS

A fierce wind from the rapidly intensifying hurricane-buffeted the Lincoln Navigator and threatened to hurl it off the road.

I struggled with the steering wheel which had a mind of its own. Ahead, a cop blocked the entrance to the bridge. I rolled down the window and took a blast of rain full in the face.

"You gotta turn back. We're going to close the bridge."

I shrugged and dangled a $100 bill out the window. It flapped in the wind before it disappeared into his pocket.

He stepped aside and let me through. I pushed the pedal to the metal and the beast shot forward, climbing up the roadway toward the crest two hundred feet above the river. I tried not to think about the drop but my vertigo went into overdrive. My arms and legs turned to rubber. Time and space compressed and a shrieking mongoose clawed at my forehead from the inside. At the height of my panic, the obvious suddenly occurred to me.

Why the fuck hadn't I let Wilma drive?

Just as we reached the top of the span, a ferocious blast of wind lifted the heavy SUV up and slammed it back down. The shocks screamed in agony as the wind shoved us toward the railing and the river two hundred feet below.

In an unreasoning panic, I mashed my foot down on the accelerator and the car fishtailed on the slick surface. The Navigator did three complete donuts on the down ramp before I got it under control.

"Slow down!" Donald screamed. He sat beside me clutching the Poe sealed in its waterproof package, which was a good thing because he was on the verge of throwing up.

Lifting my foot off the gas, I let the Lincoln drift to a stop at the bottom.

Wilma continued to nonchalantly watch the debris fly past the window. An airborne stop sign cut a slash across the hood while the car was relentlessly battered by palm fronds.

I got my breathing under control again, but my heart was still racing from our close call on the bridge. I tried to focus on my driving, but couldn't shake the feeling this caper was not going to end well.

A few blocks from the compound I pulled over and helped Wilma attach her special rig to the underside of the Lincoln. It had lots of ground clearance. She climbed into the rig and hung from the bottom of the car. Dressed in her Zentai suit, she would be invisible even if they pushed a mirror under the chassis.

~

They didn't.

In fact, the guards at the gate were so preoccupied with the approaching storm they hardly glanced at us. They just waved me through and I drove slowly toward the main house.

I pulled over to let Wilma use the quick release on her harness to escape from under the car. She disappeared between the large enclosures where D'Urberville kept his private zoo.

"What do you think they're going to do with the animals?" I asked Donald.

Donald pointed toward the canal which was just visible between the driving sheets of rain.

"He has an ark."

"An ark? Like in the Bible?"

"Yes, just like Noah. It's built to withstand heavy seas. They put the animals on board and then tow it offshore and anchor it. The animals will ride out the storm."

I grimaced at the thought of the poor zoo keepers who would have the unpleasant task of taking care of a bunch of seasick animals as I watched as one of them lead a skittish giraffe toward the dock.

I was now entirely convinced that Tesla D'Urberville was insane.

At the same time, I was questioning my *own* sanity for coming after him on a night like this. The only saving grace in all this mayhem was that everyone was distracted.

A guard walked to the car and tapped on the window.

I rolled it down a crack.

"Why the fuck are you stopping here?" the guard demanded.

"We're waiting for the giraffe to cross," I told him with a smile, and then shot him between the eyes. The thud of my suppressor was lost in the howl of the wind.

"It's going to get messy from here on," I said to Donald as I rolled the window back up. "Better keep your head down."

He wrapped his arms around the book even more protectively.

~

Once inside the house, I shot my way through a few more of D'Urberville's goons.

Finally, we reached the enormous living room where the man himself sat cross-legged on the couch staring out the window defying the hurricane to come and get him.

I recognized him from his reality show and numerous appearances on FAUX News.

D'Urberville looked at me in disgust as I dripped seawater on his million-dollar Persian rug.

The room was elegant, spectacular actually, with windows running its entire length. Original works of art covered one wall, many of which I'd seen in books.

I pointed to one of the canvases. "Is that a Matisse?"

Anger flared in D'Urberville's eyes. "I lost a perfectly good Godzilla costume and my house because of you. And do you have any idea how much that pendulum cost?" He shook his head. "You keep finding new ways to annoy me."

With a loud rustling, a dozen guards filled the room, guns pointed at us.

"And I am extremely disappointed in *you*," he said stabbing a finger in Donald's direction.

His men grabbed Donald roughly and snatched the book away.

D'Urberville unfolded himself from the couch. He took the book and unwrapped it with a smile. "This will help defray some of my losses."

He pried the gun from my hand.

I looked at him defiantly. "Planning to ride out the storm? I understand this place is supposed to be hurricane proof. Man enough to test it?" I taunted.

His smile broadened. "Unfortunately, not this time. I'm needed elsewhere."

"I'm not part of this," Donald blubbered. "He forced me at gunpoint."

I appreciated Donald's survival instincts but, unfortunately, D'Urberville wasn't buying it.

"You're such an odd couple." He nodded to the guards. "Introduce them to Felix and Oscar."

~

It was a Three Stooges short outside. The entire compound was in an uproar. Guards were chasing animals and animals were chasing guards.

A panicked man ran past us. "The lions and tigers are out of their pens!"

Gee, I wonder how that happened?

A huge lion leaped out of the driving rain and cornered the guy. The man turned and, in desperation, tried to shoot the big cat. The lion knocked him down and bit off his head.

Donald fainted.

In front of us, another guard backed out of the space between two buildings. He was focused on a spot in the shadows. A grizzly bear ambled out of the darkness. The screaming guard fell to his knees. One mighty swipe of the grizzly's paw sent him off to have a face-to-face with whichever God he worshiped.

Somehow this nightmare didn't deter the men guarding us. They obviously had a better disability plan or something. They dragged Donald to his feet and hustled us along to an enclosure on the far side of the compound.

We were soaked and miserable from the storm, but that was the least of our worries. We were facing a deep, dark pit and in the frequent lightning flashes I caught a glimpse of hungry yellow eyes staring up at us.

The pit was fifteen feet deep but, to my vertigo-addled brain, it looked more like two hundred.

The guard picked me up. "In you go," he laughed and tossed me in.

I landed in a muddy cesspool and Donald smashed down beside me. He curled up into a ball and whimpered.

"Now look what you've done," I shouted up at them defiantly. "You've made Donald cry."

The guards leaned over the wall waiting for the show to begin. A low menacing growl told me they wouldn't have long to wait.

A pair of Bengal tigers, who must be Felix and Oscar, emerged from one corner of the pit and circled around us. They weren't in any great hurry to eat us. Maybe they'd already had their *Frosted Flakes* for breakfast. Regardless, I didn't make any sudden moves. I rose slowly to my feet and faced them. Donald stayed on the ground and looked away.

"Donald," I hissed, "Get your ass up."

He did and stood next to me shaking uncontrollably.

I looked up at the guards to see if they were enjoying the show. They pointed excitedly at one of the tigers who was getting ready to leap.

The guard on the right let out a cry of pain and twisted around. A frenzied baboon had leaped onto his back and was ripping at the man's neck. He slapped desperately at the creature trying to dislodge it. Off-balance from the weight of the baboon, the guard stumbled over the railing and landed ten feet from us. The dazed baboon hopped off his back.

Oscar, or was it Felix, strolled casually over to the guard and clamped his massive fangs into the man's neck. The guy screamed and the tiger gave a quick shake. The guy's neck broke with a loud snap and he went limp. The tiger dragged him off to the other side of the pit. His buddy trotted after him.

Dinner time.

Above us, the other guard looked on in shock until a neat row of bullets exploded out of his chest. He flopped forward and tumbled into the pit.

Wilma looked down at us and then lowered a ladder. Donald and I scrambled up before the tigers finished their snack and came for the main course.

"Why didn't the tigers eat us?" Donald asked.

"Professional courtesy," Wilma replied.

"We need to find D'Urberville," I said.

"Do I have to do everything for you?" Wilma lifted up a flaccid Tesla D'Urberville.

"You didn't kill him, did you?"

She shook her head.

"Good. I have something special planned for him."

ENDANGERED SPECIES

Tesla D'Urberville's blissful shit-eating grin disappeared when he finally opened his eyes.

D'Urberville was propped against a wall of the rhino pen, still massively stoned from whatever Wilma had shot into him. He tried to process what was going on, but finally gave up and began to hum.

"That's annoying!" Wilma snapped.

He stopped humming and tried to touch her face. Wilma stepped back.

D'Urberville looked up at her mournfully. "You're beautiful …"

The rest of his comment was lost as I yanked him to his feet. He giggled while I stripped off his clothes.

On the other side of a low cement wall, a large rhino paced nervously. The sign on the pen's gate read **AGATHA**.

Wilma and I hoisted D'Urberville up and Donald opened the door.

The rhino shied away from us. Donald approached her and began to stroke her neck, cooing into her ear. Agatha relaxed and started to rub her head gently against Donald's chest.

"Donald, I didn't know you were the rhino whisperer," I laughed.

He smiled and continued to calm Agatha as I dragged D'Urberville around behind her.

D'Urberville rolled his head drunkenly from side to side. "Whazzzz going …"

Donald continued to work his magic on Agatha while Wilma and I hoisted D'Urberville's naked body up onto her rump.

Then I took out my tube of Krazy Glue.

~

D'Urberville returned to reality a few minutes later and found himself firmly attached to Agatha's backside.

"What the fuck!"

He struggled but the adhesive was holding him tight.

"Better be careful, Tesla, you'll get her all hot and bothered."

The corrugated steel roof above us groaned as the wind tried to tear it off. Agatha stomped her hooves in alarm. I stood beside the rhino gently patting her head to keep her calm.

"How much do you want?" D'Urberville's panic was rising like a thermometer on a stifling day.

"Oh, we've already been paid."

"For what?"

"To kill you, of course."

D'Urberville's eyes narrowed suspiciously. "Was it the fucking network? Those pricks would do anything to get out of a contract."

"No, it wasn't the network, Tesla. This is for the Judge."

D'Urberville looked confused.

"Judge? What the fuck are you talking about? What Judge?"

Wilma squeezed a blob of jelly into the palm of her hand. She walked back and slathered it all over D'Urberville's bare buttocks.

He twisted his head to see what she was up to. "What the hell are you doing?"

"Rhino pheromone," Wilma said as she wiped her hand on a rag. "It makes them really horny."

D'Urberville desperately rocked back and forth trying to tear himself loose. He screamed when the skin on his thighs started to rip and bleed.

In the next pen, Agatha's boyfriend Rodney snorted and bashed against the wooden gate separating them.

"Rhinos have such a keen sense of smell, don't they?"

Wilma and I watched Rodney battering down the gate.

D'Urberville looked back at us in dread as Rodney, consumed with insatiable lust, smashed through the barrier and charged past us, intent on the object of his affection.

I smiled at Wilma. "I think Rodney is ready to make babies. I wonder if he's going to be jealous when he discovers he's been cuckolded."

D'Urberville let out a terrified scream. It was cut off a second later by loud squishing noise.

"Animal behavior," I said in mock disgust.

~

"Where the hell is Donald?"

D'Urberville's compound was still in total chaos. Hurricane Mortimer had picked up everything that wasn't firmly attached and the air around us was filled with deadly missiles.

Donald had evidently slipped away while we conducted our animal husbandry experiment on D'Urberville. Wilma grabbed my arm and pulled me toward the Navigator, which miraculously was just where we'd left it.

One of D'Urberville's men staggered past with three monkeys riding on his back. I swear *Speak No Evil* smiled at me.

It was hell getting the car doors open. Once inside, I started the engine and cranked up the heat.

"What about Donald?" I shouted over the howling fury of the storm.

Wilma pointed toward the house just as Donald came out the front door dragging a large suitcase like a slave hauling a block of stone toward the pyramids.

When he was safely in the car, Donald patted the suitcase and smiled. "D'Urberville's collection was too good to leave."

I slammed my foot down on the accelerator.

Donald held onto the suitcase for dear life and shouted, "I couldn't find the Poe."

Wilma smiled and held up a wrapped package.

"Think you can find another buyer?"

~

Later, back at Donald's after we'd changed into dry clothes, we sat in the kitchen drinking coffee and admiring D'Urberville's books spread out on the table.

"What do you think all these are worth?"

Donald shook his head.

"Millions. I'll split it with you, of course. Unless you'd like this."

Donald opened a bag and pulled out a rolled canvas. "I had to cut it from the frame."

It was the Matisse, which would make an excellent addition to my secret gallery.

"This is fine for me. Maybe you could give Wilma some more diamonds to offset her share."

Donald smiled and went to get the diamonds.

"Now, we have more than enough to retire," Wilma grinned.

Retirement?

I hadn't given it much thought. My work is fascinating and I get to interact with all kinds of interesting people. But I had to admit the past few projects had taken a toll on my psyche.

Retirement?

What would it look like? Sitting on a beach somewhere sunny? After blizzards and hurricanes, it would be good to feel the sun on my face. Of course, if we did retire, there would be loose ends to tie up.

One of them walked into the kitchen just then and handed Wilma a packet of black diamonds.

"We're even then?" Donald looked at us hopefully." I won't have to look over my shoulder anymore?"

I thought about it. "We'll see."

"Fair enough," he nodded grimly.

With lust-filled eyes, Donald glanced down at the books anxious to examine his new treasures.

~

The road back to Folly Beach was barely passable. We learned from the radio this was only the leading edge of the storm. The worst was yet to come. Hurricane Mortimer was about to make landfall. Charleston was squarely in its sights.

Waves crashed over the causeway and threatened to drown the Navigator. With any luck, we could get back to the condo, retrieve the van, and be safely inland before Morty struck with full force.

The power was out in Folly Beach. The condo was dark and the electric door opener didn't work.

Shit!

We made a run for the front door and got drenched again. There had to be some way to open the garage manually. I grabbed a flashlight and went to check while Wilma ran upstairs to make sure she'd packed all her Costco coffee.

I shone the light around the garage. The beam illuminated a face.

Marvin Stench.

I froze and he smiled.

It *was* a trap!

I turned toward the stairs to warn Wilma.

I heard a soft *thunk* from behind me and felt the sting of a tranquilizer dart. The garage began to swirl and I collapsed.

The last thing I remembered was Stench standing over me with an evil grin spread across his lacerated face.

IN THE BELLY OF THE BEAST

Lightning flashes illuminated a dream peppered with little bits of reality.

> *The back seat of a car.*
> *An impossibly large gun barrel.*
> *Trying to strike out at someone.*
> *Being lifted and carried.*
> *The rocking deck of a large boat.*
> *Rain slashing painfully across my face.*
> *Wilma's limp head hanging down as she is dragged away.*
> *Someone using a drill next to my left ear.*
> *And then darkness again.*
> *Sweet, comforting darkness.*

~

It had been a fantastic dream. Lions and tigers were dancing together while hippos and giraffes pirouetted. Tesla D'Urberville frolicked with a smiling rhino across a sun-dappled meadow. Waves of billowy softness enveloped me and I hugged my pillow tightly and sighed contentedly.

Consciousness returned, but it was still pleasant.

I was lying on a bed covered with freshly laundered cotton sheets which were unbelievably soft. When I opened my eyes, I saw Wilma next to me. She snored gently.

Lifting the sheet, I discovered I was naked but otherwise unharmed and unencumbered. Since they hadn't bothered to tie us up, I assumed the door was locked.

Wilma groaned and rubbed her eyes.

"Don't say *where am I*," I told her.

Wilma sat up and the covers fell away revealing that she too was naked. Little Rip stirred at the sight.

Turning a lurid shade of green, Wilma pitched forward and gripped her head between her hands.

We must be on a boat.

But in a hurricane? That's insane!

"I feel …," she moaned and vomited over the side of the bed.

Little Rip did not find this erotic at all and went back into his hidey-hole.

She threw a sheet on top of the mess and got out of bed, unsteady on her feet. I wondered if they'd given her a bigger dose of whatever tranquilizer they'd used on me. They probably needed to. Wilma wouldn't have gone along without a fight.

"I think we're on a boat," she said staggering to the window.

She pulled open the curtain and gasped.

Since it took a lot to make Wilma gasp, I dreaded taking a look. But I did anyway. Insatiable curiosity has always been one of my failings.

We were on a boat all right. But we weren't *on* the water. We were *under* it.

"Didn't Promod say D'Urberville had a submarine?" I said.

I continued to look out the window in amazement. Streams of bubbles rolled past. They must have had an illuminated hull because I could see a short distance into the murky sea.

"This is nuts," I said, still trying to comprehend what was happening.

There was a loud click and the door opened. We turned to face a uniformed steward who held out some clothing. He guarded the doorway while we changed.

I watched his eyes move lasciviously over Wilma's body as she pulled on a gray jumpsuit. She caught him looking and shot him an alluring smile. Embarrassed, he glanced away and I wondered how much he would enjoy eating his eyeballs after Wilma ripped them from their sockets.

~

The interior of the submarine was the kind of luxurious you'd expect of a billionaire's yacht. The walls were paneled in teak and accented in polished brass. The floors were covered with the kind of carpet that massaged your feet when you walked on it.

We entered a large lounge and I half expected to see Captain Nemo playing the pipe organ. Instead, Marvin Stench stood looking through a large window at the dark ocean flowing past.

"I guess we're not in Kansas anymore."

For dramatic effect, he ignored me and continued to stare out the window. After a minute or so he turned and regarded us like we were pocket lint. Stench curled his lips in a smile that emphasized the tiny gray scars furrowing his cheeks.

"You're three hundred feet below the surface of the Atlantic Ocean. Heh, heh, heh…"

His voice was clipped and no-nonsense. He did, however, have a verbal tick, an annoying gasping laugh that punctuated his sentences.

It got on my nerves.

Our gray jumpsuits reminded me of the Spring Collection at Sawmill Grove Correctional Facility. The fit was better, but the inseam scratched my balls. I wished they'd included underwear.

He continued to stare at us. I couldn't tell if it was with contempt or bored amusement.

"What about the hurricane?" I asked.

The weather is always a safe topic for polite conversation.

"We're below it. It doesn't even ripple the water at this depth. Heh, heh, heh…"

I thought that you could only *ripple* the surface of the water, but I decided not to point this out to him. He looked like he had a lot on his mind.

"And where are we off to this time?"

Stench lifted a decanter from the table beside him and held it out, offering us a drink. We declined.

"*We* are going to Europe," he replied. "Unfortunately, *you* are. Heh, heh, heh…"

As he poured thick, smoky-colored liquor into a glass, Wilma lurched forward reaching for his scrawny neck. Two crew members grabbed her arms and restrained her. She continued to struggle.

"I'm sick of this supervillain shit! Why didn't you just shoot us when you had the chance?"

"That's not quite what we had in mind," said another voice from behind us.

We turned to see who it was. My heart sank. Laura Petrie, the Judge's daughter. I paused for a few seconds to let this sink in.

Nothing seemed to make sense. I looked around for the White Rabbit or the Mad Hatter to join us.

"Thanks for getting rid of D'Urberville. We owe you for that," Laura said as she walked over and stood next to Stench.

"We had planned to dispose of him anyway, he was becoming too much of a liability. He'd started to believe his own bullshit. We had something nasty planned for him, but your solution was much more amusing. Heh, heh, heh …"

"That's what we like about you," Laura added, "your resourcefulness."

"Okay, I don't mind admitting that right now I am totally fucking confused. You hire us to find your father's killers and here you are hanging out with them. I don't get it."

Laura walked to the bar and poured herself a glass of wine. She smiled at me sweetly and despite everything, Little Rip roused from his stupor.

"But to be technically correct, it was *you* who killed my father."

"Yes, but *these* assholes hired us to do it. Your father was going to sponsor a bill that would have stopped a lucrative business for them. And they used a blind cut-out, Randy Yamahaha, to make it look like mere revenge."

"And you followed the trail all the way back to the people who were *actually* responsible, didn't you?" Laura smiled. "You just didn't go far enough."

I stared at her in disbelief and then I got it. *She* was one of the people responsible.

"So why did you want your own father dead?"

A tear appeared in the corner of her left eye. She wiped it away. "I loved my father and he loved me. He just *loved* me a little too much."

An unpleasant image rode into my head and reared up like the Lone Ranger's horse.

"You should have dealt with it yourself, bitch," Wilma said.

I was surprised at Wilma's rage and wondered if she'd had similar issues. *That she* had *dealt with herself.*

"So we got rid of your daddy and D'Urberville. Now you kill us, right?"

Stench smiled and shook his head.

"D'Urberville was just a stooge. He was arrogant and stupid. He didn't even have the insight to realize how ironic his father was when he named him. I doubt that he even knew who Thomas Hardy was. Heh, heh, heh …

"No, Mr. ********, he wasn't the boss of anything. He was a public patsy who conveniently distracted everyone. Heh, heh, heh…"

I was stunned. Stench had used the name I'd been born with. It was my most carefully guarded secret. Wilma was the only person who knew it. I was naked and vulnerable.

"And you Mrs. ********," he told Wilma. "We know everything about you as well. Heh, heh, heh…"

Wilma looked as if an *ACME* anvil had clunked her on the head.

A cold trickle of fear ran along my spine.

Just who the hell were these guys?

"This was never about killing the Judge or D'Urberville. Heh, heh, heh…," Stench chuckled again, recalling D'Uberville's wild ride.

It must've been hell to extract D'Urberville from Agatha's back. I hoped it hadn't caused her too much trauma.

Do they have therapists for rhinos?

"Since we're using real names, mine is Marvin and this is Belinda. Heh, heh, heh…"

That little laugh was really beginning to fray my nerves.

"So if this isn't about avenging the Judge's killers, then what's it about?"

"What indeed. You're both clever. You even have university degrees. Why don't you give it some thought? Heh, heh, heh …"

He waited. But I was still confused. It was probably the residual effect of the tranquilizer or the disorientation of being under the ocean. My head began to ache.

Wilma stood, hands clenched at her sides, a coiled spring, dangerously over-wound.

"I look at the two of you as a Taoist expression. Heh, heh, heh …"

"Tao? Is he the one with the little red book?"

Stench frowned. "Don't pretend that you're stupid. You know what I'm talking about. The yin and the yang. Heh, heh, heh …"

"Sure, I get take out from there sometimes. They have excellent egg rolls."

Stench frowned. "We don't have a lot of time. You are the yang of course. The sunny side of the mountain, bright, shining, creative, and explosive. Heh, heh, heh …"

He turned to Wilma. "And you are the yin, the shady side, darkness, the black within the white, or the white within the black. Heh, heh, heh …"

"I don't have a fucking clue what you're talking about," Wilma told him. "Are you having a stroke?"

He laughed. "I love your defiance. In fact, I admire both of you. You're skilled, tenacious, and ruthless. Heh, heh, heh …"

"Well, since you're such a big fan of ours, maybe you'd like to enlighten us. What the fuck is going on? *Heh, heh, heh …"*

Stench looked genuinely wounded when I mimicked his verbal tick. Normally I wouldn't make fun of a handicap, but I made an exception in his case.

Heh, heh, heh …

Laura started to say something. Stench shot her a look and she clammed up.

The phone rang. Stench casually picked it up and listened for a few seconds. He set it down gently.

"We've reached our destination. Heh, heh, heh …"

"Europe?" I said.

"No. Like I told you before, you're not going quite that far. Heh, heh, heh …"

Before I had a chance to ask him why we weren't going all the way, the sub glided to a stop.

We hung in the water like my unasked question.

Then the vessel began to rise. I hoped that Stench knew what the hell he was doing. If not, we were heading into the center of a raging hurricane.

And I hadn't packed my bathing suit.

MR. RIP'S WILD RIDE

Seawater cascaded off the pilothouse window.

Stench led us out onto the bow deck which bobbed slightly in a light swell. The brilliant sunshine told me that we'd left Hurricane Mortimer far behind us.

On the surface, the sub appeared to be an ordinary run-of-the-mill luxury yacht. It wouldn't draw a second glance as it entered the harbor at Monte Carlo or Nice.

Uniformed deckhands unlocked a water-tight hanger on the bow to reveal a powerful speedboat inside.

A stiff breeze came up and ruffled Wilma's hair. She gripped the railing and tried not to throw up again. I drew in a deep breath of warm sea air. The sun felt good. I turned to face the breeze and my bowels lurched.

There was a gigantic wall of boiling black clouds off our stern and they were bearing down on us like *The Dixie Flyer*.

Jesus, the hurricane!

We were inside it.

"That is the eye of a Force 4 hurricane, with sustained winds of over 140. When the leading part of the storm passes, you think that the worst is over. But the back wall of the storm is usually more damaging than the leading edge. Heh, heh, heh …"

I looked at the monster that was approaching. I estimated it would reach us within ten minutes.

"I need to get to the point. The storm's moving at 30 miles per hour so we don't have a lot of time. We're an ancient fraternity, Mr. ********. Heh, heh, heh …"

Again I was startled to hear my birth name. I wasn't used to it.

"And like any fraternity, we need to acquire new recruits now and then. Fresh blood, as they say. But we also need to be confident that they meet our rather high standards. Heh, heh, heh …"

Realization was starting to sink in.

"This whole thing has been some sort of game?" I said incredulously.

He nodded in delight. "Actually, more of a test to see if you could make the grade. Heh, heh, heh …"

"I don't like clubs or organizations, or whatever the fuck you are," Wilma snapped. "And if I did, I'd join the Moose Lodge."

I was tempted to point out that I didn't think the Moose Lodge accepted contract killers, but I held my tongue.

"No one's inviting you to join anything. Heh, heh, heh …"

The wind was rising and the deck started heaved under us. I grabbed the railing to steady myself.

"You've proved that you have skills we may need from time to time. Call this an audition for future consideration. There is a possibility that we may never need to call on you but, if we did, it would only be as *hired help*. Heh, heh, heh …"

Again with that expression.

"We would *never* consider you as part of our group. That's reserved for a handful of very special people who, unlike yourselves, have a purpose and a philosophy. Forgive me, but while you might be useful, you are mundane. Heh, heh, heh …"

"You owe us the rest of our payment," Wilma yelled over the howling wind.

"Yes, of course. And an additional amount for helping to rid us of Mr. D'Urberville. You'll find it all in a compartment on the boat. Heh, heh, heh …"

His henchmen dragged Wilma and me to the speedboat and tossed us in. I banged my knee against the back of one of the seats. It hurt like a son of a bitch.

The hurricane was much closer now and one of the deckhands glanced nervously over his shoulder. They released the speedboat down its track. It gathered momentum and hit the water with a tremendous splash that threw us against its windshield. The boat floated free of the sub.

Stench looked over the bow rail. "You have a top speed of fifty miles an hour. I would suggest that you stay in the eye until you reach land. At that point, you are on your own. Heh, heh, heh …"

He held up a float with two keys hanging from it.

"Call this your final test. If you survive, you might be of use to us at some future date. Heh, heh, heh …" He dangled the keys from his fingers. They clinked together.

A gust of wind rocked the speedboat. I stumbled and crashed against Wilma.

I stood up and faced him defiantly. "You're just going to leave us out here to die?"

He shook his head. "No, we want you to live. And if you do, you'll be of value to us. If you don't … Well then, we'll just have to find someone else. Heh, heh, heh …"

"Fuck you!" Wilma shouted over the banshee wail of the wind.

"That's good, hold onto your anger. It will keep you focused. Heh, heh, heh …"

The wind was pushing us away from the submarine. Stench tossed the keys to me and took a final look at the approaching back wall of the hurricane's eye.

"Good luck. Heh, heh, heh …"

He waved to us and went into the deckhouse. The boat sank beneath the rising sea in a few seconds.

Wilma and I looked at each other. An understanding passed between us. We were going to survive so that we could feed that smug bastard his kidneys.

"Let's go!" she screamed.

I fumbled with the keys and tried to insert one into the ignition. It didn't fit. I shoved the other one in and twisted it. There was a loud growl from the stern of the speedboat. I pushed the throttle forward.

The boat leaped straight out of the water and then slammed down, digging into the waves. I goosed the engine and the bow rose up into full plane.

Wilma fiddled with the navigation computer and the screen came to life.

"Look for a chart," I shouted.

She rooted around and pulled out a plastic tube. Unfurling the map, she pointed to Charleston. I glanced over my shoulder. The storm seemed dangerously close. I wondered how much gas we had.

Wilma tapped coordinates into the navigation computer and the screen resolved into a line map of the coast. It looked a long way off. Even if we did make it, the storm would be on us minutes after we landed. There was no way we could escape. I looked around desperately for a solution.

I saw the keys hanging from the ignition. They clinked against the dashboard.

Why were there two keys?

I smiled grimly and tapped a spot on the map. "Put those coordinates into the GPS, that's where we're heading."

She looked at me and frowned. The storm was gaining on us. Wilma punched in the coordinates. The read-out on the screen said we were thirty miles away from shore. I did a quick calculation. It was going to be close.

I hoped we could stay ahead of the hurricane.

~

Coast Guard broadcasts were warning vessels to seek immediate shelter. *No shit.*

I kept the boat at full throttle, but the relentless storm was gaining on us. Glancing at the navigation screen, I was thankful Lumpy had given me a crash course in boating.

"You always manage to get us into interesting situations, don't you?" Wilma said.

"This is hardly what I would call *interesting*."

"It's a shame you didn't go first in Switzerland."

"Would you really have let me?"

I glanced at her and saw that she really would have.

"And then your life would have been a lot less exciting."

She laughed bitterly. "Anyway, what does it *matter*. We aren't going to make it. Even if we reach land, that storm will tear us apart."

I shook my head and gritted my teeth in determination.

Isn't that what the hero always does, grits his teeth? What a stupid expression.

"We *are* going to make it. We *always* make it. Don't worry. This time, *I've* got *your* back, *******." I'd added her real name to the end of the sentence. Hearing it didn't improve her mood.

I kept the boat pointed into the waves which were now becoming massive as we got closer to shore. The boat was tossed mercilessly about in the thrashing ocean. Rain hammered our backs and made it hard to breathe.

Hurricane Morty was tapping our shoulders to remind us that he was right there.

I risked another look and saw the swirling mass of cloud less than half a mile back. My stomach sank.

We weren't going to make it.

LAND HO!

When we reached land, the storm was less than a minute behind us.

I throttled the speedboat back and headed it straight for the canal next to the house. Pushed by the storm, the boat raced into the jetty and I cut the power. Ripping the keys from the ignition, I jumped. Wilma slipped and landed hard on the slick cement deck next to the canal. I reached out to her but the wind knocked me off my feet. I dragged myself up and braced against the blast of wind.

The house appeared to be miles away.

Where the hell was Wilma?

She'd been swallowed up by the driving wind and rain.

Jesus!

Before I could react, the full force of the storm slammed into me and bowled me over again. The wind pushed me along the slippery deck. I reached desperately for something to grab onto. My hand found one of the cleats and I held on for dear life.

If we don't get out of this swirling madness, we're going to die.

Debris whipped past me. Hurled into the air, the speedboat slammed into the cement at the end of the slip, shattering into a million fiberglass missiles.

Where the hell is Wilma?

I caught a blur of movement out of the corner of my eye. My hand shot out and grabbed Wilma as she hurtled past. Gripping her arm tightly, I pulled her close. Blood gushed from a large wound on her head. Her eyes rolled back and she sagged against me.

I screamed at her to focus, but the wind ripped the words out of my mouth. I shook Wilma trying to bring her back to consciousness. Her eyes finally fluttered open.

Wilma, we can live or die here. It's your choice.

She hugged me in a death-like grip and I staggered to my feet.

The hurricane was trying to rip us apart. I fought against it with all my strength and dragged her along. I was having trouble breathing as the wind continued to pound my chest and drive air from my lungs.

The house, still impossibly far, was shivering against the ferocious onslaught.

We had to reach it.

Then, over the sound of the screaming wind, I heard another more ominous rumbling.

Tidal surge!

"Move!" I screamed in her ear.

The water hit us just as we reached the back of the house.

I grabbed a railing with one hand and held onto Wilma with the other. She was bowled over by the rushing torrent and disappeared into it.

I felt her hand slipping from mine. I gripped it as tightly as I could and pulled against the current before she was washed away. I prayed the railing would hold.

Something popped in my shoulder and pain ripped through me. Every survival instinct screamed at me to let her go.

Instead, I pulled with all my remaining strength and Wilma came free of the water. Spitting jets of liquid, she clutched at the railing and held on.

Once we had gathered our strength, we half-climbed and half-crawled up the back stairs. Finally, we reached the door with the tidal surge right behind us. A second's hesitation and we would be swallowed up. I thought of Marvin Stench and the lovely Laura. The memory of their smug looks of superiority fueled enough anger to chase away my despair.

I reached for the door, drove the key into the lock, and turned it, willing it not to break off in my hand. The door opened a couple of inches with a soft hiss of positive pressure and I pushed against it. We fell inside and I slammed it shut just as the surge smashed into the house.

D'Urberville's sanctuary was warm and silent, an island of calm isolated from the raging madness outside.

We lay on the floor shivering for a few minutes until we got some energy back. Only the faintest sound of the wind reached us through the thick walls. The storm continued to slam against the house, trying to rip it apart. All we felt was a slight vibration from the floor.

~

The wind battered us for the whole day.

Wilma's head wound was not that severe. I cleaned it up and dressed it. Then she found us some dry clothing in D'Urberville's bedroom. I took perverse delight in wearing a pair of $600 slacks and a cheap sweatshirt that read: *You're Fired!*

The windows facing the sea were protected by thick steel shutters. I decided to risk a look outside and raised one of them a few inches. The wind had calmed down a lot, although smaller objects were still blowing around. But at this point, it wasn't much worse than your average summer thunderstorm. Still, there was no reason to go outside.

Wilma discovered a refrigerator stuffed with goodies. A generator provided power so we could watch CNN while making dinner. We hadn't eaten anything since the previous afternoon and were starving. Soon the kitchen was filled with the delicious aroma of a herbed rack of lamb.

I discovered a small wine cellar off the kitchen and rooted through the bottles. I know as much about wine as I do about building box girder bridges so Wilma walked past me and selected a bottle from the rack.

"Chateau La Mondotte Saint-Elmilion '96. Okay ... but we can do better."

Wilma looked around, selected another bottle, and smiled. "Petrus Pomerold '98. Excellent."

After her magnificent dinner and an unbelievable bottle of wine, I was comfortable and relaxed.

I swirled the last of the wine in my glass. "I'll have to pick up some of this."

"It's over $1,500 a bottle."

I drank the last of it and savored every drop.

~

We found the master bedroom and I rolled up one of the steel shutters a foot so we could watch the dying hours of the storm.

Without realizing it, I had my hand on Wilma's leg and was massaging the inside of her thigh. She reached over and pulled me close.

Little Rip felt like he'd been cast in bronze. Surviving certain death is by far the best aphrodisiac.

An instant later we were naked. I could taste the sea on her skin when I kissed her breasts. She rolled over and straddled me.

We glowed with the breath of St. Elmos's Fire.

There was no preamble, just pure unadulterated lust. We channeled the fury of the storm into a nonstop sex festival.

~

"I guess we passed their test," I told her later as I traced a finger across her belly.

She sighed.

Contented or perplexed?

"The entire thing was just an elaborate ruse to see if we measured up."

"So it was all for nothing."

I flashed back to Marvin Stench. Our final conversation triggered a memory.

"The money!"

In our desperate attempt to flee the storm, I'd forgotten to get the money from the boat. Our payment was probably miles out to sea now. That fit. This entire affair had been out to sea.

"Don't worry," Wilma smiled, "I got it."

I wasn't surprised. Wilma would never leave one dollar on the table, let alone seventy-five thousand of them.

"I can't believe they knew everything about us and we know nothing about them."

Wilma smiled again. "We know one thing about them."

"Oh? What's that?"

"They're *dead*."

I was exhausted and didn't want to think about it.

"Look, if you want to go off on some revenge mission against the Illuminati or Knights Templar or the Rotary Club, or whoever the fuck they are, count me out."

"I mean they *are* dead. Right now they're singing shanties with Davy Jones."

"Of the Monkees?"

"No, of the *Locker*." She squeezed Little Rip for emphasis.

What the fuck is she talking about?

And then I saw *THE* look, that self-satisfied little smile Wilma got when she'd done something particularly vile.

But how?

I thought back to our unpleasant sojourn on the submarine. We'd woken up in the cabin, naked. All our weapons had been taken.

There was no way …

The image of Wilma throwing up all over the floor popped into my mind. When she'd finished, she'd covered up the stinking mess with a sheet.

"What was it?"

"Nothing unusual. Just a little thermite device in a jell casing to resist the acid in my stomach. Once it was exposed to the air, however, the casing dissolved and the thermite burned through the decks like the alien's blood in that movie. When it reached seawater, the core reacted and exploded, blowing a six-inch hole in their hull."

"But what if it had gone off when we were still on board?"

Wilma shrugged.

I shivered at the possibility. How could she be so reckless and ruthless? *Oh, that's right … she's Wilma.*

"Stench said they're a big organization. They'll probably be looking to kill us now. That submarine must have cost them hundreds of millions," I said.

"Then I hope they have better luck than he did." Wilma rolled over and went to sleep.

I turned on my side and thought of Laura or Belinda or whoever she was. I saw her struggling against the rising water as the submarine fell into the darkness of a deep ocean trench. Then I saw Marvin Stench, his eyes wide open in terror watching the final oxygen bubble escape from his mouth.

I bet that wiped the smug grin off his face.

Heh, heh, heh.

THERE'S NO PLACE LIKE HOME

A few days later, the papers were filled with stories about the sinking of Tesla D'Urberville's luxury submarine off the South Carolina coast.

All hands were believed lost, including D'Urberville.

Bravo, Wilma!

While confirmation of the sinking brought joy to my heart, it didn't ease my anxiety. I had the uncomfortable feeling that Stench, Laura, and D'Urberville were only the tip of the spear. Whoever they fronted still had us in their hoary eye. I called them the *Cabal* for lack of a better name.

The Internet is filled with tons of information about mysterious groups who secretly run the world. Some are supposed to be tied in with the CIA and FBI, others with aliens, and still others with time travelers.

My personal favorite includes a conspiracy that links the Vatican and aliens to a clandestine war that has been fought for centuries.

Maybe we'd been recruited by Pope ET the Eighth.

~

Wilma and I spent four days trashing D'Urberville's home.

His well-stocked larder and excellent collection of vintage wines made our ordeal bearable. What we couldn't finish, we threw against the walls. When we weren't drinking, we had wild, passionate sex and covered every imaginative position in every conceivable place.

After CNN finally assured us the storm had passed, we left the house and surveyed the damage. D'Urberville would've been proud that his home had survived just like he'd always boasted it would.

Many other homes on Sullivan's Island were not so fortunate. They'd been blown away by the storm leaving plenty of multi-millionaires crying in their Dom Pérignon. Miraculously, one of D'Urberville's Lincoln

Navigators had survived intact and we borrowed it to get back to Folly Beach.

~

Our rented condo was still standing. The only damage was from the branch of a palm tree which had smashed in the kitchen window.

I looked at it in awe.

Hope we get our security deposit back.

Of course, the minivan had been washed away by the storm surge. Wilma contemplated the empty garage and sighed. All her Costco purchases were lost. Right now on the Ivory Coast, somebody was trying to figure out how to get all that seaweed out of an exercise machine.

Sadder, but wiser, we headed home.

~

Winter gripped Detroit by the throat, but I didn't care. It was good to be home.

The papers were still full of stories about Sparky Fletcher's personal tragedy. It was inspiring how Sparky was holding up courageously under the weight of his beloved wife's death. He'd even started a charity to support Detroit's feral felines.

No hard feelings, fellas.

All the publicity had done wonders for his flagging career. His *Greatest Hits* CD made the top ten in Billboard. An important label deal had put him back in the recording studio for the first time in fifteen years.

Sparky met me just after Christmas and paid the balance of his account.

Needless to say, he was one happy customer.

~

I continued to fret about the Cabal. It was frightening and mind-boggling how far below anyone's radar this group was.

I was forced consider different possibilities. Would they be after us for revenge or, by killing Stench and Laura, had we passed another test?

We discussed the possibility of going to ground but decided that probably wouldn't work. In the end, we figured the best strategy was to carry on with our business the way we always had. If a mysterious organization wanted to interfere, then we would just have deal with it.

So we went back to work.

~

It was a beautiful day in early May.

Huckleberry Hound sat down beside me on a bench in Riverside Park for our pre-arranged meeting. I didn't look at him. I just kept admiring the Ambassador Bridge towering over us in the background. It kind of reminded me of the iconic image of the Brooklyn Bridge from the Woody Allen movie *Manhattan.*

"Thanks for seeing me," he said with a soft British accent.

"So, Mr. Hound, what can I do for you?"

He passed me an envelope filled with $1,000 bills.

I never got tired of money.

"Well, Rip, we'd like you to kill …"

While staring at the bridge, I sat in stunned silence contemplating the magnitude of the hit he was asking me to pull off. It was impossible. There was no way we could do it and survive.

Or was there?

Maybe there was, but that's another story.

Heh, heh, heh …

ABOUT THE AUTHOR

Peter McGarvey has been a magazine columnist, radio journalist, advertising copywriter, marketing and sales executive, and filmmaker. He grew up in small town Ontario and now lives in downtown Toronto.

Peter is the author of the MOLLY PARSONS MYSTERIES, featuring a small-town police detective with a haunted past, and the RIP & WILMA HITS, the adventures of a pair of improbable contract killers.

Dark Sunset, his first novel, was called *"a near-perfect fusion of character and setting. ... a real page-turner ..."* [Don Hutchison, *The Great Pulp Heroes*]. Peter's subsequent novels, **Hair Trigger** and **Bloody Sunset**, are *"fast-paced, enjoyable crime novels that are better than many of the crime novels currently in print."* [Ray Walsh, *Curiosities*].

Peter McGarvey's new book, **Foggy Sunset**, will be released in late 2016.

Don't miss Peter McGarvey's next
Molly Parsons Mystery.

FOGGY

SUNSET

Coming soon in trade paperback,
and Kobo and Kindle eBooks
from Cliff House Publishing.

Keep reading for a preview …

ONE

Outside Pine, Michigan

Mark Barnard held the gun an inch from his sleeping father's head and thought again about pulling the trigger.

His father's death would be a sweet release from the servitude he was now resigned to. Less than a pound of pressure from his right index finger and it would all be over.

Mark's eye twitched as if something had crawled behind it and was playing with the nerve. Although barely thirty, Mark Barnard already felt like he had lived an entire lifetime. And maybe he had, with the war and then his father's ceaseless demands.

He looked down at the sleeping man and wasn't sure if his father was even still breathing. Maybe God had answered his prayers and sent the Angel of Death.

Then came the soft wheeze of the old man's next breath and Mark wanted to scream.

Once his father had been robust with the features of a Renaissance statue. Now he was shriveled and ancient. His face had collapsed in on itself and his translucent skin was so dry the epidermis was flaking away.

Robertson Barnard stirred in his sleep and Mark slid the gun into his waistband where it rubbed against the small of his back. The cold metal sent a shiver through his body.

The bedroom smelled of camphor and stale urine. Mark hardly noticed. He had smelled worse — much worse.

Outside, the day had faded into twilight. Soon it would be night and his father would wake up. Like Dracula, he would again start sucking the life out of Mark with his barrage of demands.

The pistol tucked against his spine reminded Mark how easy it would be to end the torture right there. He felt so damned conflicted; there was such a fine line between love and hate.

Age had not made the old man this way, it's how he had always been — self-centered and detached. He believed the whole universe swirled around him. And for a long time it had.

His father's story was famous. He had turned a single act of bravery during the Korean War into a bestselling memoir that in turn had powered a long, illustrious career in the Senate.

Robertson Barnard cast a long shadow which, for the most part, had left Mark and his mother in darkness. They were props in his campaign literature and at meetings and rallies. Mark had long ago learned to stay two steps behind his father, answer questions politely, and always keep a smile fixed on his face.

He had struggled to find his own light, but had failed under the inevitable comparison to his father. That had driven him into the military where three tours in Afghanistan had left him psychically shattered. After a long stay in a VA hospital, Mark returned home.

By then his mother was dead. She had been worn away by his father's constant need for care and attention. Now Mark was the prisoner, his life suspended in a familiar purgatory, knowing he would never break free while his father was still alive.

Across the yard, the automatic floodlights over the main door of the barn had come on, reminding him that it was feeding time.

Mark backed out of the room, careful not to wake up his father.

~

At the back door, he pulled on his father's waxed cotton barn coat. It smelled of gasoline and dry hay. Mark was six inches taller than his father. The jacket ended above his waist and the cold air tickled his spine. The sleeves rode up as well, exposing his wrists. His fingers were long and delicate, almost skeletal. He'd lost a lot of weight since he'd come home.

Mark left the pistol on the kitchen counter. Later he would unload it and return it to the shoebox at the back of his father's closet.

Crossing the yard to the barn, he inhaled the rich fragrance from the damp carpet of leaves. Their earthy smell was a harbinger of winter. He would need to rake them soon. He mentally added the chore to his to-do list for the morning.

~

At one time, Barnard Dairies had the largest dairy herd in this part of Michigan. Even though it was now down to six, his father was no longer able to care for the cattle. Like everything else on the farm, they were now Mark's responsibility.

It was a responsibility he did not want.

His father's lawyer had explained that Mark's power of attorney would allow him to sell the farm if he wanted to. Mark had been thinking hard about it. He couldn't imagine what life would be like without this place and their cattle, but he had no interest in running the business.

After he finished with his chores for the night, Mark turned the lights out inside the barn and slid the door shut. He began to latch it when a sharp bang threw him to his knees.

A brilliant flash of light from his father's bedroom window was followed by another loud bang.

Ambush!

He reached for his rifle but it wasn't there.

Where the fuck is my gear?

Confused, he grabbed for his sidearm.

The bedroom lit up once again, punctuated by yet another bang.

Gunshots!

Mark covered his ears and pulled himself into a protective ball.

They're over the wire and inside the camp!

He huddled, waiting for the final vicious assault. Instead, everything went dead silent. The Afghani desert faded away and he was back on the farm in Michigan.

But there was still danger.

The light at the back of the house went out. Mark crawled into the shadows and watched. A few moments later, the door opened and a figure glided out.

He strained his eyes, trying to penetrate the darkness so he could get a better look. The figure moved from the shadows near the house and out into the backyard. He could see it clearly now and gasped.

Mark was looking at something from one of his childhood nightmares — the bone white face, red painted tears, and jack-o-lantern smile of a clown.

In stunned silence, he watched as the clown twirled down the gravel driveway like a terrifying dervish until it disappeared. Only then did he exhale.

Was it a hallucination?

The doctors at the VA hospital had warned him that he might experience them.

No, it was real!

Dread washed over him.

"Dad!"

He sprinted from his hiding place and ran to the house.

~

His father had been shot twice. The body was twisted unnaturally, sprawling half off the bed. The right side of his head was gone. Blood and brain matter dripped from the curtains.

Mark stooped and picked up the gun from the rug where it had been dropped. He sat down in the armchair across from his father's body.

Cradling the pistol in his lap, Mark began to cry softly.